Coming Up for Air

Eric Arthur Blair (George Orwell) was born in 1903 in India, where his father worked for the Civil Service. The family moved to England in 1907 and in 1917 Orwell entered Eton, where he contributed regularly to the various college magazines. From 1922 to 1927 he served with the Indian Imperial Police Force in Burma, an experience that inspired his first novel, *Burmese Days* (1934). Several years of poverty followed. He lived in Paris for two years before returning to England, where he worked successively as a private tutor, schoolteacher and bookshop assistant, and contributed reviews and articles to a number of periodicals. *Down and Out in Paris and London* was published in 1933. In 1936 he was commissioned by Victor Gollancz to visit areas of mass unemployment in Lancashire and Yorkshire, and the *Road to Wigan Pier* (1937) is a powerful description of the poverty he saw there. At the end of 1936 Orwell went to Spain to fight for the Republicans and was wounded. *Homage to Catalonia* is his account of the civil war. He was admitted to a sanatorium in 1938 and from then on was never fully fit. He spent six months in Morocco and there wrote *Coming Up for Air*. During the Second World War he served in the Home Guard and worked for the BBC Eastern Service from 1941 to 1943. As literary editor of *Tribune* he contributed a regular page of political and literary commentary, and he also wrote for the *Observer* and later for the *Manchester Evening News*. His unique political allegory, *Animal Farm*, was published in 1945, and it was this novel, together with *Nineteen Eighty-Four* (1949), which brought him world-wide fame.

George Orwell died in London in January 1950. A few days before, Desmond MacCarthy had sent him a message of greeting in which he wrote: 'You have made an indelible mark on English literature ... you are among the few memorable writers of your generation.'

Peter Davison is Research Professor of English at De Montfort University, Leicester. He was born in Newcastle upon Tyne and studied for a London External BA (1954) by correspondence course. He edited an Elizabethan text for a London MA (1957) and then taught at Sydney University, where he gained a Ph.D. He was awarded a D.Litt. and an

Hon. D. Arts by De Montfort University in 1999. He has written and edited fifteen books as well as the Facsimile Edition of the manuscript of *Nineteen Eighty-Four* and the twenty volumes of Orwell's *Complete Works* (with Ian Angus and Sheila Davison). He is a Past-President of the Bibliographical Society, whose journal he edited for twelve years. He was made an OBE in 1999 for services to literature.

GEORGE ORWELL

Coming Up for Air

He's dead, but he won't lie down.
Popular Song

PENGUIN BOOKS
in association with Martin Secker & Warburg Ltd

PENGUIN BOOKS

Published by the Penguin Group
Penguin Books Ltd, 80 Strand, London WC2R 0RL, England
Penguin Putnam Inc., 375 Hudson Street, New York, New York 10014, USA
Penguin Books Australia Ltd, 250 Camberwell Road, Camberwell, Victoria 3124, Australia
Penguin Books Canada Ltd, 10 Alcorn Avenue, Toronto, Ontario, Canada M4V 3B2
Penguin Books India (P) Ltd, 11 Community Centre, Panchsheel Park, New Delhi – 110 017, India
Penguin Books (NZ) Ltd, Cnr Rosedale and Airborne Roads, Albany, Auckland, New Zealand
Penguin Books (South Africa) (Pty) Ltd, 24 Sturdee Avenue, Rosebank 2196, South Africa

Penguin Books Ltd, Registered Offices: 80 Strand, London WC2R 0RL, England

www.penguin.com

First published by Victor Gollancz 1939
Uniform Edition published by Martin Secker & Warburg Ltd 1948
Published in Penguin Books 1962
This edition first published by Martin Secker & Warburg Ltd
in the Complete Works of George Orwell series 1986
Published in Penguin Books with a new Note on the Text 1990
Reprinted in Penguin Classics 2000

028

Copyright 1939 by Eric Blair
This edition copyright © the Estate of the late Sonia Brownell Orwell, 1986
Note on the Text copyright © Peter Davison, 1990
All rights reserved

Printed and bound in Great Britain by Clays Ltd, Elcograf S.p.A.
Filmset in Monophoto Bembo

ISBN-13: 978–0–141–18569–9

www.greenpenguin.co.uk

A NOTE ON THE TEXT

Coming Up for Air presents few editorial problems though there are one or two textual points of interest. Orwell was seriously ill early in 1938 and had spent some months in a sanatorium at Aylesford, Kent. He was advised to spend the winter in a warm climate. The novelist L. H. Myers anonymously, through Dorothy Plowman, gave £300 to enable him to go. Although this was a gift, Orwell insisted on regarding it as a loan and when he could afford to repay it in 1946 he still did not know his benefactor's name; Myers had, in fact, died in 1944. Orwell went with his wife to North Africa, staying mainly in Marrakesh, from September 1938 to March 1939. Whilst he was there he wrote *Coming Up for Air*. The book was published by Gollancz on 12 June 1939 (2,000 copies) and almost immediately another 1,000 copies were called for. It was the first of Orwell's books to be printed in Secker & Warburg's Uniform Edition, 5,000 copies being published on 13 May 1948. Writing to Julian Symons on 10 May 1948, Orwell said:

> I thought it worth reprinting because it was rather killed by the outbreak of war and then blitzed out of existence, so thoroughly that in order to get a copy from which to reset it we had to steal one from a public library.

The first American edition was published by Harcourt, Brace & Company on 19 January 1950 (8,000 copies), two days before Orwell died. It was proposed in August 1939 to include *Coming Up for Air* in a series of books in English circulated on the Continent of Europe by the Albatross Press. Certain unfriendly references to Hitler were to be excised (though not all of them) and a passage of about one page in length that suggested war was imminent was to be cut out. These changes were required (and accepted by Orwell) because Albatross books were distributed chiefly in Germany. The project came to nothing because war broke out the following month, though Orwell was still making inquiries about it in December 1939.

No typescript survives of *Coming Up for Air* but there is a corrected proof of the Uniform Edition which has been claimed to be Orwell's though it more probably emanates from the publishing house. The references to 'Boars'/'Boers' on page 45 caused the printers problems. In the first edition, Lady Astor was included in the list of 'soul-savers and Nosey Parkers' on page 183, line 4, but was omitted from the Uniform Edition. For reasons explained in the Textual Note to the Complete Works edition, VII, pages 250–51 (Secker & Warburg, 1986), it is probable that this cut was made by Orwell and her name is not included in this edition.

There is one minor but curious aspect about the composition of *Coming Up for Air*. When Orwell returned his set of proofs from Jura on 22 October 1947, he told Roger Senhouse, a Director of Secker & Warburg:

> Did you know by the way that this book hasn't got a semicolon in it? I had decided about that time that the semicolon is an unnecessary stop and that I would write my next book without one.

In fact, the surviving set of proofs and the Uniform Edition include three semicolons: after 'streamlined', page 22, line 20; after 'Maybrick', page 23, line 15; and after 'Hashbadana', page 30, line 24—incorrectly given as 'Hashbadada' in 1939 and 1948. It is impossible to tell whether Orwell missed this inclusion of the semicolons, or whether he marked their omission on another set of proofs no longer extant and his instructions were ignored. Orwell did not always pick up mistakes in proof so, despite his concern about semicolons, it is quite possible he missed these rather than that Senhouse went against Orwell's wishes—for Senhouse did accept Orwell's use of 'onto' as a single word despite the former's 'archaic horror' of it being so printed. Because Orwell was so specific about the omission of semicolons, they have been left out of this edition.

Although Orwell checked the proofs for the Uniform Edition there is evidence to show that his preferences in spelling, followed in the first edition (e.g., 'further' rather than 'farther' and 'today' without a hyphen) were disregarded and that a house style of punctuation was imposed. In making such changes in 1948, Secker & Warburg were inconsistent. Thus, for example, 'streamlined' appears both as one word and hyphenated. This edition is based on that of 1939, which is, in general, closer to Orwell's styling, but it takes into account the few changes deemed to be Orwell's and his expressed wishes in the matter of semicolons and capitalisation.

PETER DAVISON
Albany, London

PART I

PART I

THE IDEA REALLY came to me the day I got my new false teeth.

I remember the morning well. At about a quarter to eight I'd nipped out of bed and got into the bathroom just in time to shut the kids out. It was a beastly January morning, with a dirty yellowish-grey sky. Down below, out of the little square of bathroom window, I could see the ten yards by five of grass, with a privet hedge round it and a bare patch in the middle, that we call the back garden. There's the same back garden, same privets and same grass, behind every house in Ellesmere Road. Only difference—where there are no kids there's no bare patch in the middle.

I was trying to shave with a bluntish razor-blade while the water ran into the bath. My face looked back at me out of the mirror, and underneath, in a tumbler of water on the little shelf over the washbasin, the teeth that belonged in the face. It was the temporary set that Warner, my dentist, had given me to wear while the new ones were being made. I haven't such a bad face, really. It's one of those bricky-red faces that go with butter-coloured hair and pale-blue eyes. I've never gone grey or bald, thank God, and when I've got my teeth in I probably don't look my age, which is forty-five.

Making a mental note to buy razor-blades, I got into the bath and started soaping. I soaped my arms (I've got those kind of pudgy arms that are freckled up to the elbow) and then took the back-brush and soaped my shoulder-blades, which in the ordinary way I can't reach. It's a nuisance, but

3

there are several parts of my body that I can't reach nowadays. The truth is that I'm inclined to be a little bit on the fat side. I don't mean that I'm like something in a sideshow at a fair. My weight isn't much over fourteen stone, and last time I measured round my waist it was either forty-eight or forty-nine, I forget which. And I'm not what they call 'disgustingly' fat, I haven't got one of those bellies that sag half-way down to the knees. It's merely that I'm a little bit broad in the beam, with a tendency to be barrel-shaped. Do you know the active, hearty kind of fat man, the athletic bouncing type that's nicknamed Fatty or Tubby and is always the life and soul of the party? I'm that type. 'Fatty', they mostly call me. Fatty Bowling. George Bowling is my real name.

But at that moment I didn't feel like the life and soul of the party. And it struck me that nowadays I nearly always do have a morose kind of feeling in the early mornings, although I sleep well and my digestion's good. I knew what it was, of course—it was those bloody false teeth. The things were magnified by the water in the tumbler, and they were grinning at me like the teeth in a skull. It gives you a rotten feeling to have your gums meet, a sort of pinched-up, withered feeling like when you've bitten into a sour apple. Besides, say what you will, false teeth are a landmark. When your last natural tooth goes, the time when you can kid yourself that you're a Hollywood sheik is definitely at an end. And I was fat as well as forty-five. As I stood up to soap my crutch I had a look at my figure. It's all rot about fat men being unable to see their feet, but it's a fact that when I stand upright I can only see the front halves of mine. No woman, I thought as I worked the soap round my belly, will ever look twice at me again, unless she's paid to. Not that at that moment I particularly wanted any woman to look twice at me.

But it struck me that this morning there were reasons

why I ought to have been in a better mood. To begin with I wasn't working today. The old car, in which I 'cover' my district (I ought to tell you that I'm in the insurance business. The Flying Salamander. Life, fire, burglary, twins, shipwreck—everything) was temporarily in dock, and though I'd got to look in at the London office to drop some papers, I was really taking the day off to go and fetch my new false teeth. And besides, there was another business that had been in and out of my mind for some time past. This was that I had seventeen quid which nobody else had heard about—nobody in the family, that is. It had happened this way. A chap in our firm, Mellors by name, had got hold of a book called *Astrology applied to Horse-racing* which proved that it's all a question of the influence of the planets on the colours the jockey is wearing. Well, in some race or other there was a mare called Corsair's Bride, a complete outsider, but her jockey's colour was green, which it seemed was just the colour for the planets that happened to be in the ascendant. Mellors, who was deeply bitten with this astrology business, was putting several quid on the horse and went down on his knees to me to do the same. In the end, chiefly to shut him up, I risked ten bob, though I don't bet as a general rule. Sure enough Corsair's Bride came home in a walk. I forget the exact odds, but my share worked out at seventeen quid. By a kind of instinct—rather queer, and probably indicating another landmark in my life—I just quietly put the money in the bank and said nothing to anybody. I'd never done anything of this kind before. A good husband and father would have spent it on a dress for Hilda (that's my wife) and boots for the kids. But I'd been a good husband and father for fifteen years and I was beginning to get fed up with it.

After I'd soaped myself all over I felt better and lay down in the bath to think about my seventeen quid and what to spend it on. The alternatives, it seemed to me, were either a week-end with a woman or dribbling it quietly away on odds and ends such as cigars and double whiskies. I'd just turned on some more hot water and was thinking about women and cigars when there was a noise like a herd of buffaloes coming down the two steps that lead to the bathroom. It was the kids, of course. Two kids in a house the size of ours is like a quart of beer in a pint mug. There was a frantic stamping outside and then a yell of agony.

'Dadda! I wanna come in!'

'Well, you can't. Clear out!'

'But dadda! I wanna go somewhere!'

'Go somewhere else, then. Hop it. I'm having my bath.'

'Dad-*da!* I wanna *go some—where!*'

No use! I knew the danger signal. The w c is in the bathroom—it would be, of course, in a house like ours. I hooked the plug out of the bath and got partially dry as quickly as I could. As I opened the door, little Billy—my youngest, aged seven—shot past me, dodging the smack which I aimed at his head. It was only when I was nearly dressed and looking for a tie that I discovered that my neck was still soapy.

It's a rotten thing to have a soapy neck. It gives you a disgusting sticky feeling, and the queer thing is that, however carefully you sponge it away, when you've once discovered that your neck is soapy you feel sticky for the rest of the day. I went downstairs in a bad temper and ready to make myself disagreeable.

Our dining-room, like the other dining-rooms in Ellesmere Road, is a poky little place, fourteen feet by twelve, or maybe it's twelve by ten, and the Japanese oak sideboard, with the two empty decanters and the silver egg-stand that Hilda's mother gave us for a wedding present, doesn't leave much room. Old Hilda was glooming behind the teapot, in her usual state of alarm and dismay because the *News Chronicle* had announced that the price of butter was going up, or something. She hadn't lighted the gas-fire, and though the windows were shut it was beastly cold. I bent down and put a match to the fire, breathing rather loudly through my nose (bending always makes me puff and blow) as a kind of hint to Hilda. She gave me the little sidelong glance that she always gives me when she thinks I'm doing something extravagant.

Hilda is thirty-nine, and when I first knew her she looked just like a hare. So she does still, but she's got very thin and rather wizened, with a perpetual brooding, worried look in her eyes, and when she's more upset than usual she's got a trick of humping her shoulders and folding her arms across her breast, like an old gypsy woman over her fire. She's one of those people who get their main kick in life out of foreseeing disasters. Only petty disasters, of course. As for wars, earthquakes, plagues, famines and revolutions, she pays no attention to them. Butter is going up, and the gas-bill is enormous, and the kids' boots are wearing out and there's another instalment due on the radio—that's Hilda's litany. She gets what I've finally decided is a definite pleasure out of rocking herself to and fro with her arms across her breast, and glooming at me, 'But, George, it's very *serious!* I don't know what we're going to *do!* I don't know where the money's coming from! You don't seem to realise how serious it *is!*' and so on and so forth. It's fixed firmly in her head that we shall end up in the workhouse. The funny thing is that if we ever do get to the workhouse Hilda won't mind it a quarter as much as I shall, in fact she'll probably rather enjoy the feeling of security.

The kids were downstairs already, having washed and dressed at lightning speed, as they always do when there's no chance to keep anyone else out of the bathroom. When I got to the breakfast table they were having an argument

7

which went to the tune of 'Yes, you did!' 'No, I didn't!' 'Yes, you did!' 'No, I didn't!' and looked like going on for the rest of the morning, until I told them to cheese it. There are only the two of them, Billy, aged seven, and Lorna, aged eleven. It's a peculiar feeling that I have towards the kids. A great deal of the time I can hardly stick the sight of them. As for their conversation, it's just unbearable. They're at that dreary bread-and-buttery age when a kid's mind revolves round things like rulers, pencil-boxes and who got top marks in French. At other times, especially when they're asleep, I have quite a different feeling. Sometimes I've stood over their cots, on summer evenings when it's light, and watched them sleeping, with their round faces and their tow-coloured hair, several shades lighter than mine, and it's given me that feeling you read about in the Bible when it says your bowels yearn. At such times I feel that I'm just a kind of dried-up seed-pod that doesn't matter twopence and that my sole importance has been to bring these creatures into the world and feed them while they're growing. But that's only at moments. Most of the time my separate existence looks pretty important to me, I feel that there's life in the old dog yet and plenty of good times ahead, and the notion of myself as a kind of tame dairy-cow for a lot of women and kids to chase up and down doesn't appeal to me.

We didn't talk much at breakfast. Hilda was in her 'I don't know what we're going to *do!*' mood, partly owing to the price of butter and partly because the Christmas holidays were nearly over and there was still five pounds owing on the school fees for last term. I ate my boiled egg and spread a piece of bread with Golden Crown marmalade. Hilda will persist in buying the stuff. It's fivepence-halfpenny a pound, and the label tells you in the smallest print the law allows that it contains 'a certain proportion of neutral fruit-juice'. This started me off, in the rather irritating way I have sometimes, talking about neutral fruit-trees, wondering what they looked like and what countries they grew in, until finally Hilda got angry. It's not that she minds me chipping her, it's only that in some obscure way she thinks it's wicked to make jokes about anything you save money on.

I had a look at the paper, but there wasn't much news. Down in Spain and over in China they were murdering one another as usual, a woman's legs had been found in a railway waiting-room and King Zog's wedding was wavering in the balance. Finally, at about ten o'clock, rather earlier than I'd intended, I started out for town. The kids had gone off to play in the public gardens. It was a beastly raw morning. As I stepped out of the front door a nasty little gust of wind caught the soapy patch on my neck and made me suddenly feel that my clothes didn't fit and that I was sticky all over.

II

Do you know the road I live in—Ellesmere Road, West Bletchley? Even if you don't, you know fifty others exactly like it.

You know how these streets fester all over the inner-outer suburbs. Always the same. Long, long rows of little semi-detached houses—the numbers in Ellesmere Road run to 212 and ours is 191—as much alike as council houses and generally uglier. The stucco front, the creosoted gate, the privet hedge, the green front door. The Laurels, The Myrtles, The Hawthorns, Mon Abri, Mon Repos, Belle Vue. At perhaps one house in fifty some anti-social type who'll probably end in the workhouse has painted his front door blue instead of green.

That sticky feeling round my neck had put me into a

9

demoralised kind of mood. It's curious how it gets you down to have a sticky neck. It seems to take all the bounce out of you, like when you suddenly discover in a public place that the sole of one of your shoes is coming off. I had no illusions about myself that morning. It was almost as if I could stand at a distance and watch myself coming down the road, with my fat red face and my false teeth and my vulgar clothes. A chap like me is incapable of looking like a gentleman. Even if you saw me at two hundred yards' distance you'd know immediately—not, perhaps, that I was in the insurance business, but that I was some kind of tout or salesman. The clothes I was wearing were practically the uniform of the tribe. Grey herringbone suit a bit the worse for wear, blue overcoat costing fifty shillings, bowler hat and no gloves. And I've got the look that's peculiar to people who sell things on commission, a kind of coarse brazen look. At my best moments, when I've got a new suit or when I'm smoking a cigar, I might pass for a bookie or a publican, and when things are very bad I might be touting vacuum cleaners, but at ordinary times you'd place me correctly. 'Five to ten quid a week', you'd say as soon as you saw me. Economically and socially I'm about at the average level of Ellesmere Road.

I had the street pretty much to myself. The men had bunked to catch the 8.21 and the women were fiddling with the gas-stoves. When you've time to look about you, and when you happen to be in the right mood, it's a thing that makes you laugh inside to walk down these streets in the inner-outer suburbs and to think of the lives that go on there. Because, after all, what *is* a road like Ellesmere Road? Just a prison with the cells all in a row. A line of semi-detached torture-chambers where the poor little five-to-ten-pound-a-weekers quake and shiver, every one of them with the boss twisting his tail and the wife riding him like the nightmare and the kids sucking his blood like leeches.

There's a lot of rot talked about the sufferings of the working class. I'm not so sorry for the proles myself. Did you ever know a navvy who lay awake thinking about the sack? The prole suffers physically, but he's a free man when he isn't working. But in every one of those little stucco boxes there's some poor bastard who's *never* free except when he's fast asleep and dreaming that he's got the boss down the bottom of a well and is bunging lumps of coal at him.

Of course the basic trouble with people like us, I said to myself, is that we all imagine we've got something to lose. To begin with, nine-tenths of the people in Ellesmere Road are under the impression that they own their houses. Ellesmere Road, and the whole quarter surrounding it, until you get to the High Street, is part of a huge racket called the Hesperides Estate, the property of the Cheerful Credit Building Society. Building societies are probably the cleverest racket of modern times. My own line, insurance, is a swindle I admit, but it's an open swindle with the cards on the table. But the beauty of the building-society swindle is that your victims think you're doing them a kindness. You wallop them, and they lick your hand. I sometimes think I'd like to have the Hesperides Estate surmounted by an enormous statue to the god of building societies. It would be a queer sort of god. Among other things it would be bi-sexual. The top half would be a managing director and the bottom half would be a wife in the family way. In one hand it would carry an enormous key—the key of the workhouse, of course—and in the other—what do they call those things like French horns with presents coming out of them?—a cornucopia, out of which would be pouring portable radios, life-insurance policies, false teeth, aspirins, French letters and concrete garden rollers.

As a matter of fact in Ellesmere Road we don't own

our houses, even when we've finished paying for them. They're not freehold, only leasehold. They're priced at five-fifty, payable over a period of sixteen years, and they're a class of house which, if you bought them for cash down, would cost round about three-eighty. That represents a profit of a hundred and seventy for the Cheerful Credit, but needless to say the Cheerful Credit makes a lot more out of it than that. Three-eighty includes the builder's profit, but the Cheerful Credit, under the name of Wilson & Bloom, builds the houses itself and scoops the builder's profit. All it has to pay for is the materials. But it also scoops the profit on the materials, because under the name of Brookes & Scatterby it sells itself the bricks, tiles, doors, window-frames, sand, cement and, I think, glass. And it wouldn't altogether surprise me to learn that under yet another alias it sells itself the timber to make the doors and window-frames. Also—and this was something which we really might have foreseen, though it gave us all a knock when we discovered it—the Cheerful Credit doesn't always keep to its end of the bargain. When Ellesmere Road was built it gave on some open fields—nothing very wonderful, but good for the kids to play in—known as Platt's Meadows. There was nothing in black and white, but it had always been understood that Platt's Meadows weren't to be built on. However, West Bletchley was a growing suburb, Rothwells' jam factory had opened in '28 and the Anglo-American All-Steel Bicycle factory started in '33, and the population was increasing and rents were going up. I've never seen Sir Hubert Crum or any other of the big noises of the Cheerful Credit in the flesh, but in my mind's eye I could see their mouths watering. Suddenly the builders arrived and houses began to go up on Platt's Meadows. There was a howl of agony from the Hesperides, and a tenants' defence association was set up. No use! Crum's lawyers had knocked the stuffing out of us in five minutes, and Platt's Meadows were built over. But the really subtle swindle, the one that makes me feel old Crum deserved his baronetcy, is the mental one. Merely because of the illusion that we own our houses and have what's called 'a stake in the country', we poor saps in the Hesperides, and in all such places, are turned into Crum's devoted slaves for ever. We're all respectable householders—that's to say Tories, yes-men and bumsuckers. Daren't kill the goose that lays the gilded eggs! And the fact that actually we aren't householders, that we're all in the middle of paying for our houses and eaten up with the ghastly fear that something might happen before we've made the last payment, merely increases the effect. We're all bought, and what's more we're bought with our own money. Every one of those poor downtrodden bastards, sweating his guts out to pay twice the proper price for a brick dolls' house that's called Belle Vue because there's no view and the bell doesn't ring—every one of those poor suckers would die on the field of battle to save his country from Bolshevism.

I turned down Walpole Road and got into the High Street. There's a train to London at 10.14. I was just passing the Sixpenny Bazaar when I remembered the mental note I'd made that morning to buy a packet of razor-blades. When I got to the soap counter the floor-manager, or whatever his proper title is, was cursing the girl in charge there. Generally there aren't many people in the Sixpenny at that hour of the morning. Sometimes if you go in just after opening-time you see all the girls lined up in a row and given their morning curse, just to get them into trim for the day. They say these big chain-stores have chaps with special powers of sarcasm and abuse who are sent from branch to branch to ginger the girls up. The floor-manager was an ugly little devil, undersized, with very square shoulders and a spiky grey moustache. He'd just pounced on her about something, some mistake in the change evidently, and was going for her with a voice like a circular saw.

'Ho, no! Course you couldn't count it! *Course* you couldn't. Too much trouble, that'd be. Ho, no!'

Before I could stop myself I'd caught the girl's eye. It wasn't so nice for her to have a fat middle-aged bloke with a red face looking on while she took her cursing. I turned away as quickly as I could and pretended to be interested in some stuff at the next counter, curtain rings or something. He was onto her again. He was one of those people who turn away and then suddenly dart back at you, like a dragon-fly.

'*Course* you couldn't count it! Doesn't matter to *you* if we're two bob out. Doesn't matter at all. What's two bob to *you*? Couldn't ask *you* to go to the trouble of counting it properly. Ho, no! Nothing matters 'ere 'cept *your* convenience. You don't think about others, do you?'

This went on for about five minutes in a voice you could hear half across the shop. He kept turning away to make her think he'd finished with her and then darting back to have another go. As I edged a bit further off I had a glance at them. The girl was a kid of about eighteen, rather fat, with a sort of moony face, the kind that would never get the change right anyway. She'd turned pale pink and she was wriggling, actually wriggling with pain. It was just the same as if he'd been cutting into her with a whip. The girls at the other counters were pretending not to hear. He was an ugly, stiff-built little devil, the sort of cock-sparrow type of man that sticks his chest out and puts his hands under his coat-tails—the type that'd be a sergeant-major only they aren't tall enough. Do you notice how often they have undersized men for these bullying jobs? He was sticking his face, moustache and all, almost into hers so as to scream at her better. And the girl all pink and wriggling.

Finally he decided that he'd said enough and strutted off like an admiral on the quarter-deck, and I came up to the counter for my razor-blades. He knew I'd heard every word, and so did she, and both of them knew I knew they knew. But the worst of it was that for my benefit she'd got to pretend that nothing had happened and put on the standoffish keep-your-distance attitude that a shopgirl's supposed to keep up with male customers. Had to act the grown-up young lady half a minute after I'd seen her cursed like a skivvy! Her face was still pink and her hands were trembling. I asked her for penny blades and she started fumbling in the threepenny tray. Then the little devil of a floor-manager turned our way and for a moment both of us thought he was coming back to begin again. The girl flinched like a dog that sees the whip. But she was looking at me out of the corner of her eye. I could see that because I'd seen her cursed she hated me like the devil. Queer!

I cleared out with my razor-blades. Why do they stand it? I was thinking. Pure funk, of course. One back-answer and you get the sack. It's the same everywhere. I thought of the lad that sometimes serves me at the chain-store grocery we deal at. A great hefty lump of twenty, with cheeks like roses and enormous fore-arms, ought to be working in a blacksmith's shop. And there he is in his white jacket, bent double across the counter, rubbing his hands together with his 'Yes, sir! Very true, sir! Pleasant weather for the time of year, sir! What can I have the pleasure of getting you today, sir?' practically asking you to kick his bum. Orders, of course. The customer is always right. The thing you can see in his face is mortal dread that you might report him for impertinence and get him sacked. Besides, how's he to know you aren't one of the narks the company sends round? Fear! We swim in it. It's our element. Everyone that isn't scared stiff of losing his job is scared stiff of war, or Fascism, or Communism, or something. Jews sweating when they think of Hitler. It crossed my mind that that little bastard with the spiky moustache was probably a damn sight more scared for his job than the girl was. Probably got a family to support. And perhaps, who knows, at home he's meek and mild, grows cucumbers in the back garden, lets his wife sit on him and the kids pull his moustache. And by the same token you never read about a Spanish Inquisitor or one of these higher-ups in the Russian Ogpu without being told that in private life he was such a good kind man, best of husbands and fathers, devoted to his tame canary and so forth.

The girl at the soap counter was looking after me as I went out of the door. She'd have murdered me if she could. How she hated me because of what I'd seen! Much more than she hated the floor-manager.

III

There was a bombing plane flying low overhead. For a minute or two it seemed to be keeping pace with the train.

Two vulgar kind of blokes in shabby overcoats, obviously commercials of the lowest type, newspaper canvassers probably, were sitting opposite me. One of them was reading the *Mail* and the other was reading the *Express*. I could see by their manner that they'd spotted me for one of their kind. Up at the other end of the carriage two lawyers' clerks with black bags were keeping up a conversation full of legal baloney that was meant to impress the rest of us and show that they didn't belong to the common herd.

I was watching the backs of the houses sliding past. The line from West Bletchley runs most of the way through slums, but it's kind of peaceful, the glimpses you get of little backyards with bits of flowers stuck in boxes and the flat roofs where the women peg out the washing and the bird-cage on the wall. The great black bombing plane swayed a little in the air and zoomed ahead so that I couldn't see it. I was sitting with my back to the engine. One of the commercials cocked his eye at it for just a second. I knew what he was thinking. For that matter it's what everybody else is thinking. You don't have to be a highbrow to think such thoughts nowadays. In two years' time, one year's time, what shall we be doing when we see one of those things? Making a dive for the cellar, wetting our bags with fright.

The commercial bloke put down his *Daily Mail*.

'Templegate's winner come in,' he said.

The lawyers' clerks were spouting some learned rot about fee-simple and peppercorns. The other commercial felt in his waistcoat pocket and took out a bent Woodbine. He felt in the other pocket and then leaned across to me.

'Got a match, Tubby?'

I felt for my matches. 'Tubby', you notice. That's interesting, really. For about a couple of minutes I stopped thinking about bombs and began thinking about my figure as I'd studied it in my bath that morning.

It's quite true I'm tubby, in fact my upper half is almost exactly the shape of a tub. But what's interesting, I think, is that merely because you happen to be a little bit fat, almost anyone, even a total stranger, will take it for granted to give you a nickname that's an insulting comment on your personal appearance. Suppose a chap was a hunchback or had a squint or a hare-lip—would you give him a nickname to remind him of it? But every fat man's labelled as a matter of course. I'm the type that people automatically slap on the back and punch in the ribs, and nearly all of them think I like it. I never go into the saloon bar of the Crown at Pudley (I pass that way once a week on business) without that ass Waters, who travels for the Seafoam Soap people but who's more or less a permanency in the saloon bar of the Crown, prodding me in the ribs and singing out 'Here a sheer hulk lies poor Tom Bowling!', which is a joke the bloody fools in the bar never get tired of. Waters has got a finger like a bar of iron. They all think a fat man doesn't have any feelings.

The commercial took another of my matches, to pick his teeth with, and chucked the box back. The train whizzed onto an iron bridge. Down below I got a glimpse of a baker's van and a long string of lorries loaded with cement. The queer thing, I was thinking, is that in a way they're right about fat men. It's a fact that a fat man, particularly a man who's been fat from birth—from child-hood, that's to say—isn't quite like other men. He goes through his life on a different plane, a sort of light-comedy plane, though in the case of blokes in side-shows at fairs, or in fact anyone over twenty stone, it isn't so much light comedy as low farce. I've been both fat and thin in my life, and I know the difference fatness makes to your outlook. It kind of prevents you from taking things too hard. I doubt whether a man who's never been anything but fat, a man who's been called Fatty ever since he could walk, even knows of the existence of any really deep emotions. How could he? He's got no experience of such things. He can't ever be present at a tragic scene, because a scene where there's a fat man present isn't tragic, it's comic. Just imagine a fat Hamlet, for instance! Or Oliver Hardy acting Romeo. Funnily enough I'd been thinking something of the kind only a few days earlier when I was reading a novel I'd got out of Boots'. *Wasted Passion*, it was called. The chap in the story finds out that his girl has gone off with another chap. He's one of these chaps you read about in novels, that have pale sensitive faces and dark hair and a private income. I remember more or less how the passage went:

David paced up and down the room, his hands pressed to his forehead. The news seemed to have stunned him. For a long time he could not believe it. Sheila untrue to him! It could not be! Suddenly realisation rushed over him, and he saw the fact in all its stark horror. It was too much. He flung himself down in a paroxysm of weeping.

Anyway, it went something like that. And even at the time it started me thinking. There you have it, you see. That's how people—some people—are expected to behave. But how about a chap like me? Suppose Hilda went off for a week-end with somebody else—not that I'd care a damn, in fact it would rather please me to find that she'd still got that much kick left in her—but suppose I did care, would I fling myself down in a paroxysm of weeping? Would anyone expect me to? You couldn't, with a figure like mine. It would be downright obscene.

The train was running along an embankment. A little below us you could see the roofs of the houses stretching on and on, the little red roofs where the bombs are going to drop, a bit lighted up at this moment because a ray of sunshine was catching them. Funny how we keep on thinking about bombs. Of course there's no question that it's coming soon. You can tell how close it is by the cheer-up stuff they're talking about it in the newspapers. I was reading a piece in the *News Chronicle* the other day where it said that bombing planes can't do any damage nowadays. The anti-aircraft guns have got so good that the bomber has to stay at twenty thousand feet. The chap thinks, you notice, that if an aeroplane's high enough the bombs don't reach the ground. Or more likely what he really meant was that they'll miss Woolwich Arsenal and only hit places like Ellesmere Road.

But taking it by and large, I thought, it's not so bad to be fat. One thing about a fat man is that he's always popular. There's really no kind of company, from bookies to bishops, where a fat man doesn't fit in and feel at home. As for women, fat men have more luck with them than people seem to think. It's all bunk to imagine, as some people do, that a woman looks on a fat man as just a joke. The truth is that a woman doesn't look on *any* man as a joke if he can kid her that he's in love with her.

Mind you, I haven't always been fat. I've been fat for eight or nine years, and I suppose I've developed most of the characteristics. But it's also a fact that internally, mentally, I'm not altogether fat. No! Don't mistake me. I'm not trying to put myself over as a kind of tender flower, the aching heart behind the smiling face and so forth. You couldn't get on in the insurance business if you were anything like that. I'm vulgar, I'm insensitive, and I fit in with my environment. So long as anywhere in the world things are being sold on commission and livings are picked up by sheer brass and lack of finer feelings, chaps like me will be doing it. In almost all circumstances I'd manage to make a living—always a living and never a fortune—and even in war, revolution, plague and famine I'd back myself to stay alive longer than most people. I'm that type. But also I've got something else inside me, chiefly a hangover from the past. I'll tell you about that later. I'm fat, but I'm thin inside. Has it ever struck you that there's a thin man inside every fat man, just as they say there's a statue inside every block of stone?

The chap who'd borrowed my matches was having a good pick at his teeth over the *Express*.

'Legs case don't seem to get much forrader,' he said.

'They'll never get 'im,' said the other. ' 'Ow could you identify a pair of legs? They're all the bleeding same, aren't they?'

'Might trace 'im through the piece of paper 'e wrapped 'em up in,' said the first.

Down below you could see the roofs of the houses stretching on and on, twisting this way and that with the streets, but stretching on and on, like an enormous plain that you could have ridden over. Whichever way you cross London it's twenty miles of houses almost without a break. Christ! how can the bombers miss us when they come? We're just one great big bull's-eye. And no warning, probably. Because who's going to be such a bloody fool as to declare war nowadays? If I was Hitler I'd send my bombers across in the middle of a disarmament conference. Some quiet morning, when the clerks are streaming across London Bridge, and the canary's singing and the old woman's pegging the bloomers on the line—zoom, whizz, plonk! Houses going up into the air, bloomers soaked with blood, canary singing on above the corpses.

Seems a pity somehow, I thought. I looked at the great sea of roofs stretching on and on. Miles and miles of streets, fried-fish shops, tin chapels, picture houses, little printing-shops up back alleys, factories, blocks of flats, whelk stalls, dairies, power stations—on and on and on. Enormous! And the peacefulness of it! Like a great wilderness with no wild beasts. No guns firing, nobody chucking pineapples, nobody beating anybody else up with a rubber truncheon. If you come to think of it, in the whole of England at this moment there probably isn't a single bedroom window from which anyone's firing a machine-gun.

But how about five years from now? Or two years? Or one year?

IV

I'd dropped my papers at the office. Warner is one of these cheap American dentists, and he has his consulting-room, or 'parlour' as he likes to call it, half-way up a big block of offices, between a photographer and a rubber-goods wholesaler. I was early for my appointment, but it was time for a bit of grub. I don't know what put it into my head to go into a milk-bar. They're places I generally avoid. We five-to-ten-pound-a-weekers aren't well served in the way of eating-places in London. If your idea of the amount to spend on a meal is one and threepence, it's either Lyons, the Express Dairy or the ABC, or else it's the kind of funeral snack they serve you in the saloon bar, a pint of bitter and a slab of cold pie, so cold that it's colder than the beer. Outside the milk-bar the boys were yelling the first editions of the evening papers.

Behind the bright red counter a girl in a tall white cap was fiddling with an ice-box, and somewhere at the back a radio was playing, plonk-tiddle-tiddle-plonk, a kind of tinny sound. Why the hell am I coming here? I thought to myself as I went in. There's a kind of atmosphere about these places that gets me down. Everything slick and shiny and streamlined, mirrors, enamel and chromium-plate whichever direction you look in. Everything spent on the decorations and nothing on the food. No real food at all. Just lists of stuff with American names, sort of phantom stuff that you can't taste and can hardly believe in the existence of. Everything comes out of a carton or a tin, or it's hauled out of a refrigerator or squirted out of a tap or squeezed out of a tube. No comfort, no privacy. Tall stools to sit on, a kind of narrow ledge to eat off, mirrors all around you. A sort of propaganda floating round, mixed up with the noise of the radio, to the effect that food doesn't matter, comfort doesn't matter, nothing matters except slickness and shininess and streamlining. Everything's streamlined nowadays, even the bullet Hitler's keeping for you. I ordered a large coffee and a couple of frankfurters. The girl in the white cap jerked them at me with about as much interest as you'd throw ants' eggs to a goldfish.

Outside the door a newsboy yelled 'Starnoosstan*nerd!*' I saw the poster flapping against his knees: LEGS. FRESH DISCOVERIES. Just 'legs', you notice. It had got down to that. Two days earlier they'd found a woman's legs in a railway waiting-room, done up in a brown-paper parcel, and what with successive editions of the papers, the whole nation was supposed to be so passionately interested in these blasted legs that they didn't need any further introduction. They were the only legs that were news at the moment. It's queer, I thought, as I ate a bit of roll, how dull the murders are getting nowadays. All this cutting people up and leaving bits of them about the countryside. Not a patch on the old domestic poisoning dramas, Crippen, Seddon, Mrs Maybrick, the truth being, I suppose, that you can't do a good murder unless you believe you're going to roast in hell for it.

At this moment I bit into one of my frankfurters, and—Christ!

I can't honestly say that I'd expected the thing to have a pleasant taste. I'd expected it to taste of nothing, like the roll. But this—well, it was quite an experience. Let me try and describe it to you.

The frankfurter had a rubber skin, of course, and my temporary teeth weren't much of a fit. I had to do a kind of sawing movement before I could get my teeth through the skin. And then suddenly—pop! The thing burst in my mouth like a rotten pear. A sort of horrible soft stuff was oozing all over my tongue. But the taste! For a moment I just couldn't believe it. Then I rolled my tongue round it again and had another try. It was *fish!* A sausage, a thing calling itself a frankfurter, filled with fish! I got up and walked straight out without touching my coffee. God knows what that might have tasted of.

Outside the newsboy shoved the *Standard* into my face

and yelled, 'Legs! 'Orrible revelations! All the winners! Legs! Legs!' I was still rolling the stuff round my tongue, wondering where I could spit it out. I remembered a bit I'd read in the paper somewhere about these food-factories in Germany where everything's made out of something else. Ersatz, they call it. I remembered reading that *they* were making sausages out of fish, and fish, no doubt, out of something different. It gave me the feeling that I'd bitten into the modern world and discovered what it was really made of. That's the way we're going nowadays. Everything slick and streamlined, everything made out of something else. Celluloid, rubber, chromium-steel everywhere, arc-lamps blazing all night, glass roofs over your head, radios all playing the same tune, no vegetation left, everything cemented over, mock-turtles grazing under the neutral fruit-trees. But when you come down to brass tacks and get your teeth into something solid, a sausage for instance, that's what you get. Rotten fish in a rubber skin. Bombs of filth bursting inside your mouth.

When I'd got the new teeth in I felt a lot better. They sat nice and smooth over the gums, and though very likely it sounds absurd to say that false teeth can make you feel younger, it's a fact that they did so. I tried a smile at myself in a shop window. They weren't half bad. Warner, though cheap, is a bit of an artist and doesn't aim at making you look like a toothpaste advert. He's got huge cabinets full of false teeth—he showed them to me once—all graded according to size and colour, and he picks them out like a jeweller choosing stones for a necklace. Nine people out of ten would have taken my teeth for natural.

I caught a full-length glimpse of myself in another window I was passing, and it struck me that really I wasn't such a bad figure of a man. A bit on the fat side, admittedly, but nothing offensive, only what the tailors call a 'full figure', and some women like a man to have a red face.

There's life in the old dog yet, I thought. I remembered my seventeen quid, and definitely made up my mind that I'd spend it on a woman. There was time to have a pint before the pubs shut, just to baptise the teeth, and feeling rich because of my seventeen quid I stopped at a tobacconist's and bought myself a sixpenny cigar of a kind I'm rather partial to. They're eight inches long and guaranteed pure Havana leaf all through. I suppose cabbages grow in Havana the same as anywhere else.

When I came out of the pub I felt quite different.

I'd had a couple of pints, they'd warmed me up inside, and the cigar smoke oozing round my new teeth gave me a fresh, clean, peaceful sort of feeling. All of a sudden I felt kind of thoughtful and philosophic. It was partly because I didn't have any work to do. My mind went back to the thoughts of war I'd been having earlier that morning, when the bomber flew over the train. I felt in a kind of prophetic mood, the mood in which you foresee the end of the world and get a certain kick out of it.

I was walking westward up the Strand, and though it was coldish I went slowly to get the pleasure of my cigar. The usual crowd that you can hardly fight your way through was streaming up the pavement, all of them with that insane fixed expression on their faces that people have in London streets, and there was the usual jam of traffic with the great red buses nosing their way between the cars and the engines roaring and horns tooting. Enough noise to waken the dead, but not to waken this lot, I thought. I felt as if I was the only person awake in a city of sleepwalkers. That's an illusion, of course. When you walk through a crowd of strangers it's next door to impossible not to imagine that they're all waxworks, but probably they're thinking just the same about you. And this kind of prophetic feeling that keeps coming over me nowadays, the feeling that war's just round the corner and that war's the end of all things, isn't peculiar to me. We've all got it, more or less. I suppose even among the people passing at that moment there must have been chaps who were seeing mental pictures of the shellbursts and the mud. Whatever thought you think there's always a million people thinking it at the same moment. But that was how I felt. We're all on the burning deck and nobody knows it except me. I looked at the dumb-bell faces streaming past. Like turkeys in November, I thought. Not a notion of what's coming to them. It was as if I'd got X-rays in my eyes and could see the skeletons walking.

I looked forward a few years. I saw this street as it'll be in five years' time, say, or three years' time (1941 they say it's booked for), after the fighting's started.

No, not all smashed to pieces. Only a little altered, kind of chipped and dirty-looking, the shop-windows almost empty and so dusty that you can't see into them. Down a side-street there's an enormous bomb-crater and a block of buildings burnt out so that it looks like a hollow tooth. Thermite. It's all curiously quiet, and everyone's very thin. A platoon of soldiers comes marching up the street. They're all as thin as rakes and their boots are dragging. The sergeant's got corkscrew moustaches and holds himself like a ramrod, but he's thin too and he's got a cough that almost tears him open. Between his coughs he's trying to bawl at them in the old parade-ground style. 'Nah then, Jones! Lift yer 'ed up! What yer keep starin' at the ground for? All them fag-ends was picked up years ago.' Suddenly a fit of coughing catches him. He tries to stop it, can't, doubles up like a ruler and almost coughs his guts out. His face turns pink and purple, his moustache goes limp and the water runs out of his eyes.

I can hear the air-raid sirens blowing and the loud-speakers bellowing that our glorious troops have taken a hundred thousand prisoners. I see a top-floor-back in

Birmingham and a child of five howling and howling for a bit of bread. And suddenly the mother can't stand it any longer, and she yells at it, 'Shut your trap, you little bastard!' and then she ups the child's frock and smacks its bottom hard, because there isn't any bread and isn't going to be any bread. I see it all. I see the posters and the food-queues, and the castor oil and the rubber truncheons and the machine-guns squirting out of bedroom windows.

Is it going to happen? No knowing. Some days it's impossible to believe it. Some days I say to myself that it's just a scare got up by the newspapers. Some days I know in my bones there's no escaping it.

When I got down near Charing Cross the boys were yelling a later edition of the evening papers. There was some more drivel about the murder. LEGS. FAMOUS SURGEON'S STATEMENT. Then another poster caught my eye: KING ZOG'S WEDDING POST-PONED. King Zog! What a name! It's next door to impossible to believe a chap with a name like that isn't a jet-black Negro.

But just at that moment a queer thing happened. King Zog's name—but I suppose, as I'd already seen the name several times that day, it was mixed up with some sound in the traffic or the smell of horse-dung or something—had started memories in me.

The past is a curious thing. It's with you all the time, I suppose an hour never passes without your thinking of things that happened ten or twenty years ago, and yet most of the time it's got no reality, it's just a set of facts that you've learned, like a lot of stuff in a history book. Then some chance sight or sound or smell, especially smell, sets you going, and the past doesn't merely come back to you, you're actually *in* the past. It was like that at this moment.

I was back in the parish church at Lower Binfield, and it was thirty-eight years ago. To outward appearances, I suppose, I was still walking down the Strand, fat and forty-five, with false teeth and a bowler hat, but inside me I was Georgie Bowling, aged seven, younger son of Samuel Bowling, corn and seed merchant, of 57 High Street, Lower Binfield. And it was Sunday morning, and I could smell the church. How I could smell it! You know the smell churches have, a peculiar, dank, dusty, decaying, sweetish sort of smell. There's a touch of candle-grease in it, and perhaps a whiff of incense and a suspicion of mice, and on Sunday mornings it's a bit overlaid by yellow soap and serge dresses, but predominantly it's that sweet dusty, musty smell that's like the smell of death and life mixed up together. It's powdered corpses, really.

In those days I was about four feet high. I was standing on the hassock so as to see over the pew in front, and I could feel Mother's black serge dress under my hand. I could also feel my stockings pulled up over my knees—we used to wear them like that then—and the saw edge of the Eton collar they used to buckle me into on Sunday mornings. And I could hear the organ wheezing and two enormous voices bellowing out the psalm. In our church there were two men who led the singing, in fact they did so much of the singing that nobody else got much of a chance. One was Shooter, the fishmonger, and the other was old Wetherall, the joiner and undertaker. They used to sit opposite one another on either side of the nave, in the pews nearest the pulpit. Shooter was a short fat man with a very pink, smooth face, a big nose, drooping moustache and a chin that kind of fell away beneath his mouth. Wetherall was quite different. He was a great, gaunt, powerful old devil of about sixty, with a face like a death's-head and stiff grey hair half an inch long all over his head. I've never seen a living man who looked so exactly like a skeleton. You could see every line of the skull in his face, his skin was like parchment, and his great lantern jaw full of yellow teeth worked up and down just like the jaw of a skeleton in an anatomical museum. And yet with all his leanness he looked as strong as iron, as though he'd live to be a hundred and make coffins for everyone in that church before he'd finished. Their voices were quite different, too. Shooter had a kind of desperate, agonised bellow, as though someone had a knife at his throat and he was just letting out his last yell for help. But Wetherall had a tremendous, churning, rumbling noise that happened deep down inside him, like enormous barrels being rolled to and fro underground. However much noise he let out, you always knew he'd got plenty more in reserve. The kids nicknamed him Rumbletummy.

They used to get up a kind of antiphonal effect, especially in the psalms. It was always Wetherall who had the last word. I suppose really they were friends in private life, but in my kid's way I used to imagine that they were deadly enemies and trying to shout one another down. Shooter would roar out 'The Lord is my shepherd', and then Wetherall would come in with 'Therefore can I lack nothing', drowning him completely. You always knew which of the two was master. I used especially to look forward to that psalm that has the bit about Sihon king of the Amorites and Og the king of Bashan (this was what King Zog's name had reminded me of). Shooter would start off with 'Sihon king of the Amorites', then perhaps for half a second you could hear the rest of the congregation singing the 'and', and then Wetherall's enormous bass would come in like a tidal wave and swallow everybody up with 'Og the king of Bashan'. I wish I could make you hear the tremendous, rumbling, subterranean barrel-noise that he could get into that word 'Og'. He even used to clip off the end of the 'and', so that when I was a very small kid I used to think it was Dog the king of Bashan. But later, when I got the names right, I formed a picture in my mind's eye of Sihon and Og. I saw them as a couple of those great Egyptian statues that I'd seen pictures of in the penny encyclopedia, enormous stone statues thirty feet high, sitting on their thrones opposite one another, with their hands on their knees and a faint mysterious smile on their faces.

How it came back to me! That peculiar feeling—it was only a feeling, you couldn't describe it as an activity—that we used to call 'Church'. The sweet corpsy smell, the rustle of Sunday dresses, the wheeze of the organ and the roaring voices, the spot of light from the hole in the window creeping slowly up the nave. In some way the grown-ups could put it across that this extraordinary performance was necessary. You took it for granted, just as you took the Bible, which you got in big doses in those days. There were texts on every wall and you knew whole chapters of the OT by heart. Even now my head's stuffed full of bits out of the Bible. And the children of Israel did evil again in the sight of the Lord. And Asher abode in his breaches. Followed them from Dan until thou come unto Beersheba. Smote him under the fifth rib, so that he died. You never understood it, you didn't try to or want to, it was just a kind of medicine, a queer-tasting stuff that you had to swallow and knew to be in some way necessary. An extraordinary rigmarole about people with names like Shimei and Nebuchadnezzar and Ahithophel and Hashbadana, people with long stiff garments and Assyrian beards, riding up and down on camels among temples and cedar trees and doing extraordinary things. Sacrificing burnt offerings, walking about in fiery furnaces, getting nailed on crosses, getting swallowed by whales. And all mixed up with the sweet graveyard smell and the serge dresses and the wheeze of the organ.

That was the world I went back to when I saw the poster about King Zog. For a moment I didn't merely remember it, I was *in* it. Of course such impressions don't last more than a few seconds. A moment later it was as though I'd opened my eyes again, and I was forty-five and there was a traffic jam in the Strand. But it had left a kind of after-effect behind. Sometimes when you come out of a train of thought you feel as if you were coming up from deep water, but this time it was the other way about, it was as though it was back in 1900 that I'd been breathing real air. Even now, with my eyes open, so to speak, all those bloody fools hustling to and fro, and the posters and the petrol-stink and the roar of the engines, seemed to me less real than Sunday morning in Lower Binfield thirty-eight years ago.

I chucked away my cigar and walked on slowly. I could smell the corpse-smell. In a manner of speaking I can smell it now. I'm back in Lower Binfield, and the year's 1900. Beside the horse-trough in the market-place the carrier's horse is having its nose-bag. At the sweet-shop on the corner Mother Wheeler is weighing out a ha'porth of brandy balls. Lady Rampling's carriage is driving by, with the tiger sitting behind in his pipeclayed breeches with his arms folded. Uncle Ezekiel is cursing Joe Chamberlain. The recruiting-sergeant in his scarlet jacket, tight blue over-alls and pillbox hat, is strutting up and down twisting his moustache. The drunks are puking in the yard behind the George. Vicky's at Windsor, God's in heaven, Christ's on the cross, Jonah's in the whale, Shadrach, Meshach and Abednego are in the fiery furnace, and Sihon king of the Amorites and Og the king of Bashan are sitting on their thrones looking at one another—not doing anything, exactly, just existing, keeping their appointed places, like a couple of fire-dogs, or the Lion and the Unicorn.

Is it gone for ever? I'm not certain. But I tell you it was a good world to live in. I belong to it. So do you.

PART II

I

THE WORLD I momentarily remembered when I saw King Zog's name on the poster was so different from the world I live in now that you might have a bit of difficulty in believing I ever belonged to it.

I suppose by this time you've got a kind of picture of me in your mind—a fat middle-aged bloke with false teeth and a red face—and subconsciously you've been imagining that I was just the same even when I was in my cradle. But forty-five years is a long time, and though some people don't change and develop, others do. I've changed a great deal, and I've had my ups and downs, mostly ups. It may seem queer, but my father would probably be rather proud of me if he could see me now. He'd think it a wonderful thing that a son of his should own a motor-car and live in a house with a bathroom. Even now I'm a little above my origin, and at other times I've touched levels that we should never have dreamed of in those old days before the war.

Before the war! How long shall we go on saying that, I wonder? How long before the answer will be 'Which war?' In my case the never-never land that people are thinking of when they say 'before the war' might almost be before the Boer War. I was born in '93, and I can actually remember the outbreak of the Boer War, because of the first-class row that Father and Uncle Ezekiel had about it. I've several other memories that would date from about a year earlier than that.

The very first thing I remember is the smell of sainfoin chaff. You went up the stone passage that led from the kitchen to the shop, and the smell of sainfoin got stronger all the way. Mother had fixed a wooden gate in the doorway to prevent Joe and myself (Joe was my elder brother) from getting into the shop. I can still remember standing there clutching the bars, and the smell of sainfoin mixed up with the damp plastery smell that belonged to the passage. It wasn't till years later that I somehow managed to crash the gate and get into the shop when nobody was there. A mouse that had been having a go at one of the meal-bins suddenly plopped out and ran between my feet. It was quite white with meal. This must have happened when I was about six.

When you're very young you seem to suddenly become conscious of things that have been under your nose for a long time past. The things round about you swim into your mind one at a time, rather as they do when you're waking from sleep. For instance, it was only when I was nearly four that I suddenly realised that we owned a dog. Nailer, his name was, an old white English terrier of the breed that's gone out nowadays. I met him under the kitchen table and in some way seemed to grasp, having only learnt it that moment, that he belonged to us and that his name was Nailer. In the same way, a bit earlier, I'd discovered that beyond the gate at the end of the passage there was a place where the smell of sainfoin came from. And the shop itself, with the huge scales and the wooden measures and the tin shovel, and the white lettering on the window, and the bullfinch in its cage—which you couldn't see very well even from the pavement, because the window was always dusty—all these things dropped into place in my mind one by one, like bits of a jigsaw puzzle.

Time goes on, you get stronger on your legs, and by degrees you begin to get a grasp of geography. I suppose Lower Binfield was just like any other market town of about two thousand inhabitants. It was in Oxfordshire—I keep saying *was*, you notice, though after all the place still exists—about five miles from the Thames. It lay in a bit of a valley, with a low ripple of hills between itself and the Thames, and higher hills behind. On top of the hills there were woods in sort of dim blue masses among which you could see a great white house with a colonnade. This was Binfield House ('The Hall', everybody called it), and the top of the hill was known as Upper Binfield, though there was no village there and hadn't been for a hundred years or more. I must have been nearly seven before I noticed the existence of Binfield House. When you're very small you don't look into the distance. But by that time I knew every inch of the town, which was shaped roughly like a cross with the market-place in the middle. Our shop was in the High Street a little before you got to the market-place, and on the corner there was Mrs Wheeler's sweet-shop where you spent a halfpenny when you had one. Mother Wheeler was a dirty old witch and people suspected her of sucking the bull's-eyes and putting them back in the bottle, though this was never proved. Further down there was the barber's shop with the advert for Abdulla cigarettes—the one with the Egyptian soldiers on it, and curiously enough they're using the same advert to this day—and the rich boozy smell of bay rum and latakia. Behind the houses you could see the chimneys of the brewery. In the middle of the market-place there was the stone horse-trough, and on top of the water there was always a fine film of dust and chaff.

Before the war, and especially before the Boer War, it was summer all the year round. I'm quite aware that that's a delusion. I'm merely trying to tell you how things come back to me. If I shut my eyes and think of Lower Binfield any time before I was, say, eight, it's always in summer weather that I remember it. Either it's the market-place at dinner-time, with a sort of sleepy dusty hush over everything and the carrier's horse with his nose dug well into his

37

nose-bag, munching away, or it's a hot afternoon in the great green juicy meadows round the town, or it's about dusk in the lane behind the allotments, and there's a smell of pipe-tobacco and night-stocks floating through the hedge. But in a sense I do remember different seasons, because all my memories are bound up with things to eat, which varied at different times of the year. Especially the things you used to find in the hedges. In July there were dewberries—but they're very rare—and the blackberries were getting red enough to eat. In September there were sloes and hazel-nuts. The best hazel-nuts were always out of reach. Later on there were beech-nuts and crab-apples. Then there were the kind of minor foods that you used to eat when there was nothing better going. Haws—but they're not much good—and hips, which have a nice sharp taste if you clean the hairs out of them. Angelica is good in early summer, especially when you're thirsty, and so are the stems of various grasses. Then there's sorrel, which is good with bread and butter, and pig-nuts, and a kind of wood shamrock which has a sour taste. Even plantain seeds are better than nothing when you're a long way from home and very hungry.

Joe was two years older than myself. When we were very small Mother used to pay Katie Simmons eighteen pence a week to take us out for walks in the afternoons. Katie's father worked in the brewery and had fourteen children, so that the family were always on the lookout for odd jobs. She was only twelve when Joe was seven and I was five, and her mental level wasn't very different from ours. She used to drag me by the arm and call me 'Baby', and she had just enough authority over us to prevent us from being run over by dogcarts or chased by bulls, but so far as conversation went we were almost on equal terms. We used to go for long, trailing kind of walks—always, of course, picking and eating things all the way—down the lane past the allotments, across Roper's Meadows and down to the Mill Farm, where there was a pool with newts and tiny carp in it (Joe and I used to go fishing there when we were a bit older), and back by the Upper Binfield Road so as to pass the sweet-shop that stood on the edge of the town. This shop was in such a bad position that anyone who took it went bankrupt, and to my own knowledge it was three times a sweet-shop, once a grocer's and once a bicycle-repair shop, but it had a peculiar fascination for children. Even when we had no money, we'd go that way so as to glue our noses against the window. Katie wasn't in the least above sharing a farthing's worth of sweets and quarrelling over her share. You could buy things worth having for a farthing in those days. Most sweets were four ounces a penny, and there was even some stuff called Paradise Mixture, mostly broken sweets from other bottles, which was six. Then there were Farthing Everlastings, which were a yard long and couldn't be finished inside half an hour. Sugar mice and sugar pigs were eight a penny, and so were liquorice pistols, popcorn was a halfpenny for a large bag, and a prize packet which contained several different kinds of sweets, a gold ring and sometimes a whistle, was a penny. You don't see prize packets nowadays. A whole lot of the kinds of sweets we had in those days have gone out. There was a kind of flat white sweet with mottoes printed on them, and also a kind of sticky pink stuff in an oval matchwood box with a tiny tin spoon to eat it with, which cost a halfpenny. Both of those have disappeared. So have Caraway Comfits, and so have chocolate pipes and sugar matches, and even Hundreds and Thousands you hardly ever see. Hundreds and Thousands were a great standby when you'd only a farthing. And what about Penny Monsters? Does one ever see a Penny Monster nowadays? It was a huge bottle, holding more than a quart of fizzy lemonade, all for a penny. That's another thing that the war killed stone dead.

It always seems to be summer when I look back. I can feel the grass round me as tall as myself, and the heat coming out of the earth. And the dust in the lane, and the warm greeny light coming through the hazel boughs. I can see the three of us trailing along, eating stuff out of the hedge, with Katie dragging at my arm and saying 'Come on, Baby!' and sometimes yelling ahead to Joe, 'Joe! You come back 'ere this minute! You'll catch it!' Joe was a hefty boy with a big, lumpy sort of head and tremendous calves, the kind of boy who's always doing something dangerous. At seven he'd already got into short trousers, with the thick black stockings drawn up over the knee and the great clumping boots that boys had to wear in those days. I was still in frocks—a kind of holland overall that Mother used to make for me. Katie used to wear a dreadful ragged parody of a grown-up dress that descended from sister to sister in her family. She had a ridiculous great hat with her pigtails hanging down behind it, and a long, draggled skirt which trailed on the ground, and button boots with the heels trodden down. She was a tiny thing, not much taller than Joe, but not bad at 'minding' children. In a family like that a child is 'minding' other children about as soon as it's weaned. At times she'd try to be grown-up and ladylike, and she had a way of cutting you short with a proverb, which to her mind was something unanswerable. If you said 'Don't care', she'd answer immediately:

> *'Don't care was made to care,*
> *Don't care was hung,*
> *Don't care was put in a pot*
> *And boiled till he was done.'*

Or if you called her names it would be 'Hard words break no bones', or, when you'd been boasting, 'Pride comes before a fall'. This came very true one day when I was strutting along pretending to be a soldier and fell into a cow-pat. Her family lived in a filthy little rat-hole of a place in the slummy street behind the brewery. The place swarmed with children like a kind of vermin. The whole family had managed to dodge going to school, which was fairly easy to do in those days, and started running errands and doing other odd jobs as soon as they could walk. One of her elder brothers got a month for stealing turnips. She stopped taking us out for walks a year later when Joe was eight and getting too tough for a girl to handle. He'd discovered that in Katie's home they slept five in a bed, and used to tease the life out of her about it.

Poor Katie! She had her first baby when she was fifteen. No one knew who was the father, and probably Katie wasn't too certain herself. Most people believed it was one of her brothers. The workhouse people took the baby, and Katie went into service in Walton. Some time afterwards she married a tinker, which even by the standards of her family was a come-down. The last time I saw her was in 1913. I was biking through Walton, and I passed some dreadful wooden shacks beside the railway line, with fences round them made out of barrel-staves, where the gypsies used to camp at certain times of the year, when the police would let them. A wrinkled-up hag of a woman, with her hair coming down and a smoky face, looking at least fifty years old, came out of one of the huts and began shaking out a rag mat. It was Katie, who must have been twenty-seven.

II

Thursday was market day. Chaps with round red faces like pumpkins and dirty smocks and huge boots covered with dry cow-dung, carrying long hazel switches, used to drive their brutes into the market-place early in the morning. For hours there'd be a terrific hullabaloo: dogs barking, pigs squealing, chaps in tradesmen's vans who wanted to get through the crush cracking their whips and cursing, and everyone who had anything to do with the cattle shouting and throwing sticks. The big noise was always when they brought a bull to market. Even at that age it struck me that most of the bulls were harmless law-abiding brutes that only wanted to get to their stalls in peace, but a bull wouldn't have been regarded as a bull if half the town hadn't had to turn out and chase it. Sometimes some terrified brute, generally a half-grown heifer, used to break loose and charge down a side-street, and then anyone who happened to be in the way would stand in the middle of the road and swing his arms backwards like the sails of a windmill, shouting 'Woo! Woo!' This was supposed to have a kind of hypnotic effect on an animal, and certainly it did frighten them.

Half-way through the morning some of the farmers would come into the shop and run samples of seed through their fingers. Actually Father did very little business with the farmers, because he had no delivery van and couldn't afford to give long credits. Mostly he did a rather petty class of business, poultry food and fodder for the tradesmen's horses and so forth. Old Brewer, of the Mill Farm, who was a stingy old bastard with a grey chin-beard, used to stand there for half an hour, fingering samples of chicken corn and letting them drop into his pocket in an absent-minded manner, after which, of course, he finally used to make off without buying anything. In the evenings the pubs were full of drunken men. In those days beer cost twopence a pint, and unlike the beer nowadays it had some guts in it. All through the Boer War the recruiting-sergeant used to be in the four-ale bar of the George every Thursday and Saturday night, dressed up to the nines and very free with his money. Sometimes next morning you'd see him leading off some great sheepish, red-faced lump of a farm lad who'd taken the shilling when he was too drunk to see and found in the morning that it would cost him twenty pounds to get out of it. People used to stand in their doorways and shake their heads when they saw them go past, almost as if it had been a funeral. 'Well now! Listed for a soldier! Just think of it! A fine young fellow like that!' It just shocked them. Listing for a soldier, in their eyes, was the exact equivalent of a girl's going on the streets. Their attitude to the war, and to the army, was very curious. They had the good old English notions that the redcoats are the scum of the earth and anyone who joins the army will die of drink and go straight to hell, but at the same time they were good patriots, stuck Union Jacks in their windows and held it as an article of faith that the English had never been beaten in battle and never could be. At that time everyone, even the Nonconformists, used to sing sentimental songs about the thin red line and the soldier boy who died on the battlefield far away. These soldier boys always used to die 'when the shot and shell were flying', I remember. It puzzled me as a kid. Shot I could understand, but it produced a queer picture in my mind to think of cockle-shells flying through the air. When Mafeking was relieved the people nearly yelled the roof off, and there were at any rate times when they believed the tales about the Boers chucking babies into the air and skewering them on their bayonets. Old Brewer got so fed up with the kids yelling 'Krooger!' after him that towards the end of the war he shaved his beard off. The people's attitude towards the Government was really the same. They were all true-blue Englishmen and swore that Vicky was the best queen that ever lived and foreigners were dirt, but at the same time nobody ever thought of paying a tax, not even a dog-licence, if there was any way of dodging it.

Before and after the war Lower Binfield was a Liberal constituency. During the war there was a by-election which the Conservatives won. I was too young to grasp what it was all about, I only knew that I was a Conservative because I liked the blue streamers better than the red ones, and I chiefly remember it because of a drunken man who fell on his nose on the pavement outside the George. In the general excitement nobody took any notice of him, and he lay there for hours in the hot sun with his blood drying round him, and when it dried it was purple. By the time the 1906 election came along I was old enough to understand it, more or less, and this time I was a Liberal because everybody else was. The people chased the Conservative candidate half a mile and threw him into a pond full of duckweed. People took politics seriously in those days. They used to begin storing up rotten eggs weeks before an election.

Very early in life, when the Boer War broke out, I remember the big row between Father and Uncle Ezekiel. Uncle Ezekiel had a little boot-shop in one of the streets off the High Street, and also did some cobbling. It was a small business and tended to get smaller, which didn't matter greatly because Uncle Ezekiel wasn't married. He was only a half-brother and much older than Father, twenty years older at least, and for the fifteen years or so that I knew him he always looked exactly the same. He was a fine-looking old chap, rather tall, with white hair and the whitest whiskers I ever saw—white as thistledown. He had a way of slapping his leather apron and standing up very straight—a reaction from bending over the last, I suppose —after which he'd bark his opinions straight in your face, ending up with a sort of ghostly cackle. He was a real old nineteenth-century Liberal, the kind that not only used to ask you what Gladstone said in '78 but could tell you the answer, and one of the very few people in Lower Binfield who stuck to the same opinions all through the war. He was always denouncing Joe Chamberlain and some gang of people that he referred to as 'the Park Lane riff-raff'. I can hear him now, having one of his arguments with Father. 'Them and their far-flung Empire! Can't fling it too far for me. He-he-he!' And then Father's voice, a quiet, worried, conscientious kind of voice, coming back at him with the white man's burden and our dooty to the pore blacks whom these here Boars treated something shameful. For a week or so after Uncle Ezekiel gave it out that he was a pro-Boer and a Little Englander they were hardly on speaking terms. They had another row when the atrocity stories started. Father was very worried by the tales he'd heard, and he tackled Uncle Ezekiel about it. Little Englander or no, surely he couldn't think it right for these here Boars to throw babies in the air and catch them on their bayonets, even if they *were* only nigger babies? But Uncle Ezekiel just laughed in his face. Father had got it all wrong! It wasn't the Boers who threw the babies in the air, it was the British soldiers! He kept grabbing hold of me—I must have been about five—to illustrate. 'Throw them in the air and skewer them like frogs, I tell you! Same as I might throw this youngster here!' And then he'd swing me up and almost let go of me, and I had a vivid picture of myself flying through the air and landing plonk on the end of a bayonet.

Father was quite different from Uncle Ezekiel. I don't know much about my grandparents, they were dead before I was born, I only know that my grandfather had been a cobbler and late in life he married the widow of a seedsman, which was how we came to have the shop. It was a job that didn't really suit Father, though he knew the business inside out and was everlastingly working. Except on Sunday and very occasionally on weekday evenings I never remember him without meal on the backs of his hands and in the lines of his face and in what was left of his hair. He'd married when he was in his thirties and must have been nearly forty when I first remember him. He was a small man, a sort of grey, quiet little man, always in shirtsleeves and white apron and always dusty-looking because of the meal. He had a round head, a blunt nose, a rather bushy moustache, spectacles and butter-coloured hair, the same colour as mine, but he'd lost most of it and it was always mealy. My grandfather had bettered himself a good deal by marrying the seedsman's widow, and Father had been educated at Walton Grammar School, where the farmers and the better-off tradesmen sent their sons, whereas Uncle Ezekiel liked to boast that he'd never been to school in his life and had taught himself to read by a tallow candle after working hours. But he was a much quicker-witted man than Father, he could argue with anybody and he used to quote Carlyle and Spencer by the yard. Father had a slow sort of mind, he'd never taken to 'book-learning', as he called it, and his English wasn't good. On Sunday afternoons, the only time when he really took things easy, he'd settle down by the parlour fireplace to have what he called a 'good read' at the Sunday paper. His favourite paper was the *People*—Mother preferred the *News of the World*, which she considered had more murders in it. I can see them now. A Sunday afternoon—summer, of course, always summer—a smell of roast pork and greens still floating in the air, and Mother on one side of the fireplace, starting off to read the latest murder but gradually falling asleep with her mouth open, and Father on the other, in slippers and spectacles, working his way slowly through yards of smudgy print. And the soft feeling of summer all round you, the geranium in the window, a starling cooing somewhere, and myself under the table with the *BOP*, making believe that the tablecloth is a tent. Afterwards, at tea, as he chewed his way through the radishes and spring onions, Father would talk in a ruminative kind of way about the stuff he'd been reading, the fires and shipwrecks and scandals in high society, and these here new flying machines and the chap (I notice that to this day he turns up in the Sunday papers about once in three years) who was swallowed by a whale in the Red Sea and taken out three days later, alive but bleached white by the whale's gastric juice. Father was always a bit sceptical of this story, and of the new flying machines, otherwise he believed everything he read. Until 1909 no one in Lower Binfield believed that human beings would ever learn to fly. The official doctrine was that if God had meant us to fly He'd have given us wings. Uncle Ezekiel couldn't help retorting that if God had meant us to ride He'd have given us wheels, but even he didn't believe in the new flying machines.

It was only on Sunday afternoons, and perhaps on the one evening a week when he looked in at the George for a half-pint, that Father turned his mind to such things. At other times he was always more or less overwhelmed by business. There wasn't really such a lot to do, but he seemed to be always busy, either in the loft behind the yard, struggling about with sacks and bales, or in the kind of dusty little cubby-hole behind the counter in the shop, adding figures up in a notebook with a stump of pencil. He was a very honest man and a very obliging man, very anxious to provide good stuff and swindle nobody, which even in those days wasn't the best way to get on in business. He would have been just the man for some small official job, a postmaster, for instance, or station-master of a country station. But he hadn't either the cheek and enterprise to borrow money and expand the business, or the imagination to think of new selling-lines. It was characteristic of him that the only streak of imagination he ever showed, the invention of a new seed mixture for cage-birds

(Bowling's Mixture it was called, and it was famous over a radius of nearly five miles) was really due to Uncle Ezekiel. Uncle Ezekiel was a bit of a bird-fancier and had quantities of goldfinches in his dark little shop. It was his theory that cage-birds lose their colour because of lack of variation in their diet. In the yard behind the shop Father had a tiny plot of ground in which he used to grow about twenty kinds of weed under wire-netting, and he used to dry them and mix their seeds with ordinary canary seed. Jackie, the bullfinch who hung in the shop-window, was supposed to be an advertisement for Bowling's Mixture. Certainly, unlike most bullfinches in cages, Jackie never turned black.

Mother was fat ever since I remember her. No doubt it's from her that I inherit my pituitary deficiency, or whatever it is that makes you get fat.

She was a largish woman, a bit taller than Father, with hair a good deal fairer than his and a tendency to wear black dresses. But except on Sundays I never remember her without an apron. It would be an exaggeration, but not a very big one, to say that I never remember her when she wasn't cooking. When you look back over a long period you seem to see human beings always fixed in some special place and some characteristic attitude. It seems to you that they were always doing exactly the same thing. Well, just as when I think of Father I remember him always behind the counter, with his hair all mealy, adding up figures with a stump of pencil which he moistens between his lips, and just as I remember Uncle Ezekiel, with his ghostly white whiskers, straightening himself out and slapping his leather apron, so when I think of Mother I remember her at the kitchen table, with her forearms covered with flour, rolling out a lump of dough.

You know the kind of kitchen people had in those days. A huge place, rather dark and low, with a great beam across the ceiling and a stone floor and cellars underneath. Everything enormous, or so it seemed to me when I was a kid. A vast stone sink which didn't have a tap but an iron pump, a dresser covering one wall and going right up to the ceiling, a gigantic range which burned half a ton a month and took God knows how long to blacklead. Mother at the table, rolling out a huge flap of dough. And myself crawling round, messing about with bundles of firewood and lumps of coal and tin beetle-traps (we had them in all the dark corners and they used to be baited with beer) and now and again coming up to the table to try and cadge a bit of food. Mother 'didn't hold with' eating between meals. You generally got the same answer: 'Get along with you, now! I'm not going to have you spoiling your dinner. Your eye's bigger than your belly.' Very occasionally, however, she'd cut you off a thin strip of candied peel.

I used to like to watch Mother rolling pastry. There's always a fascination in watching anybody do a job which he really understands. Watch a woman—a woman who really knows how to cook, I mean—rolling dough. She's got a peculiar, solemn, indrawn air, a satisfied kind of air, like a priestess celebrating a sacred rite. And in her own mind, of course, that's exactly what she is. Mother had thick, pink, strong forearms which were generally mottled with flour. When she was cooking all her movements were wonderfully precise and firm. In her hands egg-whisks and mincers and rolling-pins did exactly what they were meant to do. When you saw her cooking you knew that she was in a world where she belonged, among things she really understood. Except through the Sunday papers and an occasional bit of gossip the outside world didn't really exist for her. Although she read more easily than Father, and unlike him used to read novelettes as well as newspapers, she was unbelievably ignorant. I realised this even by the time I was ten years old. She certainly couldn't have told you whether Ireland was east or west of England, and I doubt whether any time up to the outbreak of the Great War she could have told you who was Prime Minister. Moreover she hadn't the smallest wish to know such things. Later on when I read books about Eastern countries where they practise polygamy, and the secret harems where the women are locked up with black eunuchs mounting guard over them, I used to think how shocked Mother would have been if she'd heard of it. I can almost hear her voice—'Well, now! Shutting their wives up like that! The *idea!*' Not that she'd have known what a eunuch was. But in reality she lived her life in a space that must have been as small and almost as private as the average zenana. Even in our own house there were parts where she never set foot. She never went into the loft behind the yard and very seldom into the shop. I don't think I ever remember her serving a customer. She wouldn't have known where any of the things were kept, and until they were milled into flour she probably didn't know the difference between wheat and oats. Why should she? The shop was Father's business, it was 'the man's work', and even about the money side of it she hadn't very much curiosity. Her job, 'the woman's work', was to look after the house and the meals and the laundry and the children. She'd have had a fit if she'd seen Father or anyone else of the male sex trying to sew on a button for himself.

So far as the meals and so forth went, ours was one of those houses where everything goes like clockwork. Or no, not like clockwork, which suggests something mechanical. It was more like some kind of natural process. You knew that breakfast would be on the table tomorrow morning in much the same way as you knew the sun would rise. All through her life Mother went to bed at nine and got up at five, and she'd have thought it vaguely wicked—sort of decadent and foreign and aristocratic—to keep later hours. Although she didn't mind paying Katie Simmons to take Joe and me out for walks, she would never tolerate the idea of having a woman in to help with the housework. It was her firm belief that a hired woman always sweeps the dirt under the dresser. Our meals were always ready on the tick. Enormous meals—boiled beef and dumplings, roast beef and Yorkshire, boiled mutton and capers, pig's head, apple pie, spotted dog and jam roly-poly—with grace before and after. The old ideas about bringing up children still held good, though they were going out fast. In theory children were still thrashed and put to bed on bread and water, and certainly you were liable to be sent away from table if you made too much noise eating, or choked, or refused something that was 'good for you', or 'answered back'. In practice there wasn't much discipline in our family, and of the two Mother was the firmer. Father, though he was always quoting 'Spare the rod and spoil the child', was really much too weak with us, especially with Joe, who was a hard case from the start. He was always 'going to' give Joe a good hiding, and he used to tell us stories, which I now believe were lies, about the frightful thrashings his own father used to give him with a leather strap, but nothing ever came of it. By the time Joe was twelve he was too strong for Mother to get him across her knee, and after that there was no doing anything with him.

At that time it was still thought proper for parents to say 'don't' to their children all day long. You'd often hear a man boasting that he'd 'thrash the life out of' his son if he caught him smoking, or stealing apples, or robbing a bird's nest. In some families these thrashings actually took place. Old Lovegrove, the saddler, caught his two sons, great lumps aged sixteen and fifteen, smoking in the garden shed and walloped them so that you could hear it all over the town. Lovegrove was a very heavy smoker. The thrash-ings never seemed to have any effect, all boys stole apples, robbed birds' nests and learned to smoke sooner or later, but the idea was still knocking around that children should be treated rough. Practically everything worth doing was forbidden, in theory anyway. According to Mother, everything that a boy ever wants to do was 'dangerous'. Swimming was dangerous, climbing trees was dangerous, and so were sliding, snowballing, hanging on behind carts, using catapults and squailers and even fishing. All animals were dangerous, except Nailer, the two cats and Jackie the bullfinch. Every animal had its special recognised method of attacking you. Horses bit, bats got into your hair, earwigs got into your ears, swans broke your leg with a blow of their wings, bulls tossed you and snakes 'stung'. All snakes stung, according to Mother, and when I quoted the penny encyclopedia to the effect that they didn't sting but bit, she only told me not to answer back. Lizards, slow-worms, toads, frogs and newts also stung. All insects stung, except flies and blackbeetles. Practically all kinds of food, except the food you had at meals, were either poisonous or 'bad for you'. Raw potatoes were deadly poison, and so were mushrooms unless you bought them at the green-grocer's. Raw gooseberries gave you colic and raw rasp-berries gave you a skin-rash. If you had a bath after a meal you died of cramp, if you cut yourself between the thumb and forefinger you got lockjaw, and if you washed your hands in the water eggs were boiled in you got warts. Nearly everything in the shop was poisonous, which was why Mother had put the gate in the doorway. Cow-cake was poisonous, and so was chicken-corn, and so were mustard seed and Karswood poultry spice. Sweets were bad for you and eating between meals was bad for you, though curiously enough there were certain kinds of eating between meals that Mother always allowed. When she was making plum jam she used to let us eat the syrupy stuff that was skimmed off the top, and we used to gorge ourselves with it till we were sick. Although nearly everything in the world was either dangerous or poisonous, there were certain things that had mysterious virtues. Raw onions were a cure for almost everything. A stocking tied round your neck was a cure for a sore throat. Sulphur in a dog's drinking water acted as a tonic, and old Nailer's bowl behind the back door always had a lump of sulphur in it which stayed there year after year, never dissolving.

We used to have tea at six. By four Mother had generally finished the housework, and between four and six she used to have a quiet cup of tea and 'read her paper', as she called it. As a matter of fact she didn't often read the newspaper except on Sundays. The weekday papers only had the day's news, and it was only occasionally that there was a murder. But the editors of the Sunday papers had grasped that people don't really mind whether their murders are up to date and when there was no new murder on hand they'd hash up an old one, sometimes going as far back as Dr Palmer and Mrs Manning. I think Mother thought of the world outside Lower Binfield chiefly as a place where murders were committed. Murders had a terrible fascination for her, because, as she often said, she just didn't know how people could *be* so wicked. Cutting their wives' throats, burying their fathers under cement floors, throwing babies down wells! How anyone could *do* such things! The Jack the Ripper scare had happened about the time when Father and Mother were married, and the big wooden shutters we used to draw over the shop windows every night dated from then. Shutters for shop windows were going out, most of the shops in the High Street didn't have them, but Mother felt safer behind them. All along, she said, she'd had a dreadful feeling that Jack the Ripper was hiding in Lower Binfield. The Crippen case—but that was years later, when I was almost grown up—upset her badly. I can hear her voice now. 'Cutting his poor wife up and burying her in the coal cellar! The *idea!* What I'd do to that man if I got hold of him!' And curiously enough, when she thought of the dreadful wickedness of that little American doctor who dismembered his wife (and made a very neat job of it by taking all the bones out and chucking the head into the sea, if I remember rightly) the tears actually came into her eyes.

But what she mostly read on weekdays was *Hilda's Home Companion*. In those days it was part of the regular furnishing of any home like ours, and as a matter of fact it still exists, though it's been a bit crowded out by the more streamlined women's papers that have come up since the war. I had a look at a copy only the other day. It's changed, but less than most things. There are still the same enormous serial stories that go on for six months (and it all comes right in the end with orange blossoms to follow), and the same Household Hints, and the same ads. for sewing machines and remedies for bad legs. It's chiefly the print and the illustrations that have changed. In those days the heroine had to look like an egg-timer and now she has to look like a cylinder. Mother was a slow reader and believed in getting her threepennyworth out of *Hilda's Home Companion*. Sitting in the old yellow armchair beside the hearth, with her feet on the iron fender and the little pot of strong tea stewing on the hob, she'd work her way steadily from cover to cover, right through the serial, the two short stories, the Household Hints, the ads. for Zam-Buk and the answers to correspondents. *Hilda's Home Companion* generally lasted her the week out, and some weeks she didn't even finish it. Sometimes the heat of the fire, or the buzzing of the bluebottles on summer afternoons, would send her off into a doze, and at about a quarter to six she'd wake up with a tremendous start, glance at the clock on the mantelpiece and then get into a stew because tea was going to be late. But tea was never late.

In those days—till 1909, to be exact—Father could still afford an errand boy, and he used to leave the shop to him and come into tea with the backs of his hands all mealy. Then Mother would stop cutting slices of bread for a moment and say, 'If you'll give us grace, Father', and Father, while we all bent our heads on our chests, would mumble reverently, 'Fwat we bout to receive—Lord make us truly thankful—Amen.' Later on, when Joe was a bit older, it would be '*You* give us grace today, Joe', and Joe would pipe it out. Mother never said grace: it had to be someone of the male sex.

There were always bluebottles buzzing on summer afternoons. Ours wasn't a sanitary house, precious few houses in Lower Binfield were. I suppose the town must have contained five hundred houses and there certainly can't have been more than ten with bathrooms or fifty with what we should now describe as a w c. In summer our backyard always smelt of dustbins. And all houses had insects in them. We had blackbeetles in the wainscoting and crickets somewhere behind the kitchen range, besides, of course, the meal-worms in the shop. In those days even a house-proud woman like Mother didn't see anything to object to in blackbeetles. They were as much a part of the kitchen as the dresser or the rolling-pin. But there were insects and insects. The houses in the bad street behind the brewery, where Katie Simmons lived, were overrun by bugs. Mother or any of the shopkeepers' wives would have died of shame if they'd had bugs in the house. In fact it was considered proper to say that you didn't even know a bug by sight.

The great blue flies used to come sailing into the larder and sit longingly on the wire covers over the meat. 'Drat the flies!' people used to say, but the flies were an act of God and apart from meat-covers and fly-papers you couldn't do much about them. I said a little while back that the first thing I remember is the smell of sainfoin, but the smell of dustbins is also a pretty early memory. When I think of Mother's kitchen, with the stone floor and the beetle-traps and the steel fender and the blackleaded range, I always seem to hear the bluebottles buzzing and smell the dustbin, and also old Nailer, who carried a pretty powerful smell of dog. And God knows there are worse smells and sounds. Which would you sooner listen to, a bluebottle or a bombing plane?

III

Joe started going to Walton Grammar School two years before I did. Neither of us went there till we were nine. It meant a four-mile bike ride morning and evening, and Mother was scared of allowing us among the traffic, which by that time included a very few motor-cars.

For several years we went to the dame-school kept by old Mrs Howlett. Most of the shopkeepers' children went there, to save them from the shame and come-down of going to the board school, though everyone knew that Mother Howlett was an old impostor and worse than useless as a teacher. She was over seventy, she was very deaf, she could hardly see through her spectacles, and all she owned in the way of equipment was a cane, a blackboard, a few dog-eared grammar books and a couple of dozen smelly slates. She could just manage the girls, but the boys simply laughed at her and played truant as often as they felt like it. Once there was a frightful scandal because a boy put his hand up a girl's dress, a thing I didn't understand at the time. Mother Howlett succeeded in hushing it up. When you did something particularly bad her formula was 'I'll tell your father', and on very rare occasions she did so. But we were quite sharp enough to see that she daren't do it too often, and even when she let out at you with the cane she was so old and clumsy that it was easy to dodge.

Joe was only eight when he got in with a tough gang of boys who called themselves the Black Hand. The leader was Sid Lovegrove, the saddler's younger son, who was about thirteen, and there were two other shopkeepers' sons, an errand boy from the brewery and two farm lads who sometimes managed to cut work and go off with the gang for a couple of hours. The farm lads were great lumps bursting out of corduroy breeches, with very broad accents and rather looked down on by the rest of the gang, but they were tolerated because they knew twice as much about animals as any of the others. One of them, nick-named Ginger, would even catch a rabbit in his hands occasionally. If he saw one lying in the grass he used to fling himself on it like a spread-eagle. There was a big social distinction between the shopkeepers' sons and the sons of labourers and farm-hands, but the local boys didn't usually pay much attention to it till they were about sixteen. The gang had a secret password and an 'ordeal' which included cutting your finger and eating an earthworm, and they gave themselves out to be frightful desperadoes. Certainly they managed to make a nuisance of themselves, broke windows, chased cows, tore the knockers off doors and stole fruit by the hundredweight. Sometimes in winter they managed to borrow a couple of ferrets and go ratting, when the farmers would let them. They all had catapults and squailers, and they were always saving up to buy a saloon pistol, which in those days cost five shillings, but the savings never amounted to more than about threepence. In summer they used to go fishing and bird-nesting. When

Joe was at Mrs Howlett's he used to cut school at least once a week, and even at the Grammar School he managed it about once a fortnight. There was a boy at the Grammar School, an auctioneer's son, who could copy any handwriting and for a penny he'd forge a letter from your mother saying you'd been ill yesterday. Of course I was wild to join the Black Hand, but Joe always choked me off and said they didn't want any blasted kids hanging round.

It was the thought of going fishing that really appealed to me. At eight years old I hadn't yet been fishing, except with a penny net, with which you can sometimes catch a stickleback. Mother was always terrified of letting us go anywhere near water. She 'forbade' fishing, in the way in which parents in those days 'forbade' almost everything, and I hadn't yet grasped that grown-ups can't see round corners. But the thought of fishing sent me wild with excitement. Many a time I'd been past the pool at the Mill Farm and watched the small carp basking on the surface, and sometimes under the willow tree at the corner a great diamond-shaped carp that to my eyes looked enormous— six inches long, I suppose— would suddenly rise to the surface, gulp down a grub and sink again. I'd spent hours gluing my nose against the window of Wallace's in the High Street, where fishing tackle and guns and bicycles were sold. I used to lie awake on summer mornings thinking of the tales Joe had told me about fishing, how you mixed bread paste, how your float gives a bob and plunges under and you feel the rod bending and the fish tugging at the line. Is it any use talking about it, I wonder— the sort of fairy light that fish and fishing tackle have in a kid's eyes? Some kids feel the same about guns and shooting, some feel it about motor-bikes or aeroplanes or horses. It's not a thing that you can explain or rationalise, it's merely magic. One morning—it was in June and I must have been eight—I knew that Joe was going to cut school and go out fishing, and I made up my mind to follow. In some way Joe guessed what I was thinking about, and he started on me while we were dressing.

'Now then, young George! Don't you get thinking you're coming with the gang today. You stay back home.'

'No, I didn't. I didn't think nothing about it.'

'Yes, you did! You thought you were coming with the gang.'

'No, I didn't!'

'Yes, you did!'

'No, I didn't!'

'Yes, you did! You stay back home. We don't want any bloody kids along.'

Joe had just learned the word 'bloody' and was always using it. Father overheard him once and swore that he'd thrash the life out of Joe, but as usual he didn't do so. After breakfast Joe started off on his bike, with his satchel and his Grammar School cap, five minutes early as he always did when he meant to cut school, and when it was time for me to leave for Mother Howlett's I sneaked off and hid in the lane behind the allotments. I knew the gang were going to the pond at the Mill Farm, and I was going to follow them if they murdered me for it. Probably they'd give me a hiding, and probably I wouldn't get home to dinner, and then Mother would know that I'd cut school and I'd get another hiding, but I didn't care. I was just desperate to go fishing with the gang. I was cunning, too. I allowed Joe plenty of time to make a circuit round and get to the Mill Farm by road, and then I followed down the lane and skirted round the meadows on the far side of the hedge, so as to get almost to the pond before the gang saw me. It was a wonderful June morning. The buttercups were up to my knees. There was a breath of wind just stirring the tops of the elms, and the great green clouds of leaves were sort of soft and rich like silk. And it was nine in the morning and I was eight years old, and all round me it was early summer, with great tangled hedges where the wild roses were still in bloom, and bits of soft white cloud drifting overhead, and in the distance the low hills and the dim blue masses of the woods round Upper Binfield. And I didn't give a damn for any of it. All I was thinking of was the green pool and the carp and the gang with their hooks and lines and bread paste. It was as though they were in paradise and I'd got to join them. Presently I managed to sneak up on them—four of them, Joe and Sid Love-grove and the errand boy and another shopkeeper's son, Harry Barnes I think his name was.

Joe turned and saw me. 'Christ!' he said. 'It's the kid.' He walked up to me like a tom-cat that's going to start a fight. 'Now then, you! What'd I tell you? You get back 'ome double quick.'

Both Joe and I were inclined to drop our aitches if we were at all excited. I backed away from him.

'I'm not going back 'ome.'

'Yes you are.'

'Clip his ear, Joe,' said Sid. 'We don't want no kids along.'

'*Are* you going back 'ome?' said Joe.

'No.'

'Righto, my boy! Right-*ho!*'

Then he started on me. The next minute he was chasing me round, catching me one clip after another. But I didn't run away from the pool, I ran in circles. Presently he'd caught me and got me down, and then he knelt on my upper arms and began screwing my ears, which was his favourite torture and one I couldn't stand. I was blubbing by this time, but still I wouldn't give in and promise to go home. I wanted to stay and go fishing with the gang. And suddenly the others swung round in my favour and told

Joe to get up off my chest and let me stay if I wanted to. So I stayed after all.

The others had some hooks and lines and floats and a lump of bread paste in a rag, and we all cut ourselves willow switches from the tree at the corner of the pool. The farmhouse was only about two hundred yards away, and you had to keep out of sight because old Brewer was very down on fishing. Not that it made any difference to him, he only used the pool for watering his cattle, but he hated boys. The others were still jealous of me and kept telling me to get out of the light and reminding me that I was only a kid and knew nothing about fishing. They said that I was making such a noise I'd scare all the fish away, though actually I was making about half as much noise as anyone else there. Finally they wouldn't let me sit beside them and sent me to another part of the pool where the water was shallower and there wasn't so much shade. They said a kid like me was sure to keep splashing the water and frighten the fish away. It was a rotten part of the pool, a part where no fish would ordinarily come. I knew that. I seemed to know by a kind of instinct the places where a fish would lie. Still, I was fishing at last. I was sitting on the grass bank with the rod in my hands, with the flies buzzing round and the smell of wild peppermint fit to knock you down, watching the red float on the green water, and I was happy as a tinker although the tear-marks mixed up with dirt were still all over my face.

Lord knows how long we sat there. The morning stretched out and out, and the sun got higher and higher, and nobody had a bite. It was a hot still day, too clear for fishing. The floats lay on the water with never a quiver. You could see deep down into the water as though you were looking into a kind of dark green glass. Out in the middle of the pool you could see the fish lying just under the surface, sunning themselves, and sometimes in the weeds near the side a newt would come gliding upwards and rest there with his fingers on the weeds and his nose just out of the water. But the fish weren't biting. The others kept shouting that they'd got a nibble, but it was always a lie. And the time stretched out and out and it got hotter and hotter, and the flies ate you alive and the wild peppermint under the bank smelt like Mother Wheeler's sweetshop. I was getting hungrier and hungrier, all the more because I didn't know for certain where my dinner was coming from. But I sat as still as a mouse and never took my eyes off my float. The others had given me a lump of bait about the size of a marble, telling me that would have to do for me, but for a long time I didn't even dare to re-bait my hook, because every time I pulled my line up they swore I was making enough noise to frighten every fish within five miles.

I suppose we must have been there about two hours when suddenly my float gave a quiver. I knew it was a fish. It must have been a fish that was just passing accidentally and saw my bait. There's no mistaking the movement your float gives when it's a real bite. It's quite different from the way it moves when you twitch your line accidentally. The next moment it gave a sharp bob and almost went under. I couldn't hold myself in any longer. I yelled to the others:

'I've got a bite!'

'Rats!' yelled Sid Lovegrove instantly.

But the next moment there wasn't any doubt about it. The float dived straight down, I could still see it under the water, kind of dim red, and I felt the rod tighten in my hand. Christ, that feeling! The line jerking and straining and a fish on the other end of it! The others saw my rod bending, and the next moment they'd all flung their rods down and rushed round to me. I gave a terrific haul and the fish—a great huge silvery fish—came flying up through the air. The same moment all of us gave a yell of agony. The fish had slipped off the hook and fallen into the wild peppermint under the bank. But he'd fallen into shallow water where he couldn't turn over, and for perhaps a second he lay there on his side helpless. Joe flung himself into the water, splashing us all over, and grabbed him in both hands. 'I got 'im!' he yelled. The next moment he'd flung the fish onto the grass and we were all kneeling round it. How we gloated! The poor dying brute flapped up and down and his scales glistened all the colours of the rainbow. It was a huge carp, seven inches long at least, and must have weighed a quarter of a pound. How we shouted to see him! But the next moment it was as though a shadow had fallen across us. We looked up, and there was old Brewer standing over us, with his tall billycock hat—one of those hats they used to wear that were a cross between a top-hat and a bowler—and his cowhide gaiters and a thick hazel stick in his hand.

We suddenly cowered like partridges when there's a hawk overhead. He looked from one to other of us. He had a wicked old mouth with no teeth in it, and since he'd shaved his beard off his chin looked like a nutcracker.

'What are you boys doing here?' he said.

There wasn't much doubt about what we were doing. Nobody answered.

'I'll learn 'ee come fishing in my pool!' he suddenly roared, and the next moment he was on us, whacking out in all directions.

The Black Hand broke and fled. We left all the rods behind and also the fish. Old Brewer chased us half across the meadow. His legs were stiff and he couldn't move fast, but he got in some good swipes before we were out of his reach. We left him in the middle of the field, yelling after us that he knew all our names and was going to tell our fathers. I'd been at the back and most of the wallops had landed on me. I had some nasty red weals on the calves of my legs when we got to the other side of the hedge.

I spent the rest of the day with the gang. They hadn't made up their mind whether I was really a member yet, but for the time being they tolerated me. The errand boy, who'd had the morning off on some lying pretext or other, had to go back to the brewery. The rest of us went for a long, meandering, scrounging kind of walk, the sort of walk that boys go for when they're away from home all day, and especially when they're away without permission. It was the first real boy's walk I'd had, quite different from the walks we used to go with Katie Simmons. We had our dinner in a dry ditch on the edge of the town, full of rusty cans and wild fennel. The others gave me bits of their dinner, and Sid Lovegrove had a penny, so someone fetched a Penny Monster which we had between us. It was very hot, and the fennel smelt very strong, and the gas of the Penny Monster made us belch. Afterwards we wandered up the dusty white road to Upper Binfield, the first time I'd been that way, I believe, and into the beech woods with the carpets of dead leaves and the great smooth trunks that soar up into the sky so that the birds in the upper branches look like dots. You could go wherever you liked in the woods in those days. Binfield House was shut up, they didn't preserve the pheasants any longer, and at the worst you'd only meet a carter with a load of wood. There was a tree that had been sawn down, and the rings on the trunk looked like a target, and we had shots at it with stones. Then the others had shots at birds with their catapults, and Sid Lovegrove swore he'd hit a chaffinch and it had stuck in a fork of the tree. Joe said he was lying, and they argued and almost fought. Then we went down into a chalk hollow full of beds of dead leaves and shouted to hear the echo. Someone shouted a dirty word, and then we said over all the dirty words we knew, and the others jeered at me because I only knew three. Sid Lovegrove said he knew how babies were born and it was just the same as rabbits except that the baby came out of the woman's navel. Harry Barnes started to carve the word —— on a beech tree, but got fed up with it after the first two letters. Then we went round by the lodge of Binfield House. There was a rumour that somewhere in the grounds there was a pond with enormous fish in it, but no one ever dared go inside because old Hodges, the lodge-keeper who acted as a kind of caretaker, was 'down' on boys. He was digging in his vegetable garden by the lodge when we passed. We cheeked him over the fence until he chased us off, and then we went down to the Walton Road and cheeked the carters, keeping on the other side of the hedge so that they couldn't reach us with their whips. Beside the Walton Road there was a place that had been a quarry and then a rubbish dump, and finally had got overgrown with black-berry bushes. There were great mounds of rusty old tin cans and bicycle frames and saucepans with holes in them and broken bottles with weeds growing all over them, and we spent nearly an hour and got ourselves filthy from head to foot routing out iron fence posts, because Harry Barnes swore that the blacksmith in Lower Binfield would pay sixpence a hundredweight for old iron. Then Joe found a late thrush's nest with half-fledged chicks in it in a black-berry bush. After a lot of argument about what to do with them we took the chicks out, had shots at them with stones and finally stamped on them. There were four of them, and we each had one to stamp on. It was getting on towards tea-time now. We knew that old Brewer would be as good as his word and there was a hiding ahead of us, but we were getting too hungry to stay out much longer. Finally we trailed home, with one more row on the way, because when we were passing the allotments we saw a rat and chased it with sticks, and old Bennet the station-master, who worked at his allotment every night and was very proud of it, came after us in a tearing rage because we'd trampled on his onion-bed.

I'd walked ten miles and I wasn't tired. All day I'd trailed after the gang and tried to do everything they did, and they'd called me 'the kid' and snubbed me as much as they could, but I'd more or less kept my end up. I had a wonderful feeling inside me, a feeling you can't know about unless you've had it—but if you're a man you'll have had it some time. I knew that I wasn't a kid any longer, I was a boy at last. And it's a wonderful thing to be a boy, to go roaming where grown-ups can't catch you, and to chase rats and kill birds and shy stones and cheek carters and shout dirty words. It's a kind of strong, rank feeling, a feeling of knowing everything and fearing nothing, and it's all bound up with breaking rules and killing things. The white dusty roads, the hot sweaty feeling of one's clothes, the smell of fennel and wild peppermint, the dirty words, the sour stink of the rubbish dump, the taste of fizzy lemonade and the gas that made one belch, the stamping on the young birds, the feel of the fish straining on the line—it was all part of it. Thank God I'm a man, because no woman ever has that feeling.

Sure enough, old Brewer had sent round and told everybody. Father looked very glum, fetched a strap out of the shop and said he was going to 'thrash the life out of' Joe. But Joe struggled and yelled and kicked, and in the end Father didn't get in more than a couple of whacks at him. However, he got a caning from the headmaster of the Grammar School next day. I tried to struggle too, but I was small enough for Mother to get me across her knee, and she gave me what-for with the strap. So I'd had three hidings that day, one from Joe, one from old Brewer and one from Mother. Next day the gang decided that I wasn't really a member yet and that I'd got to go through the 'ordeal' (a word they'd got out of the Red Indian stories) after all. They were very strict in insisting that you had to bite the worm before you swallowed it. Moreover, because I was the youngest and they were jealous of me for being the only one to catch anything, they all made out afterwards that the fish I'd caught wasn't really a big one. In a general way the tendency of fish, when people talk about them, is to get bigger and bigger, but this one got smaller and smaller, until to hear the others talk you'd have thought it was no bigger than a minnow.

But it didn't matter. I'd been fishing. I'd seen the float dive under the water and felt the fish tugging at the line, and however many lies they told they couldn't take that away from me.

IV

For the next seven years, from when I was eight to when I was fifteen, what I chiefly remember is fishing.

Don't think that I did nothing else. It's only that when you look back over a long period of time, certain things seem to swell up till they overshadow everything else. I left Mother Howlett's and went to the Grammar School, with a leather satchel and a black cap with yellow stripes, and got my first bicycle and a long time afterwards my first long trousers. My first bike was a fixed-wheel—free-wheel bikes were very expensive then. When you went downhill you put your feet up on the front rests and let the pedals go whizzing round. That was one of the characteristic sights of the early nineteen hundreds—a boy sailing downhill with his head back and his feet up in the air. I went to the Grammar School in fear and trembling, because of the frightful tales Joe had told me about old Whiskers (his name was Wicksey) the headmaster, who was certainly a dreadful-looking little man, with a face just like a wolf, and at the end of the big schoolroom he had a glass case with canes in it, which he'd sometimes take out and swish through the air in a terrifying manner. But to my surprise I did rather well at school. It had never occurred to me that I might be cleverer than Joe, who was two years older than me and had bullied me ever since he could walk. Actually Joe was an utter dunce, got the cane about once a week and stayed somewhere near the bottom of the school till he was sixteen. My second term I took a prize in arithmetic and another in some queer stuff that was mostly concerned with pressed flowers and went by the name of Science, and by the time I was fourteen Whiskers was talking about scholarships and Reading University. Father, who had ambitions for Joe and me in those days, was very anxious that I should go to 'college'. There was an idea floating round that I was to be a schoolteacher and Joe was to be an auctioneer.

But I haven't many memories connected with school. When I've mixed with chaps from the upper classes, as I did during the war, I've been struck by the fact that they never really get over that frightful drilling they go through at public schools. Either it flattens them out into half-wits or they spend the rest of their lives kicking against it. It wasn't so with boys of our class, the sons of shopkeepers and farmers. You went to the Grammar School and you stayed there till you were sixteen, just to show that you weren't a prole, but school was chiefly a place that you wanted to get away from. You'd no sentiment of loyalty, no goofy feeling about the old grey stones (and they *were* old, right enough, the school had been founded by Cardinal Wolsey), and there was no Old Boys' tie and not even a school song. You had your half-holidays to yourself, because games weren't compulsory and as often as not you cut them. We played football in braces, and though it was considered proper to play cricket in a belt, you wore your ordinary shirt and trousers. The only game I really cared about was the stump cricket we used to play in the gravel yard during the break, with a bat made out of a bit of packing case and a compo ball.

But I remember the smell of the big schoolroom, a smell of ink and dust and boots, and the stone in the yard that had been a mounting block and was used for sharpening knives on, and the little baker's shop opposite where they sold a kind of Chelsea bun, twice the size of the Chelsea buns you get nowadays, which were called Lardy Busters and cost a halfpenny. I did all the things you do at school. I carved my name on a desk and got the cane for it—you were always caned for it if you were caught, but it was the etiquette that you had to carve your name. And I got inky fingers and bit my nails and made darts out of penholders and played conkers and passed round dirty stories and learned to masturbate and cheeked old Blowers, the English master, and bullied the life out of little Willy Simeon, the undertaker's son, who was half-witted and believed everything you told him. Our favourite trick was to send him to shops to buy things that didn't exist. All the old gags—the ha'porth of penny stamps, the rubber hammer, the left-handed screwdriver, the pot of striped paint—poor Willy fell for all of them. We had grand sport one afternoon, putting him in a tub and telling him to lift himself up by the handles. He ended up in an asylum, poor Willy. But it was in the holidays that one really lived.

There were good things to do in those days. In winter we used to borrow a couple of ferrets—Mother would never let Joe and me keep them at home, 'nasty smelly things' she called them—and go round the farms and ask leave to do a bit of ratting. Sometimes they let us, sometimes they told us to hook it and said we were more trouble than the rats. Later in winter we'd follow the threshing machine and help kill the rats when they threshed the stacks. One winter, 1908 it must have been, the Thames flooded and then froze and there was skating for weeks on end, and Harry Barnes broke his collar-bone on the ice. In early spring we went after squirrels with squailers, and later on we went birdnesting. We had a theory that birds can't count and it's all right if you leave one egg, but we were cruel little beasts and sometimes we'd just knock the nest down and trample on the eggs or chicks. There was another game we had when the toads were spawning. We used to catch toads, ram the nozzle of a bicycle pump up their backsides and blow them up till they burst. That's what boys are like, I don't know why. In summer we used to bike over to Burford Weir and bathe. Wally Lovegrove, Sid's young cousin, was drowned in 1906. He got tangled in the weeds at the bottom, and when the drag-hooks brought his body to the surface his face was jet black.

But fishing was the real thing. We went many a time to old Brewer's pool, and took tiny carp and tench out of it, and once a whopping eel, and there were other cow-ponds that had fish in them and were within walking distance on Saturday afternoons. But after we got bicycles we started fishing in the Thames below Burford Weir. It seemed more grown-up than fishing in cow-ponds. There were no farmers chasing you away, and there are some thumping fish in the Thames—though, so far as I know, nobody's ever been known to catch one.

It's queer, the feeling I had for fishing—and still have, really. I can't call myself a fisherman. I've never in my life caught a fish two feet long, and it's thirty years now since I've had a rod in my hands. And yet when I look back the whole of my boyhood from eight to fifteen seems to have revolved round the days when we went fishing. Every detail has stuck clear in my memory. I can remember individual days and individual fish, there isn't a cow-pond or a backwater that I can't see a picture of if I shut my eyes and think. I could write a book on the technique of fishing. When we were kids we didn't have much in the way of tackle, it cost too much and most of our threepence a week (which was the usual pocket-money in those days) went on sweets and Lardy Busters. Very small kids generally fish with a bent pin, which is too blunt to be much use, but you can make a pretty good hook (though of course it's got no barb) by bending a needle in a candle flame with a pair of pliers. The farm lads knew how to plait horsehair so that it was almost as good as gut, and you can take a small fish on a single horsehair. Later we got to having two-shilling fishing-rods and even reels of sorts. God, what hours I've spent gazing into Wallace's window! Even the .410 guns and saloon pistols didn't thrill me so much as the fishing tackle. And the copy of Gamage's catalogue that I picked up somewhere, on a rubbish dump I think, and studied as though it had been the Bible! Even now I could give you all the details about gut-substitute and gimp and Limerick hooks and priests and disgorgers and Notting-ham reels and God knows how many other technicalities.

Then there were the kinds of bait we used to use. In our shop there were always plenty of mealworms, which were good but not very good. Gentles were better. You had to beg them off old Gravitt, the butcher, and the gang used to draw lots or do ena-mena-mina-mo to decide who should go and ask, because Gravitt wasn't usually too pleasant about it. He was a big, rough-faced old devil with a voice like a mastiff, and when he barked, as he generally did when speaking to boys, all the knives and steels on his blue apron would give a jangle. You'd go in with an empty treacle-tin in your hand, hang round till any customers had disappeared and then say very humbly:

'Please, Mr Gravitt, y'got any gentles today?'

Generally he'd roar out: 'What! Gentles! Gentles in my

71

shop! Ain't seen such a thing in years. Think I got blow-flies in my shop?'

He had, of course. They were everywhere. He used to deal with them with a strip of leather on the end of a stick, with which he could reach out to enormous distances and smack a fly into paste. Sometimes you had to go away without any gentles, but as a rule he'd shout after you just as you were going:

' 'Ere! Go round the backyard an' 'ave a look. P'raps you might find one or two if you looked careful.'

You used to find them in little clusters everywhere. Gravitt's backyard smelt like a battlefield. Butchers didn't have refrigerators in those days. Gentles live longer if you keep them in sawdust.

Wasp grubs are good, though it's hard to make them stick on the hook, unless you bake them first. When someone found a wasps' nest we'd go out at night and pour turpentine down it and plug up the hole with mud. Next day the wasps would all be dead and you could dig out the nest and take the grubs. Once something went wrong, the turps missed the hole or something, and when we took the plug out the wasps, which had been shut up all night, came out all together with a zoom. We weren't very badly stung, but it was a pity there was no one standing by with a stop-watch. Grasshoppers are about the best bait there is, especially for chub. You stick them on the hook without any shot and just flick them to and fro on the surface—'dapping', they call it. But you can never get more than two or three grasshoppers at a time. Greenbottle flies, which are also damned difficult to catch, are the best bait for dace, especially on clear days. You want to put them on the hook alive, so that they wriggle. A chub will even take a wasp, but it's a ticklish job to put a live wasp on the hook.

God knows how many other baits there were. Bread

paste you make by squeezing water through white bread in a rag. Then there are cheese paste and honey paste and paste with aniseed in it. Boiled wheat isn't bad for roach. Redworms are good for gudgeon. You find them in very old manure heaps. And you also find another kind of worm called a brandling, which is striped and smells like an earwig, and which is very good bait for perch. Ordinary earthworms are good for perch. You have to put them in moss to keep them fresh and lively. If you try to keep them in earth they die. Those brown flies you find on cow-dung are pretty good for roach. You can take a chub on a cherry, so they say, and I've seen a roach taken with a currant out of a bun.

In those days, from the sixteenth of June (when the coarse-fishing season starts) till mid-winter I wasn't often without a tin of worms or gentles in my pocket. I had some fights with Mother about it, but in the end she gave in, fishing came off the list of forbidden things and Father even gave me a two-shilling fishing-rod for Christmas in 1903. Joe was barely fifteen when he started going after girls, and from then on he seldom came out fishing, which he said was a kid's game. But there were about half a dozen others who were as mad on fishing as I was. Christ, those fishing days! The hot sticky afternoons in the big schoolroom when I've sprawled across my desk, with old Blowers's voice grating away about predicates and subjunctives and relative clauses, and all that's in my mind is the backwater near Burford Weir and the green pool under the willows with the dace gliding to and fro. And then the terrific rush on bicycles after tea, up Chamford Hill and down to the river to get in an hour's fishing before dark. The still summer evening, the faint splash of the weir, the rings on the water where the fish are rising, the midges eating you alive, the shoals of dace swarming round your hook and never biting. And the kind of passion with which you'd watch the black backs of the fish swarming round, hoping and praying (yes, literally praying) that one of them would change his mind and grab your bait before it got too dark. And then it was always 'Let's have five minutes more', and then 'Just five minutes more', until in the end you had to walk your bike into the town because Towler, the copper, was prowling round and you could be 'had up' for riding without a light. And the times in the summer holidays when we went out to make a day of it with boiled eggs and bread and butter and a bottle of lemonade, and fished and bathed and then fished again and did occasionally catch something. At night you'd come home with filthy hands and so hungry that you'd eaten what was left of your bread paste, with three or four smelly dace wrapped up in your handkerchief. Mother always refused to cook the fish I brought home. She would never allow that river fish were edible, except trout and salmon. 'Nasty muddy things', she called them. The fish I remember best of all are the ones I didn't catch. Especially the monstrous fish you always used to see when you went for a walk along the towpath on Sunday afternoons and hadn't a rod with you. There was no fishing on Sundays, even the Thames Conservancy Board didn't allow it. On Sundays you had to go for what was called a 'nice walk' in your thick black suit and the Eton collar that sawed your head off. It was on a Sunday that I saw a pike a yard long asleep in shallow water by the bank and nearly got him with a stone. And sometimes in the green pools on the edge of the reeds you'd see a huge Thames trout go sailing past. The trout grow to vast sizes in the Thames, but they're practically never caught. They say that one of the real Thames fishermen, the old bottle-nosed blokes that you see muffled up in overcoats on camp-stools with twenty-foot roach-poles at all seasons of the year, will willingly give up a year of his life to catching a Thames trout. I don't blame them, I see their point entirely, and still better I saw it then.

Of course other things were happening. I grew three inches in a year, got my long trousers, won some prizes at school, went to confirmation classes, told dirty stories, took to reading and had crazes for white mice, fretwork and postage stamps. But it's always fishing that I remember. Summer days, and the flat water-meadows and the blue hills in the distance, and the willows up the backwater and the pools underneath like a kind of deep green glass. Summer evenings, the fish breaking the water, the night-jars hawking round your head, the smell of night-stocks and latakia. Don't mistake what I'm talking about. It's not that I'm trying to put across any of that poetry of childhood stuff. I know that's all baloney. Old Porteous (a friend of mine, a retired schoolmaster, I'll tell you about him later) is great on the poetry of childhood. Sometimes he reads me stuff about it out of books. Wordsworth. Lucy Gray. There was a time when meadow, grove and all that. Needless to say he's got no kids of his own. The truth is that kids aren't in any way poetic, they're merely savage little animals, except that no animal is a quarter as selfish. A boy isn't interested in meadows, groves and so forth. He never looks at a landscape, doesn't give a damn for flowers, and unless they affect him in some way, such as being good to eat, he doesn't know one plant from another. Killing things—that's about as near to poetry as a boy gets. And yet all the while there's that peculiar intensity, the power of longing for things as you can't long when you're grown up, and the feeling that time stretches out and out in front of you and that whatever you're doing you could go on for ever.

I was rather an ugly little boy, with butter-coloured hair which was always cropped short except for a quiff in front. I don't idealise my childhood, and unlike many people I've

75

no wish to be young again. Most of the things I used to care for would leave me something more than cold. I don't care if I never see a cricket ball again, and I wouldn't give you threepence for a hundredweight of sweets. But I've still got, I've always had, that peculiar feeling for fishing. You'll think it damned silly, no doubt, but I've actually half a wish to go fishing even now, when I'm fat and forty-five and got two kids and a house in the suburbs. Why? Because in a manner of speaking I *am* sentimental about my childhood—not my own particular childhood, but the civilisation which I grew up in and which is now, I suppose, just about at its last kick. And fishing is somehow typical of that civilisation. As soon as you think of fishing you think of things that don't belong to the modern world. The very idea of sitting all day under a willow tree beside a quiet pool—and being able to find a quiet pool to sit beside—belongs to the time before the war, before the radio, before aeroplanes, before Hitler. There's a kind of peacefulness even in the names of English coarse fish. Roach, rudd, dace, bleak, barbel, bream, gudgeon, pike, chub, carp, tench. They're solid kind of names. The people who made them up hadn't heard of machine-guns, they didn't live in terror of the sack or spend their time eating aspirins, going to the pictures and wondering how to keep out of the concentration camp.

Does anyone go fishing nowadays, I wonder? Anywhere within a hundred miles of London there are no fish left to catch. A few dismal fishing-clubs plant themselves in rows along the banks of canals, and millionaires go trout-fishing in private waters round Scotch hotels, a sort of snobbish game of catching hand-reared fish with artificial flies. But who fishes in mill-streams or moats or cowponds any longer? Where are the English coarse fish now? When I was a kid every pond and stream had fish in it. Now all the ponds are drained, and when the streams aren't poisoned with chemicals from factories they're full of rusty tins and motor-bike tyres.

My best fishing-memory is about some fish that I never caught. That's usual enough, I suppose.

When I was about fourteen Father did a good turn of some kind to old Hodges, the caretaker at Binfield House. I forget what it was—gave him some medicine that cured his fowls of the worms, or something. Hodges was a crabby old devil, but he didn't forget a good turn. One day a little while afterwards when he'd been down to the shop to buy chicken-corn he met me outside the door and stopped me in his surly way. He had a face like something carved out of a bit of root, and only two teeth, which were dark brown and very long.

'Hey, young 'un! Fisherman, ain't you?'

'Yes.'

'Thought you was. You listen, then. If so be you wanted to, you could bring your line and have a try in that they pool up ahind the Hall. There's plenty bream and jack in there. But don't you tell no one as I told you. And don't you go for to bring any of them other young whelps, or I'll beat the skin off their backs.'

Having said this he hobbled off with his sack of corn over his shoulder, as though feeling that he'd said too much already. The next Saturday afternoon I biked up to Binfield House with my pockets full of worms and gentles, and looked for old Hodges at the lodge. At that time Binfield House had already been empty for ten or twenty years. Mr Farrel, the owner, couldn't afford to live in it and either couldn't or wouldn't let it. He lived in London on the rent of his farms and let the house and grounds go to the devil. All the fences were green and rotting, the park was a mass of nettles, the plantations were like a jungle and even the gardens had gone back to meadow, with only a few old gnarled rose-bushes to show you where the beds had been. But it was a very beautiful house, especially from a distance. It was a great white place with colonnades and long-shaped windows, which had been built, I suppose, about Queen Anne's time by someone who'd travelled in Italy. If I went there now I'd probably get a certain kick out of wandering round the general desolation and thinking about the life that used to go on there, and the people who built such places because they imagined that the good days would last for ever. As a boy I didn't give either the house or the grounds a second look. I dug out old Hodges, who'd just finished his dinner and was a bit surly, and got him to show me the way down to the pool. It was several hundred yards behind the house and completely hidden in the beech woods, but it was a good-sized pool, almost a lake, about a hundred and fifty yards across. It was astonishing, and even at that age it astonished me, that there, a dozen miles from Reading and not fifty from London, you could have such solitude. You felt as much alone as if you'd been on the banks of the Amazon. The pool was ringed completely round by the enormous beech trees, which in one place came down to the edge and were reflected in the water. On the other side there was a patch of grass where there was a hollow with beds of wild peppermint, and up at one end of the pool an old wooden boathouse was rotting among the bulrushes.

The pool was swarming with bream, small ones, about four to six inches long. Every now and again you'd see one of them turn half over and gleam reddy-brown under the water. There were pike there too, and they must have been big ones. You never saw them, but sometimes one that was basking among the weeds would turn over and plunge with a splash that was like a brick being bunged into the water. It was no use trying to catch them, though of course I always tried every time I went there. I tried them with dace and minnows I'd caught in the Thames and kept alive in a jam-jar, and even with a spinner made out of a bit of tin. But they were gorged with fish and wouldn't bite, and in any case they'd have broken any tackle I possessed. I never came back from the pool without at least a dozen small bream. Sometimes in the summer holidays I went there for a whole day, with my fishing-rod and a copy of *Chums* or the *Union Jack* or something, and a hunk of bread and cheese which Mother had wrapped up for me. And I've fished for hours and then lain in the grass hollow and read the *Union Jack*, and then the smell of my bread paste and the plop of a fish jumping somewhere would send me wild again, and I'd go back to the water and have another go, and so on all through a summer's day. And the best of all was to be alone, utterly alone, though the road wasn't a quarter of a mile away. I was just old enough to know that it's good to be alone occasionally. With the trees all round you it was as though the pool belonged to you, and nothing ever stirred except the fish ringing the water and the pigeons passing overhead. And yet, in the two years or so that I went fishing there, how many times did I really go, I wonder? Not more than a dozen. It was a three-mile bike ride from home and took up a whole afternoon at least. And sometimes other things turned up, and sometimes when I'd meant to go it rained. You know the way things happen.

One afternoon the fish weren't biting and I began to explore at the end of the pool furthest from Binfield House. There was a bit of an overflow of water and the ground was boggy, and you had to fight your way through a sort of jungle of blackberry bushes and rotten boughs that had fallen off the trees. I struggled through it for about fifty yards, and then suddenly there was a clearing and I came to another pool which I had never known existed. It was a small pool not more than twenty yards wide, and rather dark because of the boughs that overhung it. But it was very clear water and immensely deep. I could see ten or fifteen feet down into it. I hung about for a bit, enjoying the dampness and the rotten boggy smell, the way a boy does. And then I saw something that almost made me jump out of my skin.

It was an enormous fish. I don't exaggerate when I say it was enormous. It was almost the length of my arm. It glided across the pool, deep under water, and then became a shadow and disappeared into the darker water on the other side. I felt as if a sword had gone through me. It was far the biggest fish I'd ever seen, dead or alive. I stood there without breathing, and in a moment another huge thick shape glided through the water, and then another and then two more close together. The pool was full of them. They were carp, I suppose. Just possibly they were bream or tench, but more probably carp. Bream or tench wouldn't grow so huge. I knew what had happened. At some time this pool had been connected with the other, and then the stream had dried up and the woods had closed round the small pool and it had just been forgotten. It's a thing that happens occasionally. A pool gets forgotten somehow, nobody fishes in it for years and decades and the fish grow to monstrous sizes. The brutes that I was watching might be a hundred years old. And not a soul in the world knew about them except me. Very likely it was twenty years since anyone had so much as looked at the pool, and probably even old Hodges and Mr Farrel's bailiff had forgotten its existence.

Well, you can imagine what I felt. After a bit I couldn't even bear the tantalisation of watching. I hurried back to the other pool and got my fishing things together. It was no use trying for those colossal brutes with the tackle I had. They'd snap it as if it had been a hair. And I couldn't go on fishing any longer for the tiny bream. The sight of the big carp had given me a feeling in my stomach almost as if I was going to be sick. I got onto my bike and whizzed down the hill and home. It was a wonderful secret for a boy to have. There was the dark pool hidden away in the woods and the monstrous fish sailing round it—fish that had never been fished for and would grab the first bait you offered them. It was only a question of getting hold of a line strong enough to hold them. Already I'd made all the arrangements. I'd buy the tackle that would hold them if I had to steal the money out of the till. Somehow, God knew how, I'd get hold of half a crown and buy a length of silk salmon line and some thick gut or gimp and Number 5 hooks, and come back with cheese and gentles and paste and mealworms and brandlings and grasshoppers and every mortal bait a carp might look at. The very next Saturday afternoon I'd come back and try for them.

But as it happened I never went back. One never does go back. I never stole the money out of the till or bought the bit of salmon line or had a try for those carp. Almost immediately afterwards something turned up to prevent me, but if it hadn't been that it would have been something else. It's the way things happen.

I know, of course, that you think I'm exaggerating about the size of those fish. You think, probably, that they were just medium-sized fish (a foot long, say) and that they've swollen gradually in my memory. But it isn't so. People tell lies about the fish they've caught and still more about the fish that are hooked and get away, but I never caught any of these or even tried to catch them, and I've no motive for lying. I tell you they were enormous.

V

Fishing!

Here I'll make a confession, or rather two. The first is
that when I look back through my life I can't honestly say
that anything I've ever done has given me quite such a kick
as fishing. Everything else has been a bit of a flop in
comparison, even women. I don't set up to be one of those
men that don't care about women. I've spent plenty of
time chasing them, and I would even now if I had the
chance. Still, if you gave me the choice of having any
woman you care to name, but I mean *any* woman, or
catching a ten-pound carp, the carp would win every time.
And the other confession is that after I was sixteen I never
fished again.

Why? Because that's how things happen. Because in this
life we lead—I don't mean human life in general, I mean
life in this particular age and this particular country—we
don't do the things we want to do. It isn't because we're
always working. Even a farm-hand or a Jew tailor isn't
always working. It's because there's some devil in us that
drives us to and fro on everlasting idiocies. There's time for
everything except the things worth doing. Think of something you really care about. Then add hour to hour and
calculate the fraction of your life that you've actually spent
in doing it. And then calculate the time you've spent on
things like shaving, riding to and fro on buses, waiting in
railway junctions, swapping dirty stories and reading the
newspapers.

After I was sixteen I didn't go fishing again. There never
seemed to be time. I was at work, I was chasing girls, I was
wearing my first button boots and my first high collars
(and for the collars of 1909 you needed a neck like a giraffe),
I was doing correspondence courses in salesmanship and
accountancy and 'improving my mind'. The great fish

were gliding round in the pool behind Binfield House. Nobody knew about them except me. They were stored away in my mind; some day, some bank holiday perhaps, I'd go back and catch them. But I never went back. There was time for everything except that. Curiously enough, the only time between then and now when I did very nearly go fishing was during the war.

It was in the autumn of 1916, just before I was wounded. We'd come out of trenches to a village behind the line, and though it was only September we were covered with mud from head to foot. As usual we didn't know for certain how long we were going to stay there or where we were going afterwards. Luckily the CO was a bit off-colour, a touch of bronchitis or something, and so didn't bother about driving us through the usual parades, kit-inspections, football matches and so forth which were supposed to keep up the spirits of the troops when they were out of the line. We spent the first day sprawling about on piles of chaff in the barns where we were billeted and scraping the mud off our putties, and in the evening some of the chaps started queueing up for a couple of wretched worn-out whores who were established in a house at the end of the village. In the morning, although it was against orders to leave the village, I managed to sneak off and wander round the ghastly desolation that had once been fields. It was a damp, wintry kind of morning. All round, of course, was the awful muck and litter of war, the sort of filthy sordid mess that's actually worse than a battlefield of corpses. Trees with boughs torn off them, old shell-holes that had partly filled up again, tin cans, turds, mud, weeds, clumps of rusty barbed wire with weeds growing through them. You know the feeling you had when you came out of the line. A stiffened feeling in all your joints, and inside you a kind of emptiness, a feeling that you'd never again have any interest in anything. It was partly fear and exhaustion but mainly boredom. At that time no one saw any reason why the war shouldn't go on for ever. Today or tomorrow or the day after you were going back to the line, and maybe next week a shell would blow you to potted meat, but that wasn't so bad as the ghastly boredom of the war stretching out for ever.

I was wandering up the side of a hedge when I ran into a chap in our company whose surname I don't remember but who was nicknamed Nobby. He was a dark, slouching, gypsy-looking chap, a chap who even in uniform always gave the impression that he was carrying a couple of stolen rabbits. By trade he was a coster and he was a real Cockney, but one of those Cockneys that make part of their living by hop-picking, bird-catching, poaching and fruit-stealing in Kent and Essex. He was a great expert on dogs, ferrets, cage-birds, fighting-cocks and that kind of thing. As soon as he saw me he beckoned to me with his head. He had a sly, vicious way of talking:

' 'Ere, George!' (The chaps still called me George—I hadn't got fat in those days.) 'George! Ja see that clump of poplars acrost the field?'

'Yes.'

'Well, there's a pool on t'other side of it, and it's full of bleeding great fish.'

'Fish? Garn!'

'I tell you it's bleeding full of 'em. Perch, they are. As good fish as ever I got my thumbs on. Com'n see f'yerself, then.'

We trudged over the mud together. Sure enough, Nobby was right. On the other side of the poplars there was a dirty-looking pool with sandy banks. Obviously it had been a quarry and had got filled up with water. And it was swarming with perch. You could see their dark-blue stripy backs gliding everywhere just under water, and some of them must have weighed a pound. I suppose in

84

two years of war they hadn't been disturbed and had had time to multiply. Probably you can't imagine what the sight of those perch had done to me. It was as though they'd suddenly brought me to life. Of course there was only one thought in both our minds—how to get hold of a rod and line.

'Christ!' I said. 'We'll have some of those.'

'You bet we f—— well will. C'mon back to the village and let's get 'old of some tackle.'

'OK. You want to watch out, though. If the sergeant gets to know we'll cop it.'

'Oh, f—— the sergeant. They can 'ang, drore and quarter me if they want to. I'm going to 'ave some of them bleeding fish.'

You can't know how wild we were to catch those fish. Or perhaps you can, if you've ever been at war. You know the frantic boredom of war and the way you'll clutch at almost any kind of amusement. I've seen two chaps in a dugout fight like devils over half of a threepenny magazine. But there was more to it than that. It was the thought of escaping, for perhaps a whole day, right out of the atmosphere of war. To be sitting under the poplar trees, fishing for perch, away from the Company, away from the noise and the stink and the uniforms and the officers and the saluting and the sergeant's voice! Fishing is the opposite of war. But it wasn't at all certain that we could bring it off. That was the thought that sent us into a kind of fever. If the sergeant found out he'd stop us as sure as fate, and so would any of the officers, and the worst of all was that there was no knowing how long we were going to stay at the village. We might stay there a week, we might march off in two hours. Meanwhile we'd no fishing tackle of any kind, not even a pin or a bit of string. We had to start from scratch. And the pool was swarming with fish! The first thing was a rod. A willow wand is best, but of course there wasn't a willow tree anywhere this side of the horizon. Nobby shinned up one of the poplars and cut off a small bough which wasn't actually good but was better than nothing. He trimmed it down with his jack-knife till it looked something like a fishing-rod, and then we hid it in the weeds near the bank and managed to sneak back into the village without being seen.

The next thing was a needle to make a hook. Nobody had a needle. One chap had some darning needles, but they were too thick and had blunt ends. We daren't let anyone know what we wanted it for, for fear the sergeant should hear about it. At last we thought of the whores at the end of the village. They were pretty sure to have a needle. When we got there—you had to go round to the back door through a mucky courtyard—the house was shut up and the whores were having a sleep which they'd no doubt earned. We stamped and yelled and banged on the door until after about ten minutes a fat ugly woman in a wrapper came down and screamed at us in French. Nobby shouted at her:

'Needle! Needle! You got a needle?'

Of course she didn't know what he was talking about. Then Nobby tried pidgin English, which he expected her as a foreigner to understand:

'Wantee needle! Sewee clothee! Likee thisee!'

He made gestures which were supposed to represent sewing. The whore misunderstood him and opened the door a bit wider to let us in. Finally we made her understand and got a needle from her. By this time it was dinnertime.

After dinner the sergeant came round the barn where we were billeted looking for men for a fatigue. We managed to dodge him just in time by getting under a pile of chaff. When he was gone we got a candle alight, made the needle red-hot and managed to bend it into a kind of hook. We

86

didn't have any tools except jack-knives, and we burned our fingers badly. The next thing was a line. Nobody had any string except thick stuff, but at last we came across a fellow who had a reel of sewing thread. He didn't want to part with it and we had to give him a whole packet of fags for it. The thread was much too thin, but Nobby cut it into three lengths, tied them to a nail in the wall and carefully plaited them. Meanwhile after searching all over the village I'd managed to find a cork, and I cut it in half and stuck a match through it to make a float. By this time it was evening and getting on towards dark.

We'd got the essentials now, but we could do with some gut. There didn't seem much hope of getting any until we thought of the hospital orderly. Surgical gut wasn't part of his equipment, but it was just possible that he might have some. Sure enough, when we asked him, we found he'd a whole hank of medical gut in his haversack. It had taken his fancy in some hospital or other and he'd pinched it. We swapped another packet of fags for ten lengths of gut. It was rotten brittle stuff, in pieces about six inches long. After dark Nobby soaked them till they were pliable and tied them end to end. So now we'd got everything—hook, rod, line, float and gut. We could dig up worms anywhere. And the pool was swarming with fish! Huge great stripy perch crying out to be caught! We lay down to kip in such a fever that we didn't even take our boots off. Tomorrow! If we could just have tomorrow! If the war would forget about us for just a day! We made up our minds that as soon as roll-call was over we'd hook it and stay away all day, even if they gave us Field Punishment No. 1 for it when we came back.

Well, I expect you can guess the rest. At roll-call orders were to pack all kits and be ready to march in twenty minutes. We marched nine miles down the road and then got onto lorries and were shot off to another part of the line. As for the pool under the poplar trees, I never saw or heard of it again. I expect it got poisoned with mustard gas later on.

Since then I've never fished. I never seemed to get the chance. There was the rest of the war, and then like everyone else I was fighting for a job, and then I'd got a job and the job had got me. I was a promising young fellow in an insurance office—one of those keen young businessmen with firm jaws and good prospects that you used to read about in the Clark's College adverts—and then I was the usual down-trodden five-to-ten-pound-a-weeker in a semi-detached villa in the inner-outer suburbs. Such people don't go fishing, any more than stockbrokers go out picking primroses. It wouldn't be suitable. Other recreations are provided for them.

Of course I have my fortnight's holiday every summer. You know the kind of holiday. Margate, Yarmouth, Eastbourne, Hastings, Bournemouth, Brighton. There's a slight variation according to whether or not we're flush that year. With a woman like Hilda along, the chief feature of a holiday is endless mental arithmetic to decide how much the boarding-house keeper is swindling you. That and telling the kids, No, they can't have a new sand-bucket. A few years back we were at Bournemouth. One fine afternoon we loitered down the pier, which must be about half a mile long, and all the way along it chaps were fishing with stumpy sea-rods with little bells on the end and their lines stretching fifty yards out to sea. It's a dull kind of fishing, and they weren't catching anything. Still, they were fishing. The kids soon got bored and clamoured to go back to the beach, and Hilda saw a chap sticking a lobworm on his hook and said it made her feel sick, but I kept loitering up and down for a little while longer. And suddenly there was a tremendous ringing from a bell and a chap was winding in his line. Everyone stopped to watch.

And sure enough, in it came, the wet line and the lump of lead and on the end a great flat-fish (a flounder, I think) dangling and wriggling. The chap dumped it onto the planks of the pier, and it flapped up and down, all wet and gleaming, with its grey warty back and its white belly and the fresh salty smell of the sea. And something kind of moved inside me.

As we moved off I said casually, just to test Hilda's reaction:

'I've half a mind to do a bit of fishing myself while we're here.'

'What! *You* go fishing, George? But you don't even know how, do you?'

'Oh, I used to be a great fisherman,' I told her.

She was vaguely against it, as usual, but didn't have many ideas one way or the other, except that if I went fishing she wasn't coming with me to watch me put those nasty squashy things on the hook. Then suddenly she got onto the fact that if I was to go fishing the set-out that I'd need, rod and reel and so forth, would cost round about a quid. The rod alone would cost ten bob. Instantly she flew into a temper. You haven't seen old Hilda when there's talk of wasting ten bob. She burst out at me:

'The *idea* of wasting all that money on a thing like that! Absurd! And how they *dare* charge ten shillings for one of those silly little fishing-rods! It's disgraceful. And fancy you going fishing at your age! A great big grown-up man like you. Don't be such a *baby*, George.'

Then the kids got onto it. Lorna sidled up to me and asked in that silly pert way she has, 'Are you a baby, Daddy?' and little Billy, who at that time didn't speak quite plain, announced to the world in general, 'Farver's a baby.' Then suddenly they were both dancing round me, rattling their sand-buckets and chanting:

'Far-ver's a baby! Far-ver's a baby!'
Unnatural little bastards!

VI

And besides fishing there was reading.

I've exaggerated if I've given the impression that fishing was the *only* thing I cared about. Fishing certainly came first, but reading was a good second. I must have been either ten or eleven when I started reading—reading voluntarily, I mean. At that age it's like discovering a new world. I'm a considerable reader even now, in fact there aren't many weeks in which I don't get through a couple of novels. I'm what you might call the typical Boots' Library subscriber, I always fall for the best-seller of the moment (*The Good Companions*, *Bengal Lancer*, *Hatter's Castle*—I fell for every one of them), and I've been a member of the Left Book Club for a year or more. And in 1918, when I was twenty-five, I had a sort of debauch of reading that made a certain difference to my outlook. But nothing is ever like those first years when you suddenly discover that you can open a penny weekly paper and plunge straight into thieves' kitchens and Chinese opium dens and Polynesian islands and the forests of Brazil.

It was from when I was eleven to when I was about sixteen that I got my biggest kick out of reading. At first it was always the boys' penny weeklies—little thin papers with vile print and an illustration in three colours on the cover—and a bit later it was books. *Sherlock Holmes*, *Dr Nikola*, *The Iron Pirate*, *Dracula*, *Raffles*. And Nat Gould and Ranger Gull and a chap whose name I forget who wrote boxing stories almost as rapidly as Nat Gould wrote racing ones. I suppose if my parents had been a little better educated I'd have had 'good' books shoved down my throat, Dickens and Thackeray and so forth, and in fact they did drive us through *Quentin Durward* at school and Uncle Ezekiel sometimes tried to incite me to read Ruskin and Carlyle. But there were practically no books in our house. Father had never read a book in his life, except the Bible and Smiles's *Self Help*, and I didn't of my own accord read a 'good' book till much later. I'm not sorry it happened that way. I read the things I wanted to read, and I got more out of them than I ever got out of the stuff they taught me at school.

The old penny dreadfuls were already going out when I was a kid, and I can barely remember them, but there was a regular line of boys' weeklies, some of which still exist. The Buffalo Bill stories have gone out, I think, and Nat Gould probably isn't read any longer, but Nick Carter and Sexton Blake seem to be still the same as ever. The *Gem* and the *Magnet*, if I'm remembering rightly, started about 1905. The *BOP* was still rather pi in those days, but *Chums*, which I think must have started about 1903, was splendid. Then there was an encyclopedia—I don't remember its exact name—which was issued in penny numbers. It never seemed quite worth buying, but a boy at school used to give away back numbers sometimes. If I now know the length of the Mississippi or the difference between an octopus and a cuttle-fish or the exact composition of bell-metal, that's where I learned it from.

Joe never read. He was one of those boys who can go through years of schooling and at the end of it are unable to read ten lines consecutively. The sight of print made him feel sick. I've seen him pick up one of my numbers of *Chums*, read a paragraph or two and then turn away with just the same movement of disgust as a horse when it smells stale hay. He tried to kick me out of reading, but Mother and Father, who had decided that I was 'the clever one', backed me up. They were rather proud that I showed a taste for 'book-learning', as they called it. But it was typical of both of them that they were vaguely upset by my reading things like *Chums* and the *Union Jack*, thought that I ought to read something 'improving' but didn't know enough about books to be sure which books were 'improving'. Finally Mother got hold of a second-hand copy of Foxe's *Book of Martyrs*, which I didn't read, though the illustrations weren't half bad.

All through the winter of 1905 I spent a penny on *Chums* every week. I was following up their serial story, *Donovan the Dauntless*. Donovan the Dauntless was an explorer who was employed by an American millionaire to fetch incredible things from various corners of the earth. Sometimes it was diamonds the size of golf balls from the craters of volcanoes in Africa, sometimes it was petrified mammoths' tusks from the frozen forests of Siberia, sometimes it was buried Inca treasures from the lost cities of Peru. Donovan went on a new journey every week, and he always made good. My favourite place for reading was the loft behind the yard. Except when Father was getting out fresh sacks of grain it was the quietest place in the house. There were huge piles of sacks to lie on, and a sort of plastery smell mixed up with the smell of sainfoin, and bunches of cobwebs in all the corners, and just over the place where I used to lie there was a hole in the ceiling and a lath sticking out of the plaster. I can feel the feeling of it now. A winter day, just warm enough to lie still. I'm lying on my belly with *Chums* open in front of me. A mouse runs up the side of a sack like a clockwork toy, then suddenly stops dead and watches me with his little eyes like tiny jet beads. I'm twelve years old, but I'm Donovan the Dauntless. Two thousand miles up the Amazon I've just pitched my tent, and the roots of the mysterious orchid that blooms once in a hundred years are safe in the tin box under my camp bed. In the forests all round the Hopi-Hopi

Indians, who paint their teeth scarlet and skin white men alive, are beating their war-drums. I'm watching the mouse and the mouse is watching me, and I can smell the dust and sainfoin and the cool plastery smell, and I'm up the Amazon, and it's bliss, pure bliss.

VII

That's all, really.

I've tried to tell you something about the world before the war, the world I got a sniff of when I saw King Zog's name on the poster, and the chances are that I've told you nothing. Either you remember before the war and don't need to be told about it, or you don't remember, and it's no use telling you. So far I've only spoken about the things that happened to me before I was sixteen. Up to that time things had gone pretty well with the family. It was a bit before my sixteenth birthday that I began to get glimpses of what people call 'real life', meaning unpleasantness.

About three days after I'd seen the big carp at Binfield House, Father came in to tea looking very worried and even more grey and mealy than usual. He ate his way solemnly through his tea and didn't talk much. In those days he had a rather preoccupied way of eating, and his moustache used to work up and down with a sidelong movement, because he hadn't many back teeth left. I was just getting up from table when he called me back.

'Wait a minute, George, my boy. I got suthing to say to you. Sit down jest a minute. Mother, you heard what I got to say last night.'

Mother, behind the huge brown teapot, folded her hands in her lap and looked solemn. Father went on, speaking very seriously but rather spoiling the effect by trying to deal with a crumb that had lodged somewhere in what was left of his back teeth:

'George, my boy, I got suthing to say to you. I been thinking it over, and it's about time you left school. 'Fraid you'll have to get to work now and start earning a bit to bring home to your mother. I wrote to Mr Wicksey last night and told him as I should have to take you away.'

Of course this was quite according to precedent—his writing to Mr Wicksey before telling me, I mean. Parents in those days, as a matter of course, always arranged everything over their children's heads.

Father went on to make some rather mumbling and worried explanations. He'd 'had bad times lately', things had 'been a bit difficult', and the upshot was that Joe and I would have to start earning our living. At that time I didn't either know or greatly care whether the business was really in a bad way or not. I hadn't even enough commercial instinct to see the reason why things were 'difficult'. The fact was that Father had been hit by competition. Sarazins', the big retail seedsmen who had branches all over the home counties, had stuck a tentacle into Lower Binfield. Six months earlier they'd taken the lease of a shop in the market-place and dolled it up until what with bright green paint, gilt lettering, gardening tools painted red and green and huge advertisements for sweet peas, it hit you in the eye at a hundred yards' distance. Sarazins', besides selling flower seeds, described themselves as 'universal poultry and livestock providers', and apart from wheat and oats and so forth they went in for patent poultry mixtures, bird-seed done up in fancy packets, dog-biscuits of all shapes and colours, medicines, embrocations and conditioning powders, and branched off into such things as rat-traps, dog-chains, incubators, sanitary eggs, bird-netting, bulbs, weed-killer, insecticide and even, in some branches, into what they called a 'livestock department', meaning rabbits and day-old chicks. Father, with his dusty old shop and his refusal to stock new lines, couldn't compete with that kind of thing and didn't want to. The tradesmen with their van-horses, and such of the farmers as dealt with the retail seedsmen, fought shy of Sarazins', but in six months they'd gathered in the petty gentry of the neighbourhood, who in those days had carriages or dogcarts and therefore horses. This meant a big loss of trade for Father and the other corn merchant, Winkle. I didn't grasp any of this at the time. I had a boy's attitude towards it all. I'd never taken any interest in the business. I'd never or hardly ever served in the shop, and when, as occasionally happened, Father wanted me to run an errand or give a hand with something, such as hoisting sacks of grain up to the loft or down again, I'd always dodged it whenever possible. Boys in our class aren't such complete babies as public schoolboys, they know that work is work and sixpence is sixpence, but it seems natural for a boy to regard his father's business as a bore. Up till that time fishing-rods, bicycles, fizzy lemonade and so forth had seemed to me a good deal more real than anything that happened in the grown-up world.

Father had already spoken to old Grimmett, the grocer, who wanted a smart lad and was willing to take me into the shop immediately. Meanwhile Father was going to get rid of the errand-boy, and Joe was to come home and help with the shop till he got a regular job. Joe had left school some time back and had been more or less loafing ever since. Father had sometimes talked of 'getting him into' the accounts department at the brewery, and earlier had even had thoughts of making him into an auctioneer. Both were completely hopeless because Joe, at seventeen, wrote a hand like a ploughboy and couldn't repeat the multiplication table. At present he was supposed to be 'learning the trade' at a big bicycle shop on the outskirts of Walton.

Tinkering with bicycles suited Joe, who, like most half-wits, had a slight mechanical turn, but he was quite incapable of working steadily and spent all his time loafing about in greasy overalls, smoking Woodbines, getting into fights, drinking (he'd started that already), getting 'talked of' with one girl after another and sticking Father for money. Father was worried, puzzled and vaguely resentful. I can see him yet, with the meal on his bald head, and the bit of grey hair over his ears, and his spectacles and his grey moustache. He couldn't understand what was happening to him. For years his profits had gone up, slowly and steadily, ten pounds this year, twenty pounds that year, and now suddenly they'd gone down with a bump. He couldn't understand it. He'd inherited the business from his father, he'd done an honest trade, worked hard, sold sound goods, swindled nobody—and his profits were going down. He said a number of times, between sucking at his teeth to get the crumb out, that times were very bad, trade seemed very slack, he couldn't think what had come over people, it wasn't as if the horses didn't have to eat. Perhaps it was these here motors, he decided finally. 'Nasty smelly things!' Mother put in. She was a little worried, and knew that she ought to be more so. Once or twice while Father was talking there was a far-away look in her eyes and I could see her lips moving. She was trying to decide whether it should be a round of beef and carrots tomorrow or another leg of mutton. Except when there was something in her own line that needed foresight, such as buying linen or saucepans, she wasn't really capable of thinking beyond tomorrow's meals. The shop was giving trouble and Father was worried—that was about as far as she saw into it. None of us had any grasp of what was happening. Father had had a bad year and lost money, but was he really frightened by the future? I don't think so. This was 1909, remember. He didn't know what was happening to him, he wasn't capable of foreseeing that these Sarazin people would systematically undersell him, ruin him and eat him up. How could he? Things hadn't happened like that when he was a young man. All he knew was that times were bad, trade was very 'slack', very 'slow' (he kept repeating these phrases), but probably things would 'look up presently'.

It would be nice if I could tell you that I was a great help to my father in his time of trouble, suddenly proved myself a man and developed qualities which no one had suspected in me—and so on and so forth, like the stuff you used to read in the uplift novels of thirty years ago. Or alternatively I'd like to be able to record that I bitterly resented having to leave school, my eager young mind, yearning for knowledge and refinement, recoiled from the soulless mechanical job into which they were thrusting me—and so on and so forth, like the stuff you read in the uplift novels today. Both would be complete bunkum. The truth is that I was pleased and excited at the idea of going to work, especially when I grasped that old Grimmett was going to pay me real wages, twelve shillings a week, of which I could keep four for myself. The big carp at Binfield House, which had filled my mind for three days past, faded right out of it. I'd no objection to leaving school a few terms early. It generally happened the same way with boys at our school. A boy was always 'going to' go to Reading University, or study to be an engineer, or 'go into business' in London, or run away to sea—and then suddenly, at two days' notice, he'd disappear from school, and a fortnight later you'd meet him on a bicycle, delivering vegetables. Within five minutes of Father telling me that I should have to leave school I was wondering about the new suit I should wear to go to work in. I instantly started demanding a 'grown-up suit', with a kind of coat that was fashionable at that time, a 'cutaway', I think it was called. Of course both Mother and Father were scandalised and said they'd 'never heard of such a thing'. For some reason that I've never fully fathomed, parents in those days always tried to prevent their children wearing grown-up clothes as long as possible. In every family there was a stand-up fight before a boy had his first tall collars or a girl put her hair up.

So the conversation veered away from Father's business troubles and degenerated into a long, nagging kind of argument, with Father gradually getting angry and repeating over and over—dropping an aitch now and again, as he was apt to do when he got angry—'Well, you can't 'ave it. Make up your mind to that—you can't 'ave it'. So I didn't have my 'cutaway', but went to work for the first time in a ready-made black suit and a broad collar in which I looked an overgrown lout. Any distress I felt over the whole business really arose from that. Joe was even more selfish about it. He was furious at having to leave the bicycle shop, and for the short time that he remained at home he merely loafed about, made a nuisance of himself and was no help to Father whatever.

I worked in old Grimmett's shop for nearly six years. Grimmett was a fine, upstanding, white-whiskered old chap, like a rather stouter version of Uncle Ezekiel, and like Uncle Ezekiel a good Liberal. But he was less of a firebrand and more respected in the town. He'd trimmed his sails during the Boer War, he was a bitter enemy of trade unions and once sacked an assistant for possessing a photograph of Keir Hardie, and he was 'chapel'—in fact he was a big noise, literally, in the Baptist Chapel, known locally as the Tin Tab—whereas my family were 'church' and Uncle Ezekiel was an infidel at that. Old Grimmett was a town councillor and an official of the local Liberal Party. With his white whiskers, his canting talk about liberty of conscience and the Grand Old Man, his thumping bank balance and the extempore prayers you could sometimes hear him letting loose when you passed the Tin Tab, he was a little like the legendary Nonconformist grocer in the story—you've heard it, I expect:

'James!'

'Yessir!'

'Have you sanded the sugar?'

'Yessir!'

'Have you watered the treacle?'

'Yessir!'

'Then come up to prayers.'

God knows how often I heard that story whispered in the shop. We did actually start the day with a prayer before we put up the shutters. Not that old Grimmett sanded the sugar. He knew that that doesn't pay. But he was a sharp man in business, he did all the high-class grocery trade of Lower Binfield and the country round, and he had three assistants in the shop besides the errand-boy, the van-man and his own daughter (he was a widower) who acted as cashier. I was the errand-boy for my first six months. Then one of the assistants left to 'set up' in Reading and I moved into the shop and wore my first white apron. I learned to tie a parcel, pack a bag of currants, grind coffee, work the bacon-slicer, carve ham, put an edge on a knife, sweep the floor, dust eggs without breaking them, pass off an inferior article as a good one, clean a window, judge a pound of cheese by eye, open a packing-case, whack a slab of butter into shape and—what was a good deal the hardest—remember where the stock was kept. I haven't such detailed memories of grocering as I have of fishing, but I remember a good deal. To this day I know the trick of snapping a bit of string in my fingers. If you put me in front of a bacon-slicer I could work it better than I can a typewriter. I could spin you some pretty fair technicalities about grades of China tea and what margarine is made of and the average weight of eggs and the price of paper bags per thousand.

Well, for more than five years that was me—an alert young chap with a round, pink, snubby kind of face and butter-coloured hair (no longer cut short but carefully greased and slicked back in what people used to call a 'smarm'), hustling about behind the counter in a white apron with a pencil behind my ear, tying up bags of coffee like lightning and jockeying the customer along with 'Yes, ma'am! Certainly, ma'am! *And* the next order, ma'am!' in a voice with just a trace of a Cockney accent. Old Grimmett worked us pretty hard, it was an eleven-hour day except on Thursdays and Sundays, and Christmas week was a nightmare. Yet it's a good time to look back on. Don't think that I had no ambitions. I knew I wasn't going to remain a grocer's assistant for ever, I was merely 'learning the trade'. Some time, somehow or other, there'd be enough money for me to 'set up' on my own. That was how people felt in those days. This was before the war, remember, and before the slumps and before the dole. The world was big enough for everyone. Anyone could 'set up in trade', there was always room for another shop. And time was slipping on. 1909, 1910, 1911. King Edward died and the papers came out with a black border round the edge. Two cinemas opened in Walton. The cars got commoner on the roads and cross-country motor-buses began to run. An aeroplane—a flimsy, rickety-looking thing with a chap sitting in the middle on a kind of chair—flew over Lower Binfield and the whole town rushed out of their houses to yell at it. People began to say rather vaguely that this here German Emperor was getting too big for his boots and 'it' (meaning war with Germany) was 'coming some time'. My wages went gradually up, until finally, just before the war, they were twenty-eight shillings a week. I paid Mother ten shillings a week for my board, and later, when times got worse, fifteen shillings, and even that left me feeling richer than I've felt since. I grew another inch, my moustache began to sprout, I wore button boots and collars three inches high. In church on Sundays, in my natty dark-grey suit, with my bowler hat and black dogskin gloves on the pew beside me, I looked the perfect gent, so that Mother could hardly contain her pride in me. In between work and 'walking out' on Thursdays, and thinking about clothes and girls, I had fits of ambition and saw myself developing into a Big Business Man like Lever or William Whiteley. Between sixteen and eighteen I made serious efforts to 'improve my mind' and train myself for a business career. I cured myself of dropping aitches and got rid of most of my Cockney accent. (In the Thames Valley the country accents were going out. Except for the farm lads, nearly everyone who was born later than 1890 talked Cockney.) I did a correspondence course with Littleburns' Commercial Academy, learnt book-keeping and business English, read solemnly through a book of frightful blah called *The Art of Salesmanship*, and improved my arithmetic and even my handwriting. When I was as old as seventeen I've sat up late at night with my tongue hanging out of my mouth, practising copperplate by the little oil-lamp on the bedroom table. At times I read enormously, generally crime and adventure stories, and sometimes paper-covered books which were furtively passed round by the chaps at the shop and described as 'hot'. (They were translations of Maupassant and Paul de Kock.) But when I was eighteen I suddenly turned highbrow, got a ticket for the County Library and began to stodge through books by Marie Corelli and Hall Caine and Anthony Hope. It was at about that time that I joined the Lower Binfield Reading Circle, which was run by the vicar and met one evening a week all through the winter for what was called 'literary discussion'. Under pressure from the vicar I read bits of *Sesame and Lilies* and even had a go at Browning.

And time was slipping away. 1910, 1911, 1912. And Father's business was going down—not slumping suddenly into the gutter, but it was going down. Neither Father nor Mother was ever quite the same after Joe ran away from home. This happened not long after I went to work at Grimmett's.

Joe, at eighteen, had grown into an ugly ruffian. He was a hefty chap, much bigger than the rest of the family, with tremendous shoulders, a big head and a sulky, lowering kind of face on which he already had a respectable moustache. When he wasn't in the tap-room of the George he was loafing in the shop doorway, with his hands dug deep into his pockets, scowling at the people who passed, except when they happened to be girls, as though he'd like to knock them down. If anyone came into the shop he'd move aside just enough to let them pass, and, without taking his hands out of his pockets, yell over his shoulder, 'Da-ad! Shop!' This was as near as he ever got to helping. Father and Mother said despairingly that they 'didn't know what to do with him', and he was costing the devil of a lot with his drinking and endless smoking. Late one night he walked out of the house and was never heard of again. He'd prised open the till and taken all the money that was in it, luckily not much, about eight pounds. That was enough to get him a steerage passage to America. He'd always wanted to go to America, and I think he probably did so, though we never knew for certain. It made a bit of a scandal in the town. The official theory was that Joe had bolted because he'd put a girl in the family way. There was a girl named Sally Chivers who lived in the same street as the Simmonses and was going to have a baby, and Joe had certainly been with her, but so had about a dozen others, and nobody knew whose baby it was. Mother and Father accepted the baby theory and even, in private, used it to excuse their 'poor boy' for stealing the eight pounds and running away. They weren't capable of grasping that Joe had cleared out because he couldn't stand a decent respectable life in a little country town and wanted a life of loafing, fights and women. We never heard of him again. Perhaps he went utterly to the bad, perhaps he was killed in the war, perhaps he merely didn't bother to write. Luckily the baby was born dead, so there were no complications. As for the fact that Joe had stolen the eight pounds, Mother and Father managed to keep it a secret till they died. In their eyes it was a much worse disgrace than Sally Chivers's baby.

The trouble over Joe aged Father a great deal. To lose Joe was merely to cut a loss, but it hurt him and made him ashamed. From that time forward his moustache was much greyer and he seemed to have grown a lot smaller. Perhaps my memory of him as a little grey man, with a round, lined, anxious face and dusty spectacles, really dates from that time. By slow degrees he was getting more and more involved in money worries and less and less interested in other things. He talked less about politics and the Sunday papers, and more about the badness of trade. Mother seemed to have shrunk a little, too. In my childhood I'd known her as something vast and overflowing, with her yellow hair and her beaming face and her enormous bosom, a sort of great opulent creature like the figurehead of a battleship. Now she'd got smaller and more anxious and older than her years. She was less lordly in the kitchen, went in more for neck of mutton, worried over the price of coal and began to use margarine, a thing which in the old days she'd never have allowed into the house. After Joe had gone Father had to hire an errand-boy again, but from then on he employed very young boys whom he only kept for a year or two and who couldn't lift heavy weights. I sometimes lent him a hand when I was at home. I was too selfish to do it regularly. I can still see him working his way slowly across the yard, bent double and almost hidden under an enormous sack, like a snail under its shell. The huge, monstrous sack, weighing a hundred and fifty pounds, I suppose, pressing his neck and shoulders almost to the ground, and the anxious, spectacled face looking up from underneath it. In 1911 he ruptured himself and had to spend weeks in hospital and hire a temporary manager for the shop, which ate another hole in his capital. A small shopkeeper going down the hill is a dreadful thing to watch, but it isn't sudden and obvious like the fate of a working man who gets the sack and promptly finds himself on the dole. It's just a gradual chipping away of trade, with little ups and downs, a few shillings to the bad here, a few sixpences to the good there. Somebody who's dealt with you for years suddenly deserts and goes to Sarazins'. Somebody else buys a dozen hens and gives you a weekly order for corn. You can still keep going. You're still 'your own master', always a little more worried and a little shabbier, with your capital shrinking all the time. You can go on like that for years, for a lifetime if you're lucky. Uncle Ezekiel died in 1911, leaving £120 which must have made a lot of difference to Father. It wasn't till 1913 that he had to mortgage his life-insurance policy. That I didn't hear about at the time, or I'd have understood what it meant. As it was I don't think I ever got further than realising that Father 'wasn't doing well', trade was 'slack', there'd be a bit longer to wait before I had the money to 'set up'. Like Father himself, I looked on the shop as something permanent, and I was a bit inclined to be angry with him for not managing things better. I wasn't capable of seeing, and neither was he nor anyone else, that he was being slowly ruined, that his business would never pick up again and if he lived to be seventy he'd certainly end in the workhouse. Many a time I've passed Sarazins' shop in the market-place and merely thought how much I preferred their slick window-front to Father's dusty old shop, with the 'S. Bowling' which you could hardly read, the chipped white lettering and the faded packets of bird-seed. It didn't occur to me that Sarazins' were tapeworms who were eating him alive. Sometimes I used to repeat to him some of the stuff I'd been reading in my correspondence-course textbooks, about salesmanship and modern methods. He never paid much attention. He'd inherited an old-established business, he'd always worked hard, done a fair trade and supplied sound goods, and things would look up presently. It's a fact that very few shopkeepers in those days actually ended in the workhouse. With any luck you died with a few pounds still your own. It was a race between death and bankruptcy, and, thank God, death got Father first, and Mother too.

1911, 1912, 1913. I tell you it was a good time to be alive. It was late in 1912, through the vicar's Reading Circle, that I first met Elsie Waters. Till then, although, like all the rest of the boys in the town, I'd gone out looking for girls and occasionally managed to connect up with this girl or that and 'walk out' a few Sunday afternoons, I'd never really had a girl of my own. It's a queer business, that chasing of girls when you're about sixteen. At some recognised part of the town the boys stroll up and down in pairs, watching the girls, and the girls stroll up and down in pairs, pretending not to notice the boys, and presently some kind of contact is established and instead of twos they're trailing along in fours, all four utterly speechless. The chief feature of those walks—and it was worse the second time, when you went out with the girl alone—was the ghastly failure to make any kind of conversation. But Elsie Waters seemed different. The truth was that I was growing up.

I don't want to tell the story of myself and Elsie Waters, even if there was any story to tell. It's merely that she's part of the picture, part of 'before the war'. Before the war it was always summer—a delusion, as I've remarked before, but that's how I remember it. The white dusty road stretching out between the chestnut trees, the smell of night-stocks, the green pools under the willows, the splash of Burford Weir—that's what I see when I shut my eyes and think of 'before the war', and towards the end Elsie Waters is part of it.

I don't know whether Elsie would be considered pretty now. She was then. She was tall for a girl, about as tall as I am, with pale gold, heavy kind of hair which she wore somehow plaited and coiled round her head, and a delicate, curiously gentle face. She was one of those girls that always look their best in black, especially the very plain black dresses they made them wear in the drapery—she worked at Lilywhite's, the drapers, though she came originally from London. I suppose she would have been two years older than I was.

I'm grateful to Elsie, because she was the first person who taught me to care about a woman. I don't mean women in general, I mean an individual woman. I'd met her at the Reading Circle and hardly noticed her, and then one day I went into Lilywhite's during working hours, a thing I wouldn't normally have been able to do, but as it happened we'd run out of butter muslin and old Grimmett sent me to buy some. You know the atmosphere of a draper's shop. It's something peculiarly feminine. There's a hushed feeling, a subdued light, a cool smell of cloth and a faint whirring from the wooden balls of change rolling to and fro. Elsie was leaning against the counter, cutting off a length of cloth with the big scissors. There was something about her black dress and the curve of her breast against the counter—I can't describe it, something curiously soft, curiously feminine. As soon as you saw her you knew that you could take her in your arms and do what you wanted with her. She was really deeply feminine, very gentle, very submissive, the kind that would always do what a man told her, though she wasn't either small or weak. She wasn't even stupid, only rather silent and, at times, dreadfully refined. But in those days I was rather refined myself.

We were living together for about a year. Of course in a town like Lower Binfield you could only live together in a figurative sense. Officially we were 'walking out', which was a recognised custom and not quite the same as being engaged. There was a road that branched off from the road to Upper Binfield and ran along under the edge of the hills. There was a long stretch of it, nearly a mile, that was quite straight and fringed with enormous horse-chestnut trees, and on the grass at the side there was a footpath under the boughs that was known as Lovers' Lane. We used to go there on the May evenings, when the chestnuts were in blossom. Then the short nights came on, and it was light for hours after we'd left the shop. You know the feeling of a June evening. The kind of blue twilight that goes on and on, and the air brushing against your face like silk. Sometimes on Sunday afternoons we went over Chamford Hill and down to the water-meadows along the Thames. 1913! My God! 1913! The stillness, the green water, the rushing of the weir! It'll never come again. I don't mean that 1913 will never come again. I mean the feeling inside you, the feeling of not being in a hurry and not being frightened, the feeling you've either had and don't need to be told about, or haven't had and won't ever have the chance to learn.

It wasn't till late summer that we began what's called living together. I'd been too shy and clumsy to begin, and too ignorant to realise that there'd been others before me. One Sunday afternoon we went into the beech woods round Upper Binfield. Up there you could always be alone. I wanted her very badly, and I knew quite well that she was only waiting for me to begin. Something, I don't know what, put it into my head to go into the grounds of Binfield House. Old Hodges, who was past seventy and getting very crusty, was capable of turning us out, but he'd probably be asleep on a Sunday afternoon. We slipped through a gap in the fence and down the footpath between the beeches to the big pool. It was four years or more since I'd been that way. Nothing had changed. Still the utter solitude, the hidden feeling with the great trees all round you, the old boat-house rotting among the bulrushes. We lay down in the little grass hollow beside the wild pepper-mint, and we were as much alone as if we'd been in Central Africa. I'd kissed her God knows how many times, and then I'd got up and was wandering about again. I wanted her very badly, and wanted to take the plunge, only I was half-frightened. And curiously enough there was another thought in my mind at the same time. It suddenly struck me that for years I'd meant to come back here and had never come. Now I was so near, it seemed a pity not to go down to the other pool and have a look at the big carp. I felt I'd kick myself afterwards if I missed the chance, in fact I couldn't think why I hadn't been back before. The carp were stored away in my mind, nobody knew about them except me, I was going to catch them some time. Practically they were *my* carp. I actually started wandering along the bank in that direction, and then when I'd gone about ten yards I turned back. It meant crashing your way through a kind of jungle of brambles and rotten brush-wood, and I was dressed up in my Sunday best. Dark-grey suit, bowler hat, button boots and a collar that almost cut my ears off. That was how people dressed for Sunday after-noon walks in those days. And I wanted Elsie very badly. I went back and stood over her for a moment. She was lying on the grass with her arm over her face, and she didn't stir when she heard me come. In her black dress she looked—I don't know how, kind of soft, kind of yielding, as though her body was a kind of malleable stuff that you could do what you liked with. She was mine and I could have her, this minute if I wanted to. Suddenly I stopped being frightened. I chucked my hat onto the grass (it bounced, I remember), knelt down and took hold of her. I can smell the wild peppermint yet. It was my first time, but it wasn't hers, and we didn't make such a mess of it as you might expect. So that was that. The big carp faded out of my mind again, and in fact for years afterwards I hardly thought about them.

1913. 1914. The spring of 1914. First the blackthorn, then the hawthorn, then the chestnuts in blossom. Sunday afternoons along the towpath, and the wind rippling the beds of rushes so that they swayed all together in great thick masses and looked somehow like a woman's hair. The endless June evenings, the path under the chestnut trees, an owl hooting somewhere and Elsie's body against me. It was a hot July that year. How we sweated in the shop, and how the cheese and the ground coffee smelt! And then the cool of the evening outside, the smell of night-stocks and pipe-tobacco in the lane behind the allotments, the soft dust underfoot and the nightjars hawking after the cockchafers.

Christ! What's the use of saying that one oughtn't to be sentimental about 'before the war'? I *am* sentimental about it. So are you if you remember it. It's quite true that if you look back on any special period of time you tend to remember the pleasant bits. That's true even of the war. But it's also true that people then had something that we haven't got now.

What? It was simply that they didn't think of the future as something to be terrified of. It isn't that life was softer then than now. Actually it was harsher. People on the whole worked harder, lived less comfortably and died more painfully. The farm-hands worked frightful hours for fourteen shillings a week and ended up as worn-out cripples with a five-shilling old-age pension and an occasional half-crown from the parish. And what was called 'respectable' poverty was even worse. When little Watson, a small draper at the other end of the High Street, 'failed' after years of struggling, his personal assets were £2 9s 6d, and he died almost immediately of what was called 'gastric trouble', but the doctor let it out that it was starvation. Yet he'd clung to his frock coat to the last. Old Crimp, the watchmaker's assistant, a skilled workman who'd been at the job, man and boy, for fifty years, got cataract and had to go into the workhouse. His grandchildren were howling in the street when they took him away. His wife went out charring, and by desperate efforts managed to send him a shilling a week for pocket-money. You saw ghastly things happening sometimes. Small businesses sliding down the hill, solid tradesmen turning gradually into broken-down bankrupts, people dying by inches of cancer and liver disease, drunken husbands signing the pledge every Monday and breaking it every Saturday, girls ruined for life by an illegitimate baby. The houses had no bathrooms, you broke the ice in your basin on winter mornings, the back streets stank like the devil in hot weather, and the churchyard was bang in the middle of the town, so that you never went a day without remembering how you'd got to end. And yet what was it that people had in those days? A feeling of security, even when they weren't secure. More exactly, it was a feeling of continuity. All of them knew they'd got to die, and I suppose a few of them knew they were going to go bankrupt, but what they didn't know was that the order of things could change. Whatever might happen to themselves, things would go on as they'd known them. I don't believe it made very much difference that what's called religious belief was still prevalent in those days. It's true that nearly everyone went to church, at any rate in the country—Elsie and I still went to church as a matter of course, even when we were living in what the vicar would have called sin—and if you asked people whether they believed in a life after death they generally answered that they did. But I've never met anyone who gave me the impression of really believing in a future life. I think that, at most, people believe in that kind of thing in the same way as kids believe in Father Christmas. But it's precisely in a settled period, a period when civilisation seems to stand on its four legs like an elephant, that such things as a future life don't matter. It's easy enough to die if the things you care about are going to survive. You've had your life, you're getting tired, it's time to go underground—that's how people used to see it. Individually they were finished, but their way of life would continue. Their good and evil would remain good and evil. They didn't feel the ground they stood on shifting under their feet.

Father was failing, and he didn't know it. It was merely that times were very bad, trade seemed to dwindle and dwindle, his bills were harder and harder to meet. Thank God, he never even knew that he was ruined, never actually went bankrupt, because he died very suddenly (it was influenza that turned into pneumonia) at the beginning of 1915. To the end he believed that with thrift, hard work and fair dealing a man can't go wrong. There must have been plenty of small shopkeepers who carried that belief not merely onto bankrupt deathbeds but even into the workhouse. Even Lovegrove the saddler, with cars and motor-vans staring him in the face, didn't realise that he was as out of date as the rhinoceros. And Mother too—Mother never lived to know that the life she'd been brought up to, the life of a decent God-fearing shopkeeper's daughter and a decent God-fearing shopkeeper's wife in the reign of good Queen Vic, was finished for ever. Times were difficult and trade was bad, Father was worried and this and that was 'aggravating', but you carried on much the same as usual. The old English order of life couldn't change. For ever and ever decent God-fearing women would cook Yorkshire pudding and apple dumplings on enormous coal ranges, wear woollen underclothes and sleep on feathers, make plum jam in July and pickles in October, and read *Hilda's Home Companion* in the afternoons, with the flies buzzing round, in a sort of cosy little underworld of stewed tea, bad legs and happy endings. I don't say that either Father or Mother was quite the same to the end. They were a bit shaken, and sometimes a little dispirited. But at least they never lived to know that everything they'd believed in was just so much junk. They lived at the end of an epoch, when everything was dissolving into a sort of ghastly flux, and they didn't know it. They thought it was eternity. You couldn't blame them. That was what it felt like.

Then came the end of July, and even Lower Binfield grasped that things were happening. For days there was tremendous vague excitement and endless leading articles in the papers, which Father actually brought in from the shop to read aloud to Mother. And then suddenly the posters everywhere:

GERMAN ULTIMATUM. FRANCE MOBILISING.

For several days (four days, wasn't it? I forget the exact dates) there was a strange stifled feeling, a kind of waiting hush, like the moment before a thunderstorm breaks, as though the whole of England was silent and listening. It was very hot, I remember. In the shop it was as though we couldn't work, though already everyone in the neighbourhood who had five bob to spare was rushing in to buy quantities of tinned stuff and flour and oatmeal. It was as if we were too feverish to work, we only sweated and waited. In the evenings people went down to the railway station and fought like devils over the evening papers which arrived on the London train. And then one afternoon a boy came rushing down the High Street with an armful of papers, and people were coming into their doorways to shout across the street. Everyone was shouting 'We've come in! We've come in!' The boy grabbed a poster from his bundle and stuck it on the shop-front opposite:

ENGLAND DECLARES WAR ON GERMANY.

We rushed out onto the pavement, all three assistants, and cheered. Everybody was cheering. Yes, cheering. But old Grimmett, though he'd already done pretty well out of the war-scare, still held on to a little of his Liberal principles, 'didn't hold' with the war and said it would be a bad business.

Two months later I was in the army. Seven months later I was in France.

VIII

I wasn't wounded till late in 1916.

We'd just come out of the trenches and were marching over a bit of road a mile or so back which was supposed to be safe, but which the Germans must have got the range of some time earlier. Suddenly they started putting a few shells over—it was heavy HE stuff, and they were only firing about one a minute. There was the usual zwee-e-e-e! and then BOOM! in a field somewhere over to the right. I think it was the third shell that got me. I knew as soon as I heard it coming that it had my name written on it. They say you always know. It didn't say what an ordinary shell says. It said 'I'm after you, you b——, *you*, you b——, YOU!'—all this in the space of about three seconds. And the last YOU was the explosion.

I felt as if an enormous hand made of air were sweeping me along. And presently I came down with a sort of burst, shattered feeling among a lot of old tin cans, splinters of wood, rusty barbed wire, turds, empty cartridge cases and other muck in the ditch at the side of the road. When they'd hauled me out and cleaned some of the dirt off me they found that I wasn't very badly hurt. It was only a lot of small shell-splinters that had lodged in one side of my bottom and down the backs of my legs. But luckily I'd broken a rib in falling, which made it just bad enough to get me back to England. I spent that winter in a hospital camp on the downs near Eastbourne.

Do you remember those war-time hospital camps? The long rows of wooden huts like chicken-houses stuck right on top of those beastly icy downs—the 'south coast', people used to call it, which made me wonder what the north coast could be like—where the wind seems to blow at you from all directions at once. And the droves of blokes in their pale-blue flannel suits and red ties, wandering up and down looking for a place out of the wind and never finding one. Sometimes the kids from the slap-up boys' schools in Eastbourne used to be led round in crocodiles to hand out fags and peppermint creams to the 'wounded Tommies', as they called us. A pink-faced kid of about eight would walk up to a knot of wounded men sitting on the grass, split open a packet of Woodbines and solemnly hand one fag to each man, just like feeding the monkeys at the zoo. Anyone who was strong enough used to wander for miles over the downs in hopes of meeting girls. There were never enough girls to go round. In the valley below the camp there was a bit of a spinney, and long before dusk

114

you'd see a couple glued against every tree, and sometimes, if it happened to be a thick tree, one on each side of it. My chief memory of that time is sitting against a gorse-bush in the freezing wind, with my fingers so cold I couldn't bend them and the taste of a peppermint cream in my mouth. That's a typical soldier's memory. But I was getting away from a Tommy's life, all the same. The CO had sent my name in for a commission a little before I was wounded. By this time they were desperate for officers and anyone who wasn't actually illiterate could have a commission if he wanted one. I went straight from the hospital to an officers' training camp near Colchester.

It's very strange, the things the war did to people. It was less than three years since I'd been a spry young shop-assistant, bending over the counter in my white apron with 'Yes, madam! Certainly, madam! *And* the next order, madam?' with a grocer's life ahead of me and about as much notion of becoming an army officer as of getting a knighthood. And here I was already, swaggering about in a gorblimey hat and a yellow collar and more or less keeping my end up among a crowd of other temporary gents and some who weren't even temporary. And—this is really the point—not feeling it in any way strange. Nothing seemed strange in those days.

It was like an enormous machine that had got hold of you. You'd no sense of acting of your own free will, and at the same time no notion of trying to resist. If people didn't have some such feeling as that, no war could last three months. The armies would just pack up and go home. Why had I joined the army? Or the million other idiots who joined up before conscription came in? Partly for a lark and partly because of England my England and Britons never never and all that stuff. But how long did that last? Most of the chaps I knew had forgotten all about it long before they got as far as France. The men in the trenches weren't patriotic, didn't hate the Kaiser, didn't care a damn about gallant little Belgium and the Germans raping nuns on tables (it was always 'on tables', as though that made it worse) in the streets of Brussels. On the other hand it didn't occur to them to try and escape. The machine had got hold of you and it could do what it liked with you. It lifted you up and dumped you down among places and things you'd never dreamed of, and if it had dumped you down on the surface of the moon it wouldn't have seemed particularly strange. The day I joined the army the old life was finished. It was as though it didn't concern me any longer. I wonder if you'd believe that from that day forward I only once went back to Lower Binfield, and that was to Mother's funeral? It sounds incredible now, but it seemed natural enough at the time. Partly, I admit, it was on account of Elsie, whom, of course, I'd stopped writing to after two or three months. No doubt she'd picked up with someone else, but I didn't want to meet her. Otherwise, perhaps, when I got a bit of leave I'd have gone down and seen Mother, who'd had fits when I joined the army but would have been proud of a son in uniform.

Father died in 1915. I was in France at the time. I don't exaggerate when I say that Father's death hurts me more now than it did then. At the time it was just a bit of bad news which I accepted almost without interest, in the sort of empty-headed apathetic way in which one accepted everything in the trenches. I remember crawling into the doorway of the dugout to get enough light to read the letter, and I remember Mother's tear-stains on the letter, and the aching feeling in my knees and the smell of mud. Father's life-insurance policy had been mortgaged for most of its value, but there was a little money in the bank and Sarazins' were going to buy up the stock and even pay some tiny amount for the good-will. Anyway, Mother had a bit over two hundred pounds, besides the furniture.

She went for the time being to lodge with her cousin, the wife of a smallholder who was doing pretty well out of the war, near Doxley, a few miles the other side of Walton. It was only 'for the time being'. There was a temporary feeling about everything. In the old days, which as a matter of fact were barely a year old, the whole thing would have been an appalling disaster. With Father dead, the shop sold up and Mother with two hundred pounds in the world, you'd have seen stretching out in front of you a kind of fifteen-act tragedy, the last act being a pauper's funeral. But now the war and the feeling of not being one's own master overshadowed everything. People hardly thought in terms of things like bankruptcy and the workhouse any longer. This was the case even with Mother, who, God knows, had only very dim notions about the war. Besides, she was already dying, though neither of us knew it.

She came across to see me in the hospital at Eastbourne. It was over two years since I'd seen her, and her appearance gave me a bit of a shock. She seemed to have faded and somehow to have shrunken. Partly it was because by this time I was grown-up, I'd travelled, and everything looked smaller to me, but there was no question that she'd got thinner, and also yellower. She talked in the old rambling way about Aunt Martha (that was the cousin she was staying with), and the changes in Lower Binfield since the war, and all the boys who'd 'gone' (meaning joined the army), and her indigestion which was 'aggravating', and poor Father's tombstone and what a lovely corpse he made. It was the old talk, the talk I'd listened to for years, and yet somehow it was like a ghost talking. It didn't concern me any longer. I'd known her as a great splendid protecting kind of creature, a bit like a ship's figurehead and a bit like a broody hen, and after all she was only a little old woman in a black dress. Everything was changing and fading. That was the last time I saw her alive. I got the

wire saying she was seriously ill when I was at the training school at Colchester, and put in for a week's urgent leave immediately. But it was too late. She was dead by the time I got to Doxley. What she and everyone else had imagined to be indigestion was some kind of internal growth, and a sudden chill on the stomach put the final touch. The doctor tried to cheer me up by telling me that the growth was 'benevolent', which struck me as a queer thing to call it, seeing that it had killed her.

Well, we buried her next to Father, and that was my last glimpse of Lower Binfield. It had changed a lot, even in three years. Some of the shops were shut, some had different names over them. Nearly all the men I'd known as boys were gone, and some of them were dead. Sid Lovegrove was dead, killed on the Somme. Ginger Watson, the farm lad who'd belonged to the Black Hand years ago, the one who used to catch rabbits alive, was dead in Egypt. One of the chaps who'd worked with me at Grimmett's had lost both legs. Old Lovegrove had shut up his shop and was living in a cottage near Walton on a tiny annuity. Old Grimmett, on the other hand, was doing well out of the war and had turned patriotic and was a member of the local board which tried conscientious objectors. The thing which more than anything else gave the town an empty, forlorn kind of look was that there were practically no horses left. Every horse worth taking had been commandeered long ago. The station fly still existed, but the brute that pulled it wouldn't have been able to stand up if it hadn't been for the shafts. For the hour or so that I was there before the funeral I wandered round the town, saying how d'you do to people and showing off my uniform. Luckily I didn't run into Elsie. I saw all the changes, and yet it was as though I didn't see them. My mind was on other things, chiefly the pleasure of being seen in my second-loot's uniform, with my black armlet (a thing

which looks rather smart on khaki) and my new whipcord breeches. I distinctly remember that I was still thinking about those whipcord breeches when we stood at the grave-side. And then they chucked some earth onto the coffin and I suddenly realised what it means for your mother to be lying with seven feet of earth on top of her, and something kind of twitched behind my eyes and nose, but even then the whipcord breeches weren't altogether out of my mind.

Don't think I didn't feel for Mother's death. I did. I wasn't in the trenches any longer, I could feel sorry for a death. But the thing I didn't care a damn about, didn't even grasp to be happening, was the passing-away of the old life I'd known. After the funeral, Aunt Martha, who was rather proud of having a 'real officer' for a nephew and would have made a splash of the funeral if I'd let her, went back to Doxley on the bus and I took the fly down to the station, to get the train to London and then to Colchester. We drove past the shop. No one had taken it since Father died. It was shut up and the window-pane was black with dust, and they'd burned the 'S. Bowling' off the signboard with a plumber's blowflame. Well, there was the house where I'd been a child and a boy and a young man, where I'd crawled about the kitchen floor and smelt the sainfoin and read *Donovan the Dauntless*, where I'd done my homework for the Grammar School, mixed bread paste, mended bicycle punctures and tried on my first high collar. It had been as permanent to me as the pyramids, and now it would be just an accident if I ever set foot in it again. Father, Mother, Joe, the errand-boys, old Nailer the terrier, Spot, the one that came after Nailer, Jackie the bullfinch, the cats, the mice in the loft—all gone, nothing left but dust. And I didn't care a damn. I was sorry Mother was dead, I was even sorry Father was dead, but all the time my mind was on other things. I was a bit proud of being seen riding in a cab, a thing I hadn't yet got used to, and I was thinking of the sit of my new whipcord breeches, and my nice smooth officer's putties, so different from the gritty stuff the Tommies had to wear, and of the other chaps at Colchester and the sixty quid Mother had left and the beanos we'd have with it. Also I was thanking God that I hadn't happened to run into Elsie.

The war did extraordinary things to people. And what was more extraordinary than the way it killed people was the way it sometimes didn't kill them. It was like a great flood rushing you along to death, and suddenly it would shoot you up some backwater where you'd find yourself doing incredible and pointless things and drawing extra pay for them. There were labour battalions making roads across the desert that didn't lead anywhere, there were chaps marooned on oceanic islands to look out for German cruisers which had been sunk years earlier, there were Ministries of this and that with armies of clerks and typists which went on existing years after their function had ended, by a kind of inertia. People were shoved into meaningless jobs and then forgotten by the authorities for years on end. This was what happened to myself, or very likely I wouldn't be here. The whole sequence of events is rather interesting.

A little while after I was gazetted there was a call for officers for the ASC. As soon as the OC of the training camp heard that I knew something about the grocery trade (I didn't let on that I'd actually been behind the counter), he told me to send my name in. That went through all right, and I was just about to leave for another training-school for ASC officers somewhere in the Midlands when there was a demand for a young officer, with know-ledge of the grocery trade, to act as some kind of secretary to Sir Joseph Cheam, who was a big noise in the ASC. God knows why they picked me out, but at any rate they did so. I've since thought that they probably mixed my name up with somebody else's. Three days later I was saluting in Sir Joseph's office. He was a lean, upright, rather handsome old boy with grizzled hair and a grave-looking nose which immediately impressed me. He looked the perfect professional soldier, the KCMG, DSO with bar type, and might have been twin brother to the chap in the De Reszke advert, though in private life he was chairman of one of the big chain groceries and famous all over the world for something called the Cheam Wage-cut System. He stopped writing as I came in and looked me over.

'You a gentleman?'

'No, sir.'

'Good. Then perhaps we'll get some work done.'

In about three minutes he'd wormed out of me that I had no secretarial experience, didn't know shorthand, couldn't use a typewriter, and had worked in a grocery at twenty-eight shillings a week. However, he said that I'd do, there were too many gentlemen in this damned army and he'd been looking for somebody who could count beyond ten. I liked him and looked forward to working for him, but just at this moment the mysterious powers that seemed to be running the war drove us apart again. Something called the West Coast Defence Force was being formed, or rather was being talked about, and there was some vague idea of establishing dumps of rations and other stores at various points along the coast. Sir Joseph was supposed to be responsible for the dumps in the south-west corner of England. The day after I joined his office he sent me down to check over the stores at a place called Twelve Mile Dump, on the North Cornish Coast. Or rather, my job was to find out whether any stores existed. Nobody seemed certain about this. I'd just got there and discovered that the stores consisted of eleven tins of bully beef when a wire arrived from the War Office telling me to take charge of the stores at Twelve Mile Dump and remain there till further notice. I wired back 'No stores at Twelve Mile Dump'. Too late. Next day came the official letter informing me that I was OC Twelve Mile Dump. And that's really the end of the story. I remained OC Twelve Mile Dump for the rest of the war.

God knows what it was all about. It's no use asking me what the West Coast Defence Force was or what it was supposed to do. Even at that time nobody pretended to know. In any case it didn't exist. It was just a scheme that had floated through somebody's mind—following on some vague rumour of a German invasion via Ireland, I suppose—and the food dumps which were supposed to exist all along the coast were also imaginary. The whole thing had existed for about three days, like a sort of bubble, and then had been forgotten, and I'd been forgotten with it. My eleven tins of bully beef had been left behind by some officers who had been there earlier on some other mysterious mission. They'd also left behind a very deaf old man called Private Lidgebird. What Lidgebird was supposed to be doing there I never discovered. I wonder whether you'll believe that I remained guarding those eleven tins of bully beef from half-way through 1917 to the beginning of 1919? Probably you won't, but it's the truth. And at the time even that didn't seem particularly strange. By 1918 one had simply got out of the habit of expecting things to happen in a reasonable manner.

Once a month they sent me an enormous official form calling upon me to state the number and condition of pickaxes, entrenching tools, coils of barbed wire, blankets, waterproof groundsheets, first-aid outfits, sheets of corrugated iron and tins of plum and apple jam under my care. I just entered 'nil' against everything and sent the form back. Nothing ever happened. Up in London someone was quietly filing the forms, and sending out more forms, and filing those, and so on. It was the way things were happening. The mysterious higher-ups who were running the war had forgotten my existence. I didn't jog their memory. I was up a backwater that didn't lead anywhere, and after two years in France I wasn't so burning with patriotism that I wanted to get out of it.

It was a lonely part of the coast where you never saw a soul except a few yokels who'd barely heard there was a war on. A quarter of a mile away, down a little hill, the sea boomed and surged over enormous flats of sand. Nine months of the year it rained, and the other three a raging wind blew off the Atlantic. There was nothing there except Private Lidgebird, myself, two army huts—one of them a decentish two-roomed hut which I inhabited—and the eleven tins of bully beef. Lidgebird was a surly old devil and I could never get much out of him except the fact that he'd been a market gardener before he joined the army. It was interesting to see how rapidly he was reverting to type. Even before I got to Twelve Mile Dump he'd dug a patch round one of the huts and started planting spuds, in the autumn he dug another patch till he'd got about half an acre under cultivation, at the beginning of 1918 he started keeping hens which had got to quite a number by the end of the summer, and towards the end of the year he suddenly produced a pig from God knows where. I don't think it crossed his mind to wonder what the devil we were doing there, or what the West Coast Defence Force was and whether it actually existed. It wouldn't surprise me to hear that he's there still, raising pigs and potatoes on the spot where Twelve Mile Dump used to be. I hope he is. Good luck to him.

Meanwhile I was doing something I'd never before had the chance to do as a full-time job—reading.

The officers who'd been there before had left a few

books behind, mostly sevenpenny editions and nearly all of them the kind of tripe that people were reading in those days, Ian Hay and Sapper and the Craig Kennedy stories and so forth. But at some time or other somebody had been there who knew what books are worth reading and what are not. I myself, at the time, didn't know anything of the kind. The only books I'd ever voluntarily read were detective stories and once in a way a smutty sex book. God knows I don't set up to be a highbrow even now, but if you'd asked me *then* for the name of a 'good' book I'd have answered *The Woman Thou Gavest Me*, or (in memory of the vicar) *Sesame and Lilies*. In any case a 'good' book was a book one didn't have any intention of reading. But there I was, in a job where there was less than nothing to do, with the sea booming on the beach and the rain streaming down the window panes—and a whole row of books staring me in the face on the temporary shelf someone had rigged up against the wall of the hut. Naturally I started to read them from end to end, with, at the beginning, about as much attempt to discriminate as a pig working its way through a pail of garbage.

But in among them there were three or four books that were different from the others. No, you've got it wrong! Don't run away with the idea that I suddenly discovered Marcel Proust or Henry James or somebody. I wouldn't have read them even if I had. These books I'm speaking of weren't in the least highbrow. But now and again it so happens that you strike a book which is exactly at the mental level you've reached at the moment, so much so that it seems to have been written specially for you. One of them was H. G. Wells's *The History of Mr Polly*, in a cheap shilling edition which was falling to pieces. I wonder if you can imagine the effect it had upon me, to be brought up as I'd been brought up, the son of a shopkeeper in a country town, and then to come across a book like that?

Another was Compton Mackenzie's *Sinister Street*. It had been the scandal of the season a few years back, and I'd even heard vague rumours of it in Lower Binfield. Another was Conrad's *Victory*, parts of which bored me. But books like that started you thinking. And there was a back number of some magazine with a blue cover which had a short story of D. H. Lawrence's in it. I don't remember the name of it. It was a story about a German conscript who shoves his sergeant-major over the edge of a fortification and then does a bunk and gets caught in his girl's bedroom. It puzzled me a lot. I couldn't make out what it was all about, and yet it left me with a vague feeling that I'd like to read some others like it.

Well, for several months I had an appetite for books that was almost like physical thirst. It was the first real go-in at reading that I'd had since my Dick Donovan days. At the beginning I had no idea how to set about getting hold of books. I thought the only way was to buy them. That's interesting, I think. It shows you the difference upbringing makes. I suppose the children of the middle classes, the £500 a year middle classes, know all about Mudie's and the Times Book Club when they're in their cradles. A bit later I learned of the existence of lending libraries and took out a subscription at Mudie's and another at a library in Bristol. And what I read during the next year or so! Wells, Conrad, Kipling, Galsworthy, Barry Pain, W. W. Jacobs, Pett Ridge, Oliver Onions, Compton Mackenzie, H. Seton Merriman, Maurice Baring, Stephen McKenna, May Sinclair, Arnold Bennett, Anthony Hope, Elinor Glyn, O. Henry, Stephen Leacock, and even Silas Hocking and Gene Stratton Porter. How many of the names in that list are known to you, I wonder? Half the books that people took seriously in those days are forgotten now. But at the beginning I swallowed them all down like a whale that's got in among a shoal of shrimps. I just revelled in them.

After a bit, of course, I grew more highbrow and began to distinguish between tripe and not-tripe. I got hold of Lawrence's *Sons and Lovers* and sort of half-enjoyed it, and I got a lot of kick out of Oscar Wilde's *Dorian Gray* and Stevenson's *New Arabian Knights*. Wells was the author who made the biggest impression on me. I read George Moore's *Esther Waters* and liked it, and I tried several of Hardy's novels and always got stuck about half-way through. I even had a go at Ibsen, who left me with a vague impression that in Norway it's always raining.

It was queer, really. Even at the time it struck me as queer. I was a second-loot with hardly any Cockney accent left, I could already distinguish between Arnold Bennett and Elinor Glyn, and yet it was only four years since I'd been slicing cheese behind the counter in my white apron and looking forward to the days when I'd be a master-grocer. If I tot up the account, I suppose I must admit that the war did me good as well as harm. At any rate that year of reading novels was the only real education, in the sense of book-learning, that I've ever had. It did certain things to my mind. It gave me an attitude, a kind of questioning attitude, which I probably wouldn't have had if I'd gone through life in a normal sensible way. But–I wonder if you can understand this–the thing that really changed me, really made an impression on me, wasn't so much the books I read as the rotten meaninglessness of the life I was leading.

It really was unspeakably meaningless, that time in 1918. Here I was, sitting beside the stove in an army hut, reading novels, and a few hundred miles away in France the guns were roaring and droves of wretched children, wetting their bags with fright, were being driven into the machine-gun barrage like you'd shoot small coke into a furnace. I was one of the lucky ones. The higher-ups had taken their eye off me, and here I was in a snug little bolt-hole, drawing pay for a job that didn't exist. At times I got into a panic and made sure they'd remember about me and dig me out, but it never happened. The official forms, on gritty grey paper, came in once a month, and I filled them up and sent them back, and more forms came in, and I filled them up and sent them back, and so it went on. The whole thing had about as much sense in it as a lunatic's dream. The effect of all this, plus the books I was reading, was to leave me with a feeling of disbelief in everything.

I wasn't the only one. The war was full of loose ends and forgotten corners. By this time literally millions of people were stuck up backwaters of one kind and another. Whole armies were rotting away on fronts that people had forgotten the names of. There were huge Ministries with hordes of clerks and typists all drawing two pounds a week and upwards for piling up mounds of paper. Moreover they knew perfectly well that all they were doing was to pile up mounds of paper. Nobody believed the atrocity stories and the gallant little Belgium stuff any longer. The soldiers thought the Germans were good fellows and hated the French like poison. Every junior officer looked on the General Staff as mental defectives. A sort of wave of disbelief was moving across England, and it even got as far as Twelve Mile Dump. It would be an exaggeration to say that the war turned people into highbrows, but it did turn them into nihilists for the time being. People who in a normal way would have gone through life with about as much tendency to think for themselves as a suet pudding were turned into Bolshies just by the war. What should I be now if it hadn't been for the war? I don't know, but something different from what I am. If the war didn't happen to kill you it was bound to start you thinking. After that unspeakable idiotic mess you couldn't go on regarding society as something eternal and unquestionable, like a pyramid. You knew it was just a balls-up.

IX

The war had jerked me out of the old life I'd known, but in the queer period that came afterwards I forgot it almost completely.

I know that in a sense one never forgets anything. You remember that piece of orange-peel you saw in the gutter thirteen years ago, and that coloured poster of Torquay that you once got a glimpse of in a railway waiting-room. But I'm speaking of a different kind of memory. In a sense I remembered the old life in Lower Binfield. I remembered my fishing-rod and the smell of sainfoin and Mother behind the brown teapot and Jackie the bullfinch and the horse-trough in the market-place. But none of it was alive in my mind any longer. It was something far away, something that I'd finished with. It would never have occurred to me that some day I might want to go back to it.

It was a queer time, those years just after the war, almost queerer than the war itself, though people don't remember it so vividly. In a rather different form the sense of disbelieving in everything was stronger than ever. Millions of men had suddenly been kicked out of the army to find that the country they'd fought for didn't want them, and Lloyd George and his pals were giving the works to any illusions that still existed. Bands of ex-service men marched up and down rattling collection boxes, masked women were singing in the streets and chaps in officers' tunics were grinding barrel-organs. Everybody in England seemed to be scrambling for jobs, myself included. But I came off luckier than most. I got a small wound-gratuity, and what with that and the bit of money I'd put aside during the last year of war (not having had much opportunity to spend it), I came out of the army with no less than three hundred and fifty quid. It's rather interesting, I think, to notice my reaction. Here I was, with quite enough money to do the thing I'd been brought up to do and the thing I'd dreamed of for years—that is, start a shop. I had plenty of capital. If you bide your time and keep your eyes open you can run across quite nice little businesses for three hundred and fifty quid. And yet, if you'll believe me, the idea never occurred to me. I not only didn't make any move towards starting a shop, but it wasn't till years later, about 1925 in fact, that it even crossed my mind that I might have done so. The fact was that I'd passed right out of the shop-keeping orbit. That was what the army did to you. It turned you into an imitation gentleman and gave you a fixed idea that there'd always be a bit of money coming from somewhere. If you'd suggested to me then, in 1919, that I ought to start a shop—a tobacco- and sweet-shop, say, or a general store in some god-forsaken village—I'd just have laughed. I'd worn pips on my shoulder, and my social standards had risen. At the same time I didn't share the delusion, which was pretty common among ex-officers, that I could spend the rest of my life drinking pink gin. I knew I'd got to have a job. And the job, of course, would be 'in business'—just what kind of job I didn't know, but something high-up and important, something with a car and a telephone and if possible a secretary with a permanent wave. During the last year or so of war a lot of us had had visions like that. The chap who'd been a shopwalker saw himself as a travelling salesman, and the chap who'd been a travelling salesman saw himself as a managing director. It was the effect of army life, the effect of wearing pips and having a cheque-book and calling the evening meal dinner. All the while there'd been an idea floating round—and this applied to the men in the ranks as well as the officers—that when we came out of the army there'd be jobs waiting for us that would bring in at least as much as our army pay. Of course, if ideas like that didn't circulate, no war would ever be fought.

Well, I didn't get that job. It seemed that nobody was anxious to pay me £2,000 a year for sitting among stream-lined office furniture and dictating letters to a platinum blonde. I was discovering what three-quarters of the blokes who'd been officers were discovering—that from a financial point of view we'd been better off in the army than we were ever likely to be again. We'd suddenly changed from gentlemen holding His Majesty's commission into miserable out-of-works whom nobody wanted. My ideas soon sank from two thousand a year to three or four pounds a week. But even jobs of the three or four pounds a week kind didn't seem to exist. Every mortal job was filled already, either by men who'd been a few years too old to fight, or by boys who'd been a few months too young. The poor bastards who'd happened to be born between 1890 and 1900 were left out in the cold. And still it never occurred to me to go back to the grocering business. Probably I could have got a job as a grocer's assistant; old Grimmett, if he was still alive and in business (I wasn't in touch with Lower Binfield and didn't know), would have given me good refs. But I'd passed into a different orbit. Even if my social ideas hadn't risen, I could hardly have imagined, after what I'd seen and learned, going back to the old safe existence behind the counter. I wanted to be travelling about and pulling down the big dough. Chiefly I wanted to be a travelling salesman, which I knew would suit me.

But there were no jobs for travelling salesmen—that's to say, jobs with a salary attached. What there were, however, were on-commission jobs. That racket was just beginning on a big scale. It's a beautifully simple method of increasing your sales and advertising your stuff without taking any risks, and it always flourishes when times are bad. They keep you on a string by hinting that perhaps there'll be a salaried job going in three months' time, and when you get fed up there's always some other poor devil ready to take over. Naturally it wasn't long before I had an on-commission job, in fact I had quite a number in rapid succession. Thank God, I never came down to peddling vacuum-cleaners, or dictionaries. But I travelled in cutlery, in soap-powder, in a line of patent corkscrews, tin-openers and similar gadgets, and finally in a line of office accessories –paper-clips, carbon paper, typewriter ribbons and so forth. I didn't do so badly either. I'm the type that *can* sell things on commission. I've got the temperament and I've got the manner. But I never came anywhere near making a decent living. You can't, in jobs like that–and, of course, you aren't meant to.

I had about a year of it altogether. It was a queer time. The cross-country journeys, the godless places you fetched up in, suburbs of midland towns that you'd never hear of in a hundred normal lifetimes. The ghastly bed-and-breakfast houses where the sheets always smell faintly of slops and the fried egg at breakfast has a yolk paler than a lemon. And the other poor devils of salesmen that you're always meeting, middle-aged fathers of families in moth-eaten overcoats and bowler hats, who honestly believe that sooner or later trade will turn the corner and they'll jack their earnings up to five quid a week. And the traipsing from shop to shop, and the arguments with shopkeepers who don't want to listen, and the standing back and making yourself small when a customer comes in. Don't think that it worried me particularly. To some chaps that kind of life is torture. There are chaps who can't even walk into a shop and open their bag of samples without screwing themselves up as though they were going over the top. But I'm not like that. I'm tough, I can talk people into buying things they don't want, and even if they slam the door in my face it doesn't bother me. Selling things on commission is actually what I like doing, provided I can see my way

131

to making a bit of dough out of it. I don't know whether I learned much in that year, but I unlearned a good deal. It knocked the army nonsense out of me, and it drove into the back of my head the notions that I'd picked up during that idle year when I was reading novels. I don't think I read a single book, barring detective stories, all the time I was on the road. I wasn't a highbrow any longer. I was down among the realities of modern life. And what are the realities of modern life? Well, the chief one is an ever-lasting, frantic struggle to sell things. With most people it takes the form of selling themselves–that's to say, getting a job and keeping it. I suppose there hasn't been a single month since the war, in any trade you care to name, in which there weren't more men than jobs. It's brought a peculiar, ghastly feeling into life. It's like on a sinking ship when there are nineteen survivors and fourteen lifebelts. But is there anything particularly modern in that, you say? Has it anything to do with the war? Well, it feels as if it had. That feeling that you've got to be everlastingly fighting and hustling, that you'll never get anything unless you grab it from somebody else, that there's always somebody after your job, that next month or the month after they'll be reducing staff and it's you that'll get the bird–*that*, I swear, didn't exist in the old life before the war.

But meanwhile I wasn't badly off. I was earning a bit and I'd still got plenty of money in the bank, nearly two hundred quid, and I wasn't frightened for the future. I knew that sooner or later I'd get a regular job. And sure enough, after about a year, by a stroke of luck it happened. I say by a stroke of luck, but the fact is that I was bound to fall on my feet. I'm not the type that starves. I'm about as likely to end up in the workhouse as to end up in the House of Lords. I'm the middling type, the type that gravitates by a kind of natural law towards the five-pound-a–week level. So long as there are any jobs at all I'll back myself to get one.

It happened when I was peddling paper-clips and type-writer ribbons. I'd just dodged into a huge block of offices in Fleet Street, a building which canvassers weren't allowed into, as a matter of fact, but I'd managed to give the lift attendant the impression that my bag of samples was merely an attaché case. I was walking along one of the corridors looking for the offices of a small toothpaste firm that I'd been recommended to try, when I saw that some very big bug was coming down the corridor in the other direction. I knew immediately that it was a big bug. You know how it is with these big business men, they seem to take up more room and walk more loudly than any ordinary person, and they give off a kind of wave of money that you can feel fifty yards away. When he got nearly up to me I saw that it was Sir Joseph Cheam. He was in civvies, of course, but I had no difficulty in recognising him. I suppose he'd been there for some business conference or other. A couple of clerks, or secretaries, or something, were following after him, not actually holding up his train, because he wasn't wearing one, but you somehow felt that that was what they were doing. Of course I dodged aside instantly. But curiously enough he recognised me, though he hadn't seen me for years. To my surprise he stopped and spoke to me.

'Hullo, you! I've seen you somewhere before. What's your name? It's on the tip of my tongue.'

'Bowling, sir. Used to be in the ASC.'

'Of course. The boy that said he wasn't a gentleman. What are you doing here?'

I might have told him that I was selling typewriter ribbons, and there perhaps the whole thing would have ended. But I had one of those sudden inspirations that you get occasionally—a feeling that I might make something out of this if I handled it properly. I said instead:

'Well, sir, as a matter of fact I'm looking for a job.'

'A job, eh? Hm. Not so easy, nowadays.'

He looked me up and down for a second. The two train-bearers had kind of wafted themselves a little distance away. I saw his rather good-looking old face, with the heavy grey eyebrows and the intelligent nose, looking me over and realised that he'd decided to help me. It's queer, the power of these rich men. He'd been marching past me in his power and glory, with his underlings after him, and then on some whim or other he'd turned aside, like an emperor suddenly chucking a coin to a beggar.

'So you want a job? What can you do?'

Again the inspiration. No use, with a bloke like this, cracking up your own merits. Stick to the truth. I said: 'Nothing, sir. But I want a job as a travelling salesman.'

'Salesman? Hm. Not sure that I've got anything for you at present. Let's see.'

He pursed his lips up. For a moment, half a minute perhaps, he was thinking quite deeply. It was curious. Even at the time I realised that it was curious. This important old bloke, who was probably worth at least half a million, was actually taking thought on my behalf. I'd deflected him from his path and wasted at least three minutes of his time, all because of a chance remark I'd happened to make years earlier. I'd stuck in his memory and therefore he was willing to take the tiny bit of trouble that was needed to find me a job. I dare say the same day he gave twenty clerks the sack. Finally he said:

'How'd you like to go into an insurance firm? Always fairly safe, you know. People have got to have insurance, same as they've got to eat.'

Of course I jumped at the idea of going into an insurance firm. Sir Joseph was 'interested' in the Flying Salamander.

God knows how many companies he was 'interested' in. One of the underlings wafted himself forward with a scribbling-pad, and there and then, with the gold stylo out of his waistcoat pocket, Sir Joseph scribbled me a note to some higher-up in the Flying Salamander. Then I thanked him, and he marched on, and I sneaked off in the other direction, and we never saw one another again.

Well, I got the job, and, as I said earlier, the job got me. I've been with the Flying Salamander close on eighteen years. I started off in the office, but now I'm what's known as an Inspector, or, when there's reason to sound particularly impressive, a Representative. A couple of days a week I'm working in the district office, and the rest of the time I'm travelling around, interviewing clients whose names have been sent in by the local agents, making assessments on shops and other property, and now and again snapping up a few orders on my own account. I earn round about seven quid a week. And properly speaking that's the end of my story.

When I look back I realise that my active life, if I ever had one, ended when I was sixteen. Everything that really matters to me had happened before that date. But in a manner of speaking things were still happening—the war, for instance—up to the time when I got the job with the Flying Salamander. After that—well, they say that happy people have no histories, and neither do the blokes who work in insurance offices. From that day forward there was nothing in my life that you could properly describe as an event, except that about two and a half years later, at the beginning of '23, I got married.

X

I was living in a boarding-house in Ealing. The years were rolling on, or crawling on. Lower Binfield had passed almost out of my memory. I was the usual young city worker who scoots for the 8.15 and intrigues for the other fellow's job. I was fairly well thought of in the firm and pretty satisfied with life. The post-war success dope had caught me, more or less. You remember the line of talk. Pep, punch, grit, sand. Get on or get out. There's plenty of room at the top. You can't keep a good man down. And the ads in the magazines about the chap that the boss clapped on the shoulder, and the keen-jawed executive who's pulling down the big dough and attributes his success to so-and-so's correspondence course. It's funny how we all swallowed it, even blokes like me to whom it hadn't the smallest application. Because I'm neither a go-getter nor a down-and-out, and I'm by nature incapable of being either. But it was the spirit of the time. Get on! Make good! If you see a man down, jump on his guts before he gets up again. Of course this was in the early 'twenties, when some of the effects of the war had worn off and the slump hadn't yet arrived to knock the stuffing out of us.

I had an 'A' subscription at Boots' and went to half-crown dances and belonged to a local tennis club. You know those tennis clubs in the genteel suburbs—little wooden pavilions and high wire-netting enclosures where young chaps in rather badly cut white flannels prance up and down, shouting 'Fifteen forty!' and 'Vantage all!' in voices which are a tolerable imitation of the Upper Crust. I'd learned to play tennis, didn't dance too badly and got on well with the girls. At nearly thirty I wasn't a bad-looking chap, with my red face and butter-coloured hair, and in those days it was still a point in your favour to have fought in the war. I never, then or at any other time, succeeded in looking like a gentleman, but on the other hand you probably wouldn't have taken me for the son of a small shopkeeper in a country town. I could keep my end up in the rather mixed society of a place like Ealing, where the office-employee class overlaps with the middling-professional class. It was at the tennis club that I first met Hilda.

At that time Hilda was twenty-four. She was a small, slim, rather timid girl, with dark hair, beautiful movements and—because of having very large eyes—a distinct resemblance to a hare. She was one of those people who never say much, but remain on the edge of any conversation that's going on, and give the impression that they're listening. If she said anything at all, it was usually 'Oh, yes, I think so too', agreeing with whoever had spoken last. At tennis she hopped about very gracefully, and didn't play badly, but somehow had a helpless, childish air. Her surname was Vincent.

If you're married, there'll have been times when you've said to yourself 'Why the hell did I do it?', and God knows I've said it often enough about Hilda. And once again, looking at it across fifteen years, why *did* I marry Hilda?

Partly, of course, because she was young and in a way very pretty. Beyond that I can only say that because she came of totally different origins from myself it was very difficult for me to get any grasp of what she was really like. I had to marry her first and find out about her afterwards, whereas if I'd married, say, Elsie Waters, I'd have known what I was marrying. Hilda belonged to a class I only knew by hearsay, the poverty-stricken officer class. For generations past her family had been soldiers, sailors, clergymen, Anglo-Indian officials and that kind of thing. They'd never had any money, but on the other hand none of them had ever done anything that I should recognise as work. Say what you will, there's a kind of snob-appeal in that, if you belong as I do to the God-fearing shopkeeper class, the low-church and high-tea class. It wouldn't make any impression on me now, but it did then. Don't mistake what I'm saying. I don't mean that I married Hilda *because* she belonged to the class I'd once served across the counter, with some notion of jockeying myself up in the social scale. It was merely that I couldn't understand her and therefore was capable of being goofy about her. And one thing I certainly didn't grasp was that the girls in these penniless middle-class families will marry anything in trousers, just to get away from home.

It wasn't long before Hilda took me home to see her family. I hadn't known till then that there was a considerable Anglo-Indian colony in Ealing. Talk about discovering a new world! It was quite a revelation to me.

Do you know these Anglo-Indian families? It's almost impossible, when you get inside these people's houses, to remember that out in the street it's England and the twentieth century. As soon as you set foot inside the front door you're in India in the 'eighties. You know the kind of atmosphere. The carved teak furniture, the brass trays, the dusty tiger-skulls on the wall, the Trichinopoly cigars, the red-hot pickles, the yellow photographs of chaps in sun-helmets, the Hindustani words that you're expected to know the meaning of, the everlasting anecdotes about tiger-shoots and what Smith said to Jones in Poona in '87. It's a sort of little world of their own that they've created, like a kind of cyst. To me, of course, it was all quite new and in some ways rather interesting. Old Vincent, Hilda's father, had been not only in India but also in some even more outlandish place, Borneo or Sarawak. I forget which. He was the usual type, completely bald, almost invisible behind his moustache, and full of stories about cobras and cummerbunds and what the district collector said in '93.

Hilda's mother was so colourless that she was just like one of the faded photos on the wall. There was also a son, Harold, who had some official job in Ceylon and was home on leave at the time when I first met Hilda. They had a little dark house in one of those buried back-streets that exist in Ealing. It smelt perpetually of Trichinopoly cigars and it was so full of spears, blow-pipes, brass ornaments and the heads of wild animals that you could hardly move about in it.

Old Vincent had retired in 1910, and since then he and his wife had shown about as much activity, mental or physical, as a couple of shellfish. But at the time I was vaguely impressed by a family which had had majors, colonels and once even an admiral in it. My attitude towards the Vincents, and theirs towards me, is an interesting illustration of what fools people can be when they get outside their own line. Put me among business people—whether they're company directors or commercial travellers—and I'm a fairly good judge of character. But I had no experience whatever of the officer-rentier-clergyman class, and I was inclined to kow-tow to these decayed throw-outs. I looked on them as my social and intellectual superiors, while they on the other hand mistook me for a rising young business man who before long would be pulling down the big dough. To people of that kind, 'business', whether it's marine insurance or selling peanuts, is just a dark mystery. All they know is that it's something rather vulgar out of which you can make money. Old Vincent used to talk impressively about my being 'in business'—once, I remember, he had a slip of the tongue and said 'in trade'—and obviously didn't grasp the difference between being in business as an employee and being there on your own account. He had some vague notion that as I was 'in' the Flying Salamander I should sooner or later rise to the top of it, by a process of promotion. I think it's possible that he also had pictures of himself touching me for fivers at some future date. Harold certainly had. I could see it in his eye. In fact, even with my income being what it is, I'd probably be lending money to Harold at this moment if he were alive. Luckily he died a few years after we were married, of enteric or something, and both the old Vincents are dead too.

Well, Hilda and I were married, and right from the start it was a flop. Why did you marry her? you say. But why did you marry yours? These things happen to us. I wonder whether you'll believe that during the first two or three years I had serious thoughts of killing Hilda. Of course in practice one never does these things, they're only a kind of fantasy that one enjoys thinking about. Besides, chaps who murder their wives always get copped. However cleverly you've faked the alibi, they know perfectly well that it's you who did it, and they'll pin it onto you somehow. When a woman's bumped off, her husband is always the first suspect—which gives you a little side-glimpse of what people really think about marriage.

One gets used to everything in time. After a year or two I stopped wanting to kill her and started wondering about her. Just wondering. For hours, sometimes, on Sunday afternoons or in the evening when I've come home from work, I've lain on my bed with all my clothes on except my shoes, wondering about women. Why they're like that, how they get like that, whether they're doing it on purpose. It seems to be a most frightful thing, the sudden-ness with which some women go to pieces after they're married. It's as if they were strung up to do just that one thing, and the instant they've done it they wither off like a flower that's set its seed. What really gets me down is the dreary attitude towards life that it implies. If marriage was just an open swindle—if the woman trapped you into it and then turned round and said, 'Now, you bastard, I've caught you and you're going to work for me while I have a good time!'—I wouldn't mind so much. But not a bit of it. They don't want to have a good time, they merely want to slump into middle-age as quickly as possible. After the frightful battle of getting her man to the altar, the woman kind of relaxes, and all her youth, looks, energy and joy of life just vanish overnight. It was like that with Hilda. Here was this pretty, delicate girl, who'd seemed to me—and in fact when I first knew her she *was*—a finer type of animal than myself, and within only about three years she'd settled down into a depressed, lifeless, middle-aged frump. I'm not denying that I was part of the reason. But whoever she'd married it would have been much the same.

What Hilda lacks—I discovered this about a week after we were married—is any kind of joy in life, any kind of interest in things for their own sake. The idea of doing things because you enjoy them is something she can hardly understand. It was through Hilda that I first got a notion of what these decayed middle-class families are really like. The essential fact about them is that all their vitality has been drained away by lack of money. In families like that, which live on tiny pensions and annuities—that's to say on incomes which never get bigger and generally get smaller—there's more sense of poverty, more crust-wiping and looking twice at sixpence, than you'd find in any farm-labourer's family, let alone a family like mine. Hilda's often told me that almost the first thing she can remember is a ghastly feeling that there was never enough money for anything. Of course, in that kind of family, the lack of money is always at its worst when the kids are at the school-age. Consequently they grow up, especially the girls, with a fixed idea not only that one always *is* hard-up but that it's one's duty to be miserable about it.

At the beginning we lived in a poky little maisonette and had a job to get by on my wages. Later, when I was transferred to the West Bletchley branch, things were better, but Hilda's attitude didn't change. Always that ghastly glooming about money! The milk bill! The coal bill! The rent! The school fees! We've lived all our life together to the tune of 'Next week we'll be in the work-house'. It's not that Hilda's mean, in the ordinary sense of the word, and still less that she's selfish. Even when there happens to be a bit of spare cash knocking about I can hardly persuade her to buy herself any decent clothes. But she's got this feeling that you *ought* to be perpetually working yourself up into a stew about lack of money. Just working up an atmosphere of misery from a sense of duty. I'm not like that. I've got more the prole's attitude towards money. Life's here to be lived, and if we're going to be in the soup next week—well, next week is a long way off. What really shocks her is the fact that I refuse to worry. She's always going for me about it. 'But, George! You don't seem to *realise!* We've simply got no money at all! It's very *serious!*' She loves getting into a panic because something or other is 'serious'. And of late she's got that trick, when she's glooming about something, of kind of hunching her shoulders and folding her arms across her breast. If you made a list of Hilda's remarks throughout the day, you'd find three bracketed together at the top—'We can't afford it', 'It's a great saving' and 'I don't know where the money's to come from'. She does everything for negative reasons. When she makes a cake she's not thinking about the cake, only about how to save butter and eggs. When I'm in bed with her all she thinks about is how not to have a baby. If she goes to the pictures she's all the time writhing with indignation about the price of the seats. Her methods of housekeeping, with all the emphasis on 'using things up' and 'making things do', would have given Mother convulsions. On the other hand, Hilda isn't in the least a snob. She's never looked down on me because I'm

142

not a gentleman. On the contrary, from her point of view I'm much too lordly in my habits. We never have a meal in a teashop without a frightful row in whispers because I'm tipping the waitress too much. And it's a curious thing that in the last few years she's become much more definitely lower-middle-class, in outlook and even in appearance, than I am. Of course all this 'saving' business has never led to anything. It never does. We live just about as well or as badly as the other people in Ellesmere Road. But the everlasting stew about the gas bill and the milk bill and the awful price of butter and the kids' boots and school fees goes on and on. It's a kind of game with Hilda.

We moved to West Bletchley in '29 and started buying the house in Ellesmere Road the next year, a little before Billy was born. After I was made an Inspector I was more away from home and had more opportunities with other women. Of course I was unfaithful—I won't say all the time, but as often as I got the chance. Curiously enough, Hilda was jealous. In a way, considering how little that kind of thing means to her, I wouldn't have expected her to mind. And like all jealous women she'll sometimes show a cunning you wouldn't think her capable of. Sometimes the way she's caught me out would have made me believe in telepathy, if it wasn't that she's often been equally suspicious when I didn't happen to be guilty. I'm more or less permanently under suspicion, though, God knows, in the last few years—the last five years, anyway—I've been innocent enough. You have to be, when you're as fat as I am.

Taking it by and large, I suppose Hilda and I don't get on worse than about half the couples in Ellesmere Road. There've been times when I've thought of separation or divorce, but in our walk of life you don't do those things. You can't afford to. And then time goes on, and you kind of give up struggling. When you've lived with a woman for fifteen years, it's difficult to imagine life without her. She's part of the order of things. I dare say you might find things to object to in the sun and the moon, but do you really want to change them? Besides, there were the kids. Kids are a 'link', as they say. Or a 'tie'. Not to say a ball and fetter.

Of late years Hilda has made two great friends called Mrs Wheeler and Miss Minns. Mrs Wheeler is a widow, and I gather she's got very bitter ideas about the male sex. I can feel her kind of quivering with disapproval if I so much as come into the room. She's a faded little woman and gives you a curious impression that she's the same colour all over, a kind of greyish dust-colour, but she's full of energy. She's a bad influence on Hilda, because she's got the same passion for 'saving' and 'making things do', though in a slightly different form. With her it takes the form of thinking that you can have a good time without paying for it. She's for ever nosing out bargains and amusements that don't cost money. With people like that it doesn't matter a damn whether they want a thing or not, it's merely a question of whether they can get it on the cheap. When the big shops have their remnant sales Mrs Wheeler's always at the head of the queue, and it's her greatest pride, after a day's hard fighting round the counter, to come out without having bought anything. Miss Minns is quite a different sort. She's really a sad case, poor Miss Minns. She's a tall thin woman of about thirty-eight, with black patent-leather hair and a very *good*, trusting kind of face. She lives on some kind of tiny fixed income, an annuity or something, and I fancy she's a left-over from the old society of West Bletchley, when it was a little country town, before the suburb grew up. It's written all over her that her father was a clergyman and sat on her pretty heavily while he lived. They're a special by-product of the middle classes, these women who turn into withered hags before they even manage to escape from home. Poor old Miss Minns, for all her wrinkles, still looks exactly like a child. It's still a tremendous adventure to her not to go to church. She's always burbling about 'modern progress' and 'the woman's movement', and she's got a vague yearning to do something she calls 'developing her mind', only she doesn't quite know how to start. I think in the beginning she cottoned on to Hilda and Mrs Wheeler out of pure loneliness, but now they take her with them wherever they go.

And the times they've had together, those three! Sometimes I've almost envied them. Mrs Wheeler is the leading spirit. You couldn't name a kind of idiocy that she hasn't dragged them into at one time or another. Anything from theosophy to cat's-cradle, provided you can do it on the cheap. For months they went in for the food-crank business. Mrs Wheeler had picked up a second-hand copy of some book called *Radiant Energy* which proved that you should live on lettuces and other things that don't cost money. Of course this appealed to Hilda, who immediately began starving herself. She'd have tried it on me and the kids as well, only I put my foot down. Then they had a go at faith-healing. Then they thought of tackling Pelmanism, but after a lot of correspondence they found that they couldn't get the booklets free, which had been Mrs Wheeler's idea. Then it was hay-box cookery. Then it was some filthy stuff called bee wine, which was supposed to cost nothing at all because you made it out of water. They dropped that after they'd read an article in the paper saying that bee wine gives you cancer. Then they nearly joined one of those women's clubs which go for conducted tours round factories, but after a lot of arithmetic Mrs Wheeler decided that the free teas the factories gave you didn't quite equal the subscription. Then Mrs Wheeler scraped acquaintance with somebody who gave away free tickets for plays produced by some stage society or other. I've known the three of them sit for hours listening to some highbrow play of which they didn't even pretend to understand a word—couldn't even tell you the name of the play afterwards—but they felt that they were getting something for nothing. Once they even took up spiritualism. Mrs Wheeler had run across some down-and-out medium who was so desperate that he'd give séances for eighteen-pence, so that the three of them could have a glimpse beyond the veil for a tanner a time. I saw him once when he came to give a séance at our house. He was a seedy-looking old devil and obviously in mortal terror of DTs. He was so shaky that when he was taking his overcoat off in the hall he had a sort of spasm and a hank of butter-muslin dropped out of his trouser-leg. I managed to shove it back to him before the women saw. Buttermuslin is what they make the ectoplasm with, so I'm told. I suppose he was going on to another séance afterwards. You don't get manifestations for eighteen-pence. Mrs Wheeler's biggest find of the last few years is the Left Book Club. I think it was in '36 that the news of the Left Book Club got to West Bletchley. I joined it soon afterwards, and it's almost the only time I can remember spending money without Hilda protesting. She can see some sense in buying a book when you're getting it for a third of its proper price. These women's attitude is curious, really. Miss Minns certainly had a try at reading one or two of the books, but this wouldn't even have occurred to the other two. They've never had any direct connection with the Left Book Club or any notion what it's all about—in fact I believe at the beginning Mrs Wheeler thought it had something to do with books which had been left in railway carriages and were being sold off cheap. But they do know that it means seven-and-sixpenny books for half a crown, and so they're always saying that it's 'such a good idea'.

Now and again the local Left Book Club branch holds meetings and gets people down to speak, and Mrs Wheeler always takes the others along. She's a great one for public meetings of any kind, always provided that it's indoors and admission free. The three of them sit there like lumps of pudding. They don't know what the meeting's about and they don't care, but they've got a vague feeling, especially Miss Minns, that they're improving their minds, and it isn't costing them anything.

Well, that's Hilda. You see what she's like. Take it by and large, I suppose she's no worse than I am. Sometimes when we were first married I felt I'd like to strangle her, but later I got so that I didn't care. And then I got fat and settled down. It must have been in 1930 that I got fat. It happened so suddenly that it was as if a cannon ball had hit me and got stuck inside. You know how it is. One night you go to bed, still feeling more or less young, with an eye for the girls and so forth, and next morning you wake up in the full consciousness that you're just a poor old fatty with nothing ahead of you this side the grave except sweating your guts out to buy boots for the kids.

And now it's '38, and in every shipyard in the world they're riveting up the battleships for another war, and a name I chanced to see on a poster had stirred up in me a whole lot of stuff which ought to have been buried God knows how many years ago.

PART III

PART II.

I

WHEN I CAME HOME that evening I was still in doubt as to what I'd spend my seventeen quid on.

Hilda said she was going to the Left Book Club meeting. It seemed that there was a chap coming down from London to lecture, though needless to say Hilda didn't know what the lecture was going to be about. I told her I'd go with her. In a general way I'm not much of a one for lectures, but the visions of war I'd had that morning, starting with the bomber flying over the train, had put me into a kind of thoughtful mood. After the usual argument we got the kids to bed early and cleared off in time for the lecture, which was billed for eight o'clock.

It was a misty kind of evening, and the hall was cold and not too well lighted. It's a little wooden hall with a tin roof, the property of some Nonconformist sect or other, and you can hire it for ten bob. The usual crowd of fifteen or sixteen people had rolled up. On the front of the platform there was a yellow placard announcing that the lecture was on 'The Menace of Fascism'. This didn't altogether surprise me. Mr Witchett, who acts as chairman at these meetings and who in private life is something in an architect's office, was taking the lecturer round, introducing him to everyone as Mr So-and-so (I forget his name) 'the well-known anti-Fascist', very much as you might call somebody 'the well-known pianist'. The lecturer was a little chap of about forty, in a dark suit, with a bald head which he'd tried rather unsuccessfully to cover up with wisps of hair.

Meetings of this kind never start on time. There's always a period of hanging about on the pretence that perhaps a few more people are going to turn up. It was about twenty-five past eight when Witchett tapped on the table and did his stuff. Witchett's a mild-looking chap, with a pink, baby's bottom kind of face that's always covered in smiles. I believe he's secretary of the local Liberal Party, and he's also on the Parish Council and acts as MC at the magic lantern lectures for the Mothers' Union. He's what you might call a born chairman. When he tells you how delighted we all are to have Mr So-and-so on the platform tonight, you can see that he believes it. I never look at him without thinking that he's probably a virgin. The little lecturer took out a wad of notes, chiefly newspaper cuttings, and pinned them down with his glass of water. Then he gave a quick lick at his lips and began to shoot.

Do you ever go to lectures, public meetings and whatnot?

When I go to one myself, there's always a moment during the evening when I find myself thinking the same thought. Why the hell are we doing this? Why is it that people will turn out on a winter night for this kind of thing? I looked round the hall. I was sitting in the back row. I don't ever remember going to any kind of public meeting when I didn't sit in the back row if I could manage it. Hilda and the others had planked themselves in front, as usual. It was rather a gloomy little hall. You know the kind of place. Pitch-pine walls, corrugated iron roof and enough draughts to make you want to keep your overcoat on. The little knot of us were sitting in the light round the platform, with about thirty rows of empty chairs behind us. And the seats of all the chairs were dusty. On the platform behind the lecturer there was a huge square thing draped in dust-cloths which might have been an enormous coffin under a pall. Actually it was a piano.

At the beginning I wasn't exactly listening. The lecturer was rather a mean-looking little chap, but a good speaker.

White face, very mobile mouth, and the rather grating voice that they get from constant speaking. Of course he was pitching into Hitler and the Nazis. I wasn't particularly keen to hear what he was saying—get the same stuff in the *News Chronicle* every morning—but his voice came across to me as a kind of burr-burr-burr, with now and again a phrase that stuck out and caught my attention.

'Bestial atrocities. . . . Hideous outbursts of sadism. . . . Rubber truncheons. . . . Concentration camps. . . . Iniquitous persecution of the Jews. . . . Back to the Dark Ages. . . . European civilisation. . . . Act before it is too late. . . . Indignation of all decent peoples. . . . Alliance of the democratic nations. . . . Firm stand. . . . Defence of democracy. . . . Democracy. . . . Fascism. . . . Democracy. . . . Fascism . . . Democracy. . . .'

You know the line of talk. These chaps can churn it out by the hour. Just like a gramophone. Turn the handle, press the button and it starts. Democracy, Fascism, Democracy. But somehow it interested me to watch him. A rather mean little man, with a white face and a bald head, standing on a platform, shooting out slogans. What's he doing? Quite deliberately, and quite openly, he's stirring up hatred. Doing his damnedest to make you hate certain foreigners called Fascists. It's a queer thing, I thought, to be known as 'Mr So-and-so, the well-known anti-Fascist'. A queer trade, anti-Fascism. This fellow, I suppose, makes his living by writing books against Hitler. But what did he do before Hitler came along? And what'll he do if Hitler ever disappears? Same question applies to doctors, detectives, rat-catchers and so forth, of course. But the grating voice went on and on, and another thought struck me. He *means* it. Not faking at all—feels every word he's saying. He's trying to work up hatred in the audience, but that's nothing to the hatred he feels himself. Every slogan's gospel truth to him. If you cut him open all you'd find inside would be

Democracy-Fascism-Democracy. Interesting to know a chap like that in private life. But does he have a private life? Or does he only go round from platform to platform, working up hatred? Perhaps even his dreams are slogans.

As well as I could from the back row I had a look at the audience. I suppose, if you come to think of it, we people who'll turn out on winter nights to sit in draughty halls listening to Left Book Club lectures (and I consider that I'm entitled to the 'we', seeing that I'd done it myself on this occasion) have a certain significance. We're the West Bletchley revolutionaries. Doesn't look hopeful at first sight. It struck me as I looked round the audience that only about half a dozen of them had really grasped what the lecturer was talking about, though by this time he'd been pitching into Hitler and the Nazis for over half an hour. It's always like that with meetings of this kind. Invariably half the people come away without a notion of what it's all about. In his chair beside the table Witchett was watching the lecturer with a delighted smile, and his face looked a little like a pink geranium. You could hear in advance the speech he'd make as soon as the lecturer sat down—same speech as he makes at the end of the magic lantern lecture in aid of trousers for the Melanesians: 'Express our thanks —voicing the opinion of all of us—most interesting—give us all a lot to think about—most stimulating evening!' In the front row Miss Minns was sitting very upright, with her head cocked a little on one side, like a bird. The lecturer had taken a sheet of paper from under the tumbler and was reading out statistics about the German suicide-rate. You could see by the look of Miss Minns's long thin neck that she wasn't feeling happy. Was this improving her mind, or wasn't it? If only she could make out what it was all about! The other two were sitting there like lumps of pudding. Next to them a little woman with red hair was knitting a jumper. One plain, two purl, drop one and knit two together. The lecturer was describing how the Nazis chop people's heads off for treason and sometimes the executioner makes a bosh shot. There was one other woman in the audience, a girl with dark hair, one of the teachers at the Council School. Unlike the others she was really listening, sitting forward with her big round eyes fixed on the lecturer and her mouth a little bit open, drinking it all in.

Just behind her two old blokes from the local Labour Party were sitting. One had grey hair cropped very short, the other had a bald head and a droopy moustache. Both wearing their overcoats. You know the type. Been in the Labour Party since the year dot. Lives given up to the movement. Twenty years of being blacklisted by employers, and another ten of badgering the Council to do something about the slums. Suddenly everything's changed, the old Labour Party stuff doesn't matter any longer. Find themselves pitchforked into foreign politics —Hitler, Stalin, bombs, machine-guns, rubber truncheons, Rome-Berlin axis, Popular Front, anti-Comintern pact. Can't make head or tail of it. Immediately in front of me the local Communist Party branch were sitting. All three of them very young. One of them's got money and is something in the Hesperides Estate Company, in fact I believe he's old Crum's nephew. Another's a clerk at one of the banks. He cashes cheques for me occasionally. A nice boy, with a round, very young, eager face, blue eyes like a baby and hair so fair that you'd think he peroxided it. He only looks about seventeen, though I suppose he's twenty. He was wearing a cheap blue suit and a bright blue tie that went with his hair. Next to these three another Communist was sitting. But this one, it seems, is a different kind of Communist and not quite-quite, because he's what they call a Trotskyist. The others have got a down on him. He's even younger, a very thin, very dark, nervous-looking boy. Clever face. Jew, of course. These four were taking the lecture quite differently from the others. You knew they'd be on their feet the moment question-time started. You could see them kind of twitching already. And the little Trotskyist working himself from side to side on his bum in his anxiety to get in ahead of the others.

I'd stopped listening to the actual words of the lecture. But there are more ways than one of listening. I shut my eyes for a moment. The effect of that was curious. I seemed to see the fellow much better when I could only hear his voice.

It was a voice that sounded as if it could go on for a fortnight without stopping. It's a ghastly thing, really, to have a sort of human barrel-organ shooting propaganda at you by the hour. The same thing over and over again. Hate, hate, hate. Let's all get together and have a good hate. Over and over. It gives you the feeling that something has got inside your skull and is hammering down on your brain. But for a moment, with my eyes shut, I managed to turn the tables on him. I got inside *his* skull. It was a peculiar sensation. For about a second I was inside him, you might almost say I *was* him. At any rate, I felt what he was feeling.

I saw the vision that he was seeing. And it wasn't at all the kind of vision that can be talked about. What he's *saying* is merely that Hitler's after us and we must all get together and have a good hate. Doesn't go into details. Leaves it all respectable. But what he's *seeing* is something quite different. It's a picture of himself smashing people's faces in with a spanner. Fascist faces, of course. I *know* that's what he was seeing. It was what I saw myself for the second or two that I was inside him. Smash! Right in the middle! The bones cave in like an eggshell and what was a face a minute ago is just a great big blob of strawberry jam. Smash! There goes another! That's what's in his mind, waking and

156

sleeping, and the more he thinks of it the more he likes it. And it's all OK because the smashed faces belong to Fascists. You could hear all that in the tone of his voice.

But why? Likeliest explanation, because he's scared. Every thinking person nowadays is stiff with fright. This is merely a chap who's got sufficient foresight to be a little more frightened than the others. Hitler's after us! Quick! Let's all grab a spanner and get together, and perhaps if we smash in enough faces they won't smash ours. Gang up, choose your Leader. Hitler's black and Stalin's white. But it might just as well be the other way about, because in the little chap's mind both Hitler and Stalin are the same. Both mean spanners and smashed faces.

War! I started thinking about it again. It's coming soon, that's certain. But who's afraid of war? That's to say, who's afraid of the bombs and the machine-guns? 'You are,' you say. Yes, I am, and so's anybody who's ever seen them. But it isn't the war that matters, it's the after-war. The world we're going down into, the kind of hate-world, slogan-world. The coloured shirts, the barbed wire, the rubber truncheons. The secret cells where the electric light burns night and day, and the detectives watching you while you sleep. And the processions and the posters with enormous faces, and the crowds of a million people all cheering for the Leader till they deafen themselves into thinking that they really worship him, and all the time, underneath, they hate him so that they want to puke. It's all going to happen. Or isn't it? Some days I know it's impossible, other days I know it's inevitable. That night, at any rate, I knew it was going to happen. It was all in the sound of the little lecturer's voice.

So perhaps after all there *is* a significance in this mingy little crowd that'll turn out on a winter night to listen to a lecture of this kind. Or at any rate in the five or six who can grasp what it's all about. They're simply the outposts of an enormous army. They're the long-sighted ones, the first rats to spot that the ship is sinking. Quick, quick! The Fascists are coming! Spanners ready, boys! Smash others or they'll smash you. So terrified of the future that we're jumping straight into it like a rabbit diving down a boa-constrictor's throat.

And what'll happen to chaps like me when we get Fascism in England? The truth is it probably won't make the slightest difference. As for the lecturer and those four Communists in the audience, yes, it'll make plenty of difference to them. They'll be smashing faces, or having their own smashed, according to who's winning. But the ordinary middling chaps like me will be carrying on just as usual. And yet it frightens me—I tell you it frightens me. I'd just started to wonder why when the lecturer stopped and sat down.

There was the usual hollow little sound of clapping that you get when there are only about fifteen people in the audience, and then old Witchett said his piece, and before you could say Jack Robinson the four Communists were on their feet together. They had a good dog-fight that went on for about ten minutes, full of a lot of stuff that nobody else understood, such as dialectical materialism and the destiny of the proletariat and what Lenin said in 1918. Then the lecturer, who'd had a drink of water, stood up and gave a summing-up that made the Trotskyist wriggle about on his chair but pleased the other three, and the dog-fight went on unofficially for a bit longer. Nobody else did any talking. Hilda and the others had cleared off the moment the lecture ended. Probably they were afraid there was going to be a collection to pay for the hire of the hall. The little woman with red hair was staying to finish her row. You could hear her counting her stitches in a whisper while the others argued. And Witchett sat and beamed at whoever happened to be speaking, and you could see him thinking how interesting it all was and making mental notes, and the girl with black hair looked from one to the other with her mouth a little open, and the old Labour man, looking rather like a seal with his droopy moustache and his overcoat up to his ears, sat looking up at them, wondering what the hell it was all about. And finally I got up and began to put on my overcoat.

The dog-fight had turned into a private row between the little Trotskyist and the boy with fair hair. They were arguing about whether you ought to join the army if war broke out. As I edged my way along the row of chairs to get out, the fair-haired one appealed to me.

'Mr Bowling! Look here. If war broke out and we had the chance to smash Fascism once and for all, wouldn't you fight? If you were young, I mean.'

I suppose he thinks I'm about sixty.

'You bet I wouldn't,' I said. 'I had enough to go on with last time.'

'But to smash Fascism!'

'Oh, b—— Fascism! There's been enough smashing done already, if you ask me.'

The little Trotskyist chips in with social-patriotism and betrayal of the workers, but the other cuts him short:

'But you're thinking of 1914. That was just an ordinary imperialist war. This time it's different. Look here. When you hear about what's going on in Germany, and the concentration camps and the Nazis beating people up with rubber truncheons and making the Jews spit in each other's faces—doesn't it make your blood boil?'

They're always going on about your blood boiling. Just the same phrase during the war, I remember.

'I went off the boil in 1916,' I told him. 'And so'll you when you know what a trench smells like.'

And then all of a sudden I seemed to see him. It was as if I hadn't properly seen him till that moment.

A very young eager face, might have belonged to a good-looking schoolboy, with blue eyes and tow-coloured hair, gazing into mine, and for a moment actually he'd got tears in his eyes! Felt as strongly as all that about the German Jews! But as a matter of fact I knew just what he felt. He's a hefty lad, probably plays rugger for the bank. Got brains, too. And here he is, a bank clerk in a godless suburb, sitting behind the frosted window, entering figures in a ledger, counting piles of notes, bumsucking to the manager. Feels his life rotting away. And all the while, over in Europe, the big stuff's happening. Shells bursting over the trenches and waves of infantry charging through the drifts of smoke. Probably some of his pals are fighting in Spain. Of course he's spoiling for a war. How can you blame him? For a moment I had a peculiar feeling that he was my son, which in point of years he might have been. And I thought of that sweltering hot day in August when the newsboy stuck up the poster ENGLAND DECLARES WAR ON GERMANY, and we all rushed out onto the pavement in our white aprons and cheered.

'Listen, son,' I said, 'you've got it all wrong. In 1914 *we* thought it was going to be a glorious business. Well, it wasn't. It was just a bloody mess. If it comes again, you keep out of it. Why should you get your body plugged full of lead? Keep it for some girl. You think war's all heroism and VC charges, but I tell you it isn't like that. You don't have bayonet-charges nowadays, and when you do it isn't like you imagine. You don't feel like a hero. All you know is that you've had no sleep for three days, you stink like a polecat, you're pissing your bags with fright and your hands are so cold you can't hold your rifle. But that doesn't matter a damn, either. It's the things that happen afterwards.'

Makes no impression of course. They just think you're out of date. Might as well stand at the door of a knocking-shop handing out tracts.

The people were beginning to clear off. Witchett was taking the lecturer home. The three Communists and the little Jew went up the road together, and they were going at it again with proletarian solidarity and dialectic of the dialectic and what Trotsky said in 1917. They're all the same, really. It was a damp, still, very black night. The lamps seemed to hang in the darkness like stars and didn't light the road. In the distance you could hear the trams booming along the High Street. I wanted a drink, but it was nearly ten and the nearest pub was half a mile away. Besides, I wanted somebody to talk to, the way you can't talk in a pub. It was funny how my brain had been on the go all day. Partly the result of not working, of course, and partly of the new false teeth, which had kind of freshened me up. All day I'd been brooding on the future and the past. I wanted to talk about the bad time that's either coming or isn't coming, the slogans and the coloured shirts and the streamlined men from eastern Europe who are going to knock old England cock-eyed. Hopeless trying to talk to Hilda. Suddenly it occurred to me to go and look up old Porteous, who's a pal of mine and keeps late hours.

Porteous is a retired public-school master. He lives in rooms, which luckily are in the lower half of the house, in the old part of the town, near the church. He's a bachelor, of course. You can't imagine that kind married. Lives all alone with his books and his pipe and has a woman in to do for him. He's a learned kind of chap, with his Greek and Latin and poetry and all that. I suppose that if the local Left Book Club branch represents Progress, old Porteous stands for Culture. Neither of them cuts much ice in West Bletchley.

The light was burning in the little room where old Porteous sits reading till all hours of the night. As I tapped on the front door he came strolling out as usual, with his pipe between his teeth and his fingers in a book to keep the place. He's rather a striking-looking chap, very tall, with curly grey hair and a thin, dreamy kind of face that's a bit discoloured but might almost belong to a boy, though he must be nearly sixty. It's funny how some of these public-school and university chaps manage to look like boys till their dying day. It's something in their movements. Old Porteous has got a way of strolling up and down, with that handsome head of his, with the grey curls, held a little back, that makes you feel that all the while he's dreaming about some poem or other and isn't conscious of what's going on round him. You can't look at him without seeing the way he's lived written all over him. Public School, Oxford, and then back to his old school as a master. Whole life lived in an atmosphere of Latin, Greek and cricket. He's got all the mannerisms. Always wears an old Harris tweed jacket and old grey flannel bags which he likes you to call 'disgraceful', smokes a pipe and looks down on cigarettes, and though he sits up half the night I bet he has a cold bath every morning. I suppose from his point of view I'm a bit of a bounder. I haven't been to a public school, I don't know any Latin and don't even want to. He tells me sometimes that it's a pity I'm 'insensible to beauty', which I suppose is a polite way of saying that I've got no education. All the same I like him. He's very hospitable in the right kind of way, always ready to have you in and talk at all hours, and always got drinks handy. When you live in a house like ours, more or less infested by women and kids, it does you good to get out of it sometimes into a bachelor atmosphere, a kind of book-pipe-fire atmosphere. And the classy Oxford feeling of nothing mattering except books and poetry and Greek statues, and nothing worth mentioning having happened since the Goths sacked Rome—sometimes that's a comfort too.

He shoved me into the old leather armchair by the fire

and dished out whisky and soda. I've never seen his sitting-room when it wasn't dim with pipe-smoke. The ceiling is almost black. It's a smallish room, and except for the door and the window and the space over the fireplace, the walls are covered with books from the floor right up to the ceiling. On the mantelpiece there are all the things you'd expect. A row of old briar pipes, all filthy, a few Greek silver coins, a tobacco jar with the arms of old Porteous's college on it, and a little earthenware lamp which he told me he dug up on some mountain in Sicily. Over the mantelpiece there are photos of Greek statues. There's a big one in the middle of a woman with wings and no head who looks as if she was stepping out to catch a bus. I remember how shocked old Porteous was when the first time I saw it, not knowing any better, I asked him why they didn't stick a head on it.

Porteous started refilling his pipe from the jar on the mantelpiece.

'That intolerable woman upstairs has purchased a wire-less set,' he said. 'I had been hoping to live the rest of my life out of the sound of those things. I suppose there is nothing one can do? Do you happen to know the legal position?'

I told him there was nothing one could do. I rather like the Oxfordy way he says 'intolerable', and it tickles me, in 1938, to find someone objecting to having a radio in the house. Porteous was strolling up and down in his usual dreamy way, with his hands in his coat pockets and his pipe between his teeth, and almost instantly he'd begun talking about some law against musical instruments that was passed in Athens in the time of Pericles. It's always that way with old Porteous. All his talk is about things that hap-pened centuries ago. Whatever you start off with it always comes back to statues and poetry and the Greeks and Romans. If you mention the *Queen Mary* he'd start telling you about Phoenician triremes. He never reads a modern book, refuses to know their names, never looks at any newspaper except *The Times* and takes a pride in telling you that he's never been to the pictures. Except for a few poets like Keats and Wordsworth he thinks the modern world—and from his point of view the modern world is the last two thousand years—just oughtn't to have happened.

I'm part of the modern world myself, but I like to hear him talk. He'll stroll round the shelves and haul out first one book and then another, and now and again he'll read you a piece between little puffs of smoke, generally having to translate it from the Latin or something as he goes. It's all kind of peaceful, kind of mellow. All a little like a schoolmaster, and yet it soothes you, somehow. While you listen you aren't in the same world as trams and gas bills and insurance companies. It's all temples and olive trees, and peacocks and elephants, and chaps in the arena with their nets and tridents, and winged lions and eunuchs and galleys and catapults, and generals in brass armour galloping their horses over the soldiers' shields. It's funny that he ever cottoned on to a chap like me. But it's one of the advantages of being fat that you can fit into almost any society. Besides, we meet on common ground when it comes to dirty stories. They're the one modern thing he cares about, though, as he's always reminding me, they aren't modern. He's rather old-maidish about it, always tells a story in a veiled kind of way. Sometimes he'll pick out some Latin poet and translate a smutty rhyme, leaving a lot to your imagination, or he'll drop hints about the private lives of the Roman emperors and the things that went on in the temples of Ashtaroth. They seem to have been a bad lot, those Greeks and Romans. Old Porteous has got photographs of wall-paintings somewhere in Italy that would make your hair curl.

When I'm fed up with business and home life it's often done me a lot of good to go and have a talk with Porteous. But tonight it didn't seem to. My mind was still running on the same lines as it had been all day. Just as I'd done with the Left Book Club lecturer, I didn't exactly listen to what Porteous was saying, only to the sound of his voice. But whereas the lecturer's voice had got under my skin, old Porteous's didn't. It was too peaceful, too Oxfordy. Finally, when he was in the middle of saying something, I chipped in and said:

'Tell me, Porteous, what do you think of Hitler?'

Old Porteous was leaning in his lanky, graceful kind of way with his elbows on the mantelpiece and a foot on the fender. He was so surprised that he almost took his pipe out of his mouth.

'Hitler? This German person? My dear fellow! I *don't* think of him.'

'But the trouble is he's going to bloody well make us think about him before he's finished.'

Old Porteous shies a bit at the word 'bloody', which he doesn't like, though of course it's part of his pose never to be shocked. He begins walking up and down again, puffing out smoke.

'I see no reason for paying any attention to him. A mere adventurer. These people come and go. Ephemeral, purely ephemeral.'

I'm not certain what the word 'ephemeral' means, but I stick to my point:

'I think you've got it wrong. Old Hitler's something different. So's Joe Stalin. They aren't like these chaps in the old days who crucified people and chopped their heads off and so forth, just for the fun of it. They're after something quite new—something that's never been heard of before.'

'My dear fellow! There is nothing new under the sun.'

Of course that's a favourite saying of old Porteous's. He

won't hear of the existence of anything new. As soon as you tell him about anything that's happening nowadays he says that exactly the same thing happened in the reign of King So-and-so. Even if you bring up things like aeroplanes he tells you that they probably had them in Crete, or Mycenae or wherever it was. I tried to explain to him what I'd felt while the little bloke was lecturing and the kind of vision I'd had of the bad time that's coming, but he wouldn't listen. Merely repeated that there's nothing new under the sun. Finally he hauls a book out of the shelves and reads me a passage about some Greek tyrant back in the BCs who certainly might have been Hitler's twin brother.

The argument went on for a bit. All day I'd been wanting to talk to somebody about this business. It's funny. I'm not a fool, but I'm not a highbrow either, and God knows at normal times I don't have many interests that you wouldn't expect a middle-aged seven-pound-a-weeker with two kids to have. And yet I've enough sense to see that the old life we're used to is being sawn off at the roots. I can feel it happening. I can see the war that's coming and I can see the after-war, the food-queues and the secret police and the loudspeakers telling you what to think. And I'm not even exceptional in this. There are millions of others like me. Ordinary chaps that I meet everywhere, chaps I run across in pubs, bus drivers and travelling salesmen for hardware firms, have got a feeling that the world's gone wrong. They can feel things cracking and collapsing under their feet. And yet here's this learned chap, who's lived all his life with books and soaked himself in history till it's running out of his pores, and he can't even see that things are changing. Doesn't think Hitler matters. Refuses to believe there's another war coming. In any case, as he didn't fight in the last war, it doesn't enter much into his thoughts—he thinks it was a poor show compared with the siege of Troy. Doesn't see why one should bother about the slogans and the loudspeakers and the coloured shirts. 'What intelligent person would pay any attention to such things?' he always says. Hitler and Stalin will pass away, but something which old Porteous calls 'the eternal verities' won't pass away. This, of course, is simply another way of saying that things will always go on exactly as he's known them. For ever and ever, cultivated Oxford blokes will stroll up and down studies full of books, quoting Latin tags and smoking good tobacco out of jars with coats of arms on them. Really it was no use talking to him. I'd have got more change out of the lad with tow-coloured hair. By degrees the conversation twisted off, as it always does, to things that happened BC. Then it worked round to poetry. Finally old Porteous drags another book out of the shelves and begins reading Keats's 'Ode to a Nightingale' (or maybe it was a skylark—I forget).

So far as I'm concerned a little poetry goes a long way. But it's a curious fact that I rather like hearing old Porteous reading it aloud. There's no question that he reads well. He's got the habit, of course—used to reading to classes of boys. He'll lean up against something in his lounging way, with his pipe between his teeth and little jets of smoke coming out, and his voice goes kind of solemn and rises and falls with the line. You can see that it moves him in some way. I don't know what poetry is or what it's supposed to do. I imagine it has a kind of nervous effect on some people like music has on others. When he's reading I don't actually listen, that's to say I don't take in the words, but sometimes the sound of it brings a kind of peaceful feeling into my mind. On the whole I like it. But somehow to-night it didn't work. It was as if a cold draught had blown into the room. I just felt that this was all bunk. Poetry! What is it? Just a voice, a bit of an eddy in the air. And Gosh! what use would that be against machine-guns?

I watched him leaning up against the bookshelf. Funny, these public-school chaps. Schoolboys all their days. Whole life revolving round the old school and their bits of Latin and Greek and poetry. And suddenly I remembered that almost the first time I was here with Porteous he'd read me the very same poem. Read it in just the same way, and his voice quivered when he got to the same bit—the bit about magic casements, or something. And a curious thought struck me. *He's dead*. He's a ghost. All people like that are dead.

It struck me that perhaps a lot of the people you see walking about are dead. We say that a man's dead when his heart stops and not before. It seems a bit arbitrary. After all, parts of your body don't stop working—hair goes on growing for years, for instance. Perhaps a man really dies when his brain stops, when he loses the power to take in a new idea. Old Porteous is like that. Wonderfully learned, wonderfully good taste—but he's not capable of change. Just says the same things and thinks the same thoughts over and over again. There are a lot of people like that. Dead minds, stopped inside. Just keep moving backwards and forwards on the same little track, getting fainter all the time, like ghosts.

Old Porteous's mind, I thought, probably stopped working at about the time of the Russo-Japanese war. And it's a ghastly thing that nearly all the decent people, the people who *don't* want to go round smashing faces in with spanners, are like that. They're decent, but their minds have stopped. They can't defend themselves against what's coming to them, because they can't see it, even when it's under their noses. They think that England will never change and that England's the whole world. Can't grasp that it's just a left-over, a tiny corner that the bombs happen to have missed. But what about the new kind of men from eastern Europe, the streamlined men who think in slogans and talk in bullets? They're on our track. Not long before they catch up with us. No Marquess of Queensberry rules for those boys. And all the decent people are paralysed. Dead men and live gorillas. Doesn't seem to be anything between.

I cleared out about half an hour later, having completely failed to convince old Porteous that Hitler matters. I was still thinking the same thoughts as I walked home through the shivery streets. The trams had stopped running. The house was all dark and Hilda was asleep. I dropped my false teeth into the glass of water in the bathroom, got into my pyjamas and prised Hilda over to the other side of the bed. She rolled over without waking, and the kind of hump between her shoulders was towards me. It's funny, the tremendous gloom that sometimes gets hold of you late at night. At that moment the destiny of Europe seemed to me more important than the rent and the kids' school bills and the work I'd have to do tomorrow. For anyone who has to earn his living such thoughts are just plain foolishness. But they didn't move out of my mind. Still the vision of the coloured shirts and the machine-guns rattling. The last thing I remember wondering before I fell asleep was why the hell a chap like me should care.

II

The primroses had started. I suppose it was some time in March.

I'd driven through Westerham and was making for Pudley. I'd got to do an assessment of an ironmonger's shop, and then, if I could get hold of him, to interview a life-insurance case who was wavering in the balance. His name had been sent in by our local agent, but at the last moment he'd taken fright and begun to doubt whether he could afford it. I'm pretty good at talking people round. It's being fat that does it. It puts people in a cheery kind of mood, makes 'em feel that signing a cheque is almost a pleasure. Of course there are different ways of tackling different people. With some it's better to lay all the stress on the bonuses, others you can scare in a subtle way with hints about what'll happen to their wives if they die uninsured.

The old car switchbacked up and down the curly little hills. And by God, what a day! You know the kind of day that generally comes some time in March when winter suddenly seems to give up fighting. For days past we'd been having the kind of beastly weather that people call 'bright' weather, when the sky's a cold hard blue and the wind scrapes you like a blunt razor-blade. Then suddenly the wind had dropped and the sun got a chance. You know the kind of day. Pale yellow sunshine, not a leaf stirring, a touch of mist in the far distances where you could see the sheep scattered over the hillsides like lumps of chalk. And down in the valleys fires were burning, and the smoke twisted slowly upwards and melted into the mist. I'd got the road to myself. It was so warm you could almost have taken your clothes off.

I got to a spot where the grass beside the road was smothered in primroses. A patch of clayey soil, perhaps. Twenty yards further on I slowed down and stopped. The weather was too good to miss. I felt I'd got to get out and have a smell at the spring air, and perhaps even pick a few primroses if there was nobody coming. I even had some vague notion of picking a bunch of them to take home to Hilda.

I switched the engine off and got out. I never like leaving the old car running in neutral, I'm always half afraid she'll shake her mudguards off or something. She's a 1927 model, and she's done a biggish mileage. When you lift the bonnet and look at the engine it reminds you of the old Austrian Empire, all tied together with bits of string but somehow keeps plugging along. You wouldn't believe any machine could vibrate in so many directions at once. It's like the motion of the earth, which has twenty-two different kinds of wobble, or so I remember reading. If you look at her from behind when she's running in neutral it's for all the world like watching one of those Hawaiian girls dancing the hula-hula.

There was a five-barred gate beside the road. I strolled over and leaned across it. Not a soul in sight. I hitched my hat back a bit to get the kind of balmy feeling of the air against my forehead. The grass under the hedge was full of primroses. Just inside the gate a tramp or somebody had left the remains of a fire. A little pile of white embers, and a wisp of smoke still oozing out of them. Further along there was a little bit of a pool, covered over with duckweed. The field was winter wheat. It sloped up sharply, and then there was a fall of chalk and a little beech spinney. A kind of mist of young leaves on the trees. And utter stillness everywhere. Not even enough wind to stir the ashes of the fire. A lark singing somewhere, otherwise not a sound, not even an aeroplane.

I stayed there for a bit, leaning over the gate. I was alone, quite alone. I was looking at the field, and the field was looking at me. I felt—I wonder whether you'll understand.

What I felt was something that's so unusual nowadays that to say it sounds like foolishness. I felt *happy*. I felt that though I shan't live for ever, I'd be quite ready to. If you like you can say that that was merely because it was the first day of spring. Seasonal effect on the sex-glands, or something. But there was more to it than that. Curiously enough, the thing that had suddenly convinced me that life was worth living, more than the primroses or the young buds on the hedge, was that bit of fire near the gate. You know the look of a wood fire on a still day. The sticks that have gone all to white ash and still keep the shape of sticks, and under the ash the kind of vivid red that you can see into. It's curious that a red ember looks more alive, gives you more of a feeling of life, than any living thing. There's something about it, a kind of intensity, a vibration—I can't think of the exact words. But it lets you know that you're alive yourself. It's the spot on the picture that makes you notice everything else.

I bent down to pick a primrose. Couldn't reach it—too much belly. I squatted down on my haunches and picked a little bunch of them. Lucky there was no one to see me. The leaves were kind of crinkly and shaped like rabbits' ears. I stood up and put my bunch of primroses on the gatepost. Then on an impulse I slid my false teeth out of my mouth and had a look at them.

If I'd had a mirror I'd have looked at the whole of myself, though, as a matter of fact, I knew what I looked like already. A fat man of forty-five, in a grey herringbone suit a bit the worse for wear and a bowler hat. Wife, two kids and a house in the suburbs written all over me. Red face and boiled blue eyes. I know, you don't have to tell me. But the thing that struck me, as I gave my dental plate the once-over before slipping it back into my mouth, was that *it doesn't matter*. Even false teeth don't matter. I'm fat—yes. I look like a bookie's unsuccessful brother—yes. No woman will ever go to bed with me again unless she's paid to. I know all that. But I tell you I don't care. I don't want the women, I don't even want to be young again. I only want to be alive. And I was alive that moment when I stood looking at the primroses and the red embers under the hedge. It's a feeling inside you, a kind of peaceful feeling, and yet it's like a flame.

Further down the hedge the pool was covered with duckweed, so like a carpet that if you didn't know what duckweed was you might think it was solid and step on it. I wondered why it is that we're all such bloody fools. Why don't people, instead of the idiocies they do spend their time on, just walk round *looking* at things? That pool, for instance—all the stuff that's in it. Newts, water-snails, water-beetles, caddis-flies, leeches, and God knows how many other things that you can only see with a microscope. The mystery of their lives, down there under water. You could spend a lifetime watching them, ten lifetimes, and still you wouldn't have got to the end even of that one pool. And all the while the sort of feeling of wonder, the peculiar flame inside you. It's the only thing worth having, and we don't want it.

But I do want it. At least I thought so at that moment. And don't mistake what I'm saying. To begin with, unlike most Cockneys, I'm not soppy about 'the country'. I was brought up a damn sight too near to it for that. I don't want to stop people living in towns, or in suburbs for that matter. Let 'em live where they like. And I'm not suggesting that the whole of humanity could spend the whole of their lives wandering round picking primroses and so forth. I know perfectly well that we've got to work. It's only because chaps are coughing their lungs out in mines and girls are hammering at typewriters that anyone ever has time to pick a flower. Besides, if you hadn't a full belly and a warm house you wouldn't want to pick flowers. But that's not the point. Here's this feeling that I get inside me—not often, I admit, but now and again. I know it's a good feeling to have. What's more, so does everybody else, or nearly everybody. It's just round the corner all the time, and we all know it's there. Stop firing that machine-gun! Stop chasing whatever you're chasing! Calm down, get your breath back, let a bit of peace seep into your bones. No use. We don't do it. Just keep on with the same bloody fooleries.

And the next war coming over the horizon. 1941, they say. Three more circles of the sun, and then we whizz straight into it. The bombs diving down on you like black cigars, and the streamlined bullets streaming from the Bren machine-guns. Not that that worries me particularly. I'm too old to fight. There'll be air-raids, of course, but they won't hit everybody. Besides even if that kind of danger exists, it doesn't really enter into one's thoughts beforehand. As I've said several times already, I'm not frightened of the war, only of the after-war. And even that isn't likely to affect me personally. Because who'd bother about a chap like me? I'm too fat to be a political suspect. No one would bump me off or cosh me with a rubber truncheon. I'm the ordinary middling kind that moves on when the policeman tells him. As for Hilda and the kids, they'd probably never notice the difference. And yet it frightens me. The barbed wire! The slogans! The enormous faces! The cork-lined cellars where the executioner plugs you from behind! For that matter it frightens other chaps who are intellectually a good deal dumber than I am. But why? Because it means good-bye to this thing I've been telling you about, this special feeling inside you. Call it peace, if you like. But when I say peace I don't mean absence of war, I mean peace, a feeling in your guts. And it's gone for ever if the rubber-truncheon boys get hold of us.

I picked up my bunch of primroses and had a smell at them. I was thinking of Lower Binfield. It was funny how for two months past it had been in and out of my mind all the time, after twenty years during which I'd practically forgotten it. And just at this moment there was the zoom of a car coming up the road.

It brought me up with a kind of jolt. I suddenly realised what I was doing—wandering round picking primroses when I ought to have been going through the inventory at that ironmonger's shop in Pudley. What was more, it suddenly struck me what I'd look like if those people in the car saw me. A fat man in a bowler hat holding a bunch of primroses! It wouldn't look right at all. Fat men mustn't pick primroses, at any rate in public. I just had time to chuck them over the hedge before the car came in sight. It was a good job I'd done so. The car was full of young fools of about twenty. How they'd have sniggered if they'd seen me! They were all looking at me—you know how people look at you when they're in a car coming towards you—and the thought struck me that even now they might somehow guess what I'd been doing. Better let 'em think it was something else. Why should a chap get out of his car at the side of a country road? Obvious! As the car went past I pretended to be doing up a fly-button.

I cranked up the car (the self-starter doesn't work any longer) and got in. Curiously enough, in the very moment when I was doing up the fly-button, when my mind was about three-quarters full of those young fools in the other car, a wonderful idea had occurred to me.

I'd go back to Lower Binfield!

Why not? I thought as I jammed her into top gear. Why shouldn't I? What was to stop me? And why the hell hadn't I thought of it before? A quiet holiday in Lower Binfield —just the thing I wanted.

Don't imagine that I had any ideas of going back to *live* in Lower Binfield. I wasn't planning to desert Hilda and the kids and start life under a different name. That kind of thing only happens in books. But what was to stop me slipping down to Lower Binfield and having a week there all by myself, on the QT?

I seemed to have it all planned out in my mind already. It was all right as far as the money went. There was still twelve quid left in that secret pile of mine, and you can have a very comfortable week on twelve quid. I get a fortnight's holiday a year, generally in August or Septem-

175

ber. But if I made up some suitable story—relative dying of incurable disease, or something—I could probably get the firm to give me my holiday in two separate halves. Then I could have a week all to myself before Hilda knew what was happening. In May, for instance, when the hawthorn was in bloom. A week in Lower Binfield, with no Hilda, no kids, no Flying Salamander, no Ellesmere Road, no rumpus about the hire-purchase payments, no noise of traffic driving you silly—just a week of loafing round and listening to the quietness!

But why did I want to go back to Lower Binfield? you say. Why Lower Binfield in particular? What did I mean to do when I got there?

I didn't mean to do anything. That was part of the point. I wanted peace and quiet. Peace! We had it once, in Lower Binfield. I've told you something about our old life there, before the war. I'm not pretending it was perfect. I dare say it was a dull, sluggish, vegetable kind of life. You can say we were like turnips, if you like. But turnips don't live in terror of the boss, they don't lie awake at night thinking about the next slump and the next war. We had peace inside us. Of course I knew that even in Lower Binfield life would have changed. But the place itself wouldn't have. There'd still be the beech woods round Binfield House, and the towpath down by Burford Weir, and the horse-trough in the market-place. I wanted to get back there, just for a week, and let the feeling of it soak into me. It was a bit like one of these Eastern sages retiring into a desert. And I should think, the way things are going, there'll be a good many people retiring into the desert during the next few years. It'll be like the time in ancient Rome that old Porteous was telling me about, when there were so many hermits that there was a waiting list for every cave.

But it wasn't that I wanted to watch my navel. I only wanted to get my nerve back before the bad times begin.

Because does anyone who isn't dead from the neck up doubt that there's a bad time coming? We don't even know what it'll be, and yet we know it's coming. Perhaps a war, perhaps a slump—no knowing, except that it'll be something bad. Wherever we're going, we're going downwards. Into the grave, into the cesspool—no knowing. And you can't face that kind of thing unless you've got the right feeling inside you. There's something that's gone out of us in these twenty years since the war. It's a kind of vital juice that we've squirted away until there's nothing left. All this rushing to and fro! Everlasting scramble for a bit of cash. Everlasting din of buses, bombs, radios, telephone bells. Nerves worn all to bits, empty places in our bones where the marrow ought to be.

I shoved my foot down on the accelerator. The very thought of going back to Lower Binfield had done me good already. You know the feeling I had. Coming up for air! Like the big sea-turtles when they come paddling up to the surface, stick their noses out and fill their lungs with a great gulp before they sink down again among the seaweed and the octopuses. We're all stifling at the bottom of a dustbin, but I'd found the way to the top. Back to Lower Binfield! I kept my foot on the accelerator until the old car worked up to her maximum speed of nearly forty miles an hour. She was rattling like a tin tray full o crockery, and under cover of the noise I nearly started singing.

Of course the fly in the milk-jug was Hilda. That thought pulled me up a bit. I slowed down to about twenty to think it over.

There wasn't much doubt Hilda would find out sooner or later. As to getting only a week's holiday in August, I might be able to pass that off all right. I could tell her the firm were only giving me a week this year. Probably she wouldn't ask too many questions about that, because she'd jump at the chance of cutting down the holiday expenses. The kids, in any case, always stay at the seaside for a month. Where the difficulty came in was finding an alibi for that week in May. I couldn't just clear off without notice. Best thing, I thought, would be to tell her a good while ahead that I was being sent on some special job to Nottingham, or Derby, or Bristol, or some other place a good long way away. If I told her about it two months ahead it would look as if I hadn't anything to hide.

But of course she'd find out sooner or later. Trust Hilda! She'd start off by pretending to believe it, and then, in that quiet, obstinate way she has, she'd nose out the fact that I'd never been to Nottingham or Derby or Bristol or wherever it might be. It's astonishing how she does it. Such perseverance! She lies low till she's found out all the weak points in your alibi, and then suddenly, when you've put your foot in it by some careless remark, she starts on you. Suddenly comes out with the whole dossier of the case. 'Where did you spend Saturday night? That's a lie! You've been off with a woman. Look at these hairs I found when I was brushing your waistcoat. Look at them! Is my hair that colour?' And then the fun begins. Lord knows how many times it's happened. Sometimes she's been right about the woman and sometimes she's been wrong, but the after-effects are always the same. Nagging for weeks on end! Never a meal without a row – and the kids can't make out what it's all about. The one completely hopeless thing would be to tell her just where I'd spent that week, and why. If I explained till the Day of Judgment she'd never believe that.

But, hell! I thought, why bother? It was a long way off. You know how different these things seem before and after. I shoved my foot down on the accelerator again. I'd had another idea, almost bigger than the first. I wouldn't go in May. I'd go in the second half of June, when the coarse-fishing season had started, and I'd go fishing!

Why not, after all? I wanted peace, and fishing is peace. And then the biggest idea of all came into my head and very nearly made me swing the car off the road.

I'd go and catch those big carp in the pool at Binfield House!

And once again, why not? Isn't it queer how we go through life, always thinking that the things we want to do are the things that can't be done? Why shouldn't I catch those carp? And yet, as soon as the idea's mentioned, doesn't it sound to you like something impossible, something that just couldn't happen? It seemed so to me, even at that moment. It seemed to me a kind of dope-dream, like the ones you have of sleeping with film stars or winning the heavyweight championship. And yet it wasn't in the least impossible, it wasn't even improbable. Fishing can be rented. Whoever owned Binfield House now would probably let the pool if they got enough for it. And Gosh! I'd be glad to pay five pounds for a day's fishing in that pool. For that matter it was quite likely that the house was still empty and nobody even knew that the pool existed.

I thought of it in the dark place among the trees, waiting for me all those years. And the huge black fish still gliding round it. Jesus! If they were that size thirty years ago, what would they be like now?

III

It was June the seventeenth, Friday, the second day of the coarse-fishing season.

I hadn't had any difficulty in fixing things with the firm. As for Hilda, I'd fitted her up with a story that was all shipshape and watertight. I'd fixed on Birmingham for my alibi, and at the last moment I'd even told her the name of the hotel I was going to stay at, Rowbottom's Family & Commercial. I happened to know the address because I'd stayed there some years earlier. At the same time I didn't want her writing to me at Birmingham, which she might do if I was away as long as a week. After thinking it over I took young Saunders, who travels for Glisso Floor Polish, partly into my confidence. He'd happened to mention that he'd be passing through Birmingham on the eighteenth of June, and I got him to promise that he'd stop on his way and post a letter from me to Hilda, addressed from Rowbottom's. This was to tell her that I might be called away and she'd better not write. Saunders understood, or thought he did. He gave me a wink and said I was wonderful for my age. So that settled Hilda. She hadn't asked any questions, and even if she turned suspicious later, an alibi like that would take some breaking.

I drove through Westerham. It was a wonderful June morning. A faint breeze blowing, and the elm tops swaying in the sun, little white clouds streaming across the sky like a flock of sheep, and the shadows chasing each other across the fields. Outside Westerham a Wall's Ice Cream lad, with cheeks like apples, came tearing towards me on his bike, whistling so that it went through your head. It suddenly reminded me of the time when I'd been an errand-boy myself (though in those days we didn't have free-wheel bikes) and I very nearly stopped him and took one. They'd cut the hay in places, but they hadn't got it in yet. It lay drying in long shiny rows, and the smell of it drifted across the road and got mixed up with the petrol.

I drove along at a gentle fifteen. The morning had a kind of peaceful, dreamy feeling. The ducks floated about on the ponds as if they felt too satisfied to eat. In Nettlefield, the village beyond Westerham, a little man in a white apron, with grey hair and a huge grey moustache, darted across the green, planted himself in the middle of the road and began doing physical jerks to attract my attention. My car's known all along this road, of course. I pulled up. It's only Mr Weaver, who keeps the village general shop. No, he doesn't want to insure his life, nor his shop either. He's merely run out of change and wants to know whether I've got a quid's worth of 'large silver'. They never have any change in Nettlefield, not even at the pub.

I drove on. The wheat would have been as tall as your waist. It went undulating up and down the hills like a great green carpet, with the wind rippling it a little, kind of thick and silky-looking. It's like a woman, I thought. It makes you want to lie on it. And a bit ahead of me I saw the sign-post where the road forks right for Pudley and left for Oxford.

I was still on my usual beat, inside the boundary of my own 'district', as the firm calls it. The natural thing, as I was going westward, would have been to leave London along the Uxbridge Road. But by a kind of instinct I'd followed my usual route. The fact was I was feeling guilty about the whole business. I wanted to get well away before I headed for Oxfordshire. And in spite of the fact that I'd fixed things so neatly with Hilda and the firm, in spite of the twelve quid in my pocket-book and the suitcase in the back of the car, as I got nearer the crossroads I actually felt a temptation—I knew I wasn't going to succumb to it, and yet it was a temptation—to chuck the whole thing up. I had a sort of feeling that so long as I was driving along my normal beat I was still inside the law. It's not too late, I thought. There's still time to do the respectable thing. I could run into Pudley, for instance, see the manager of Barclay's Bank (he's our agent at Pudley) and find out if any new business had come in. For that matter I could even turn round, go back to Hilda and make a clean breast of the plot.

I slowed down as I got to the corner. Should I or shouldn't I? For about a second I was really tempted. But no! I tooted the klaxon and swung the car westward, on to the Oxford road.

Well, I'd done it. I was on the forbidden ground. It was true that five miles further on, if I wanted to, I could turn to the left again and get back to Westerham. But for the moment I was headed westward. Strictly speaking I was in flight. And what was curious, I was no sooner on the Oxford road than I felt perfectly certain that *they* knew all about it. When I say *they*, I mean all the people who wouldn't approve of a trip of this kind and who'd have stopped me if they could—which, I suppose, would include pretty well everybody.

What was more, I actually had a feeling that they were after me already. The whole lot of them! All the people who couldn't understand why a middle-aged man with false teeth should sneak away for a quiet week in the place where he spent his boyhood. And all the mean-minded bastards who *could* understand only too well, and who'd raise heaven and earth to prevent it. They were all on my track. It was as if a huge army was streaming up the road behind me. I seemed to see them in my mind's eye. Hilda was in front, of course, with the kids tagging after her, and Mrs Wheeler driving her forward with a grim, vindictive expression, and Miss Minns rushing along in the rear, with her pince-nez slipping down and a look of distress on her face, like the hen that gets left behind when the others have got hold of the bacon rind. And Sir Herbert Crum and the higher-ups of the Flying Salamander in their Rolls-Royces and Hispano-Suizas. And all the chaps at the office, and all the poor down-trodden pen-pushers from Ellesmere Road and from all such other roads, some of them wheeling prams and mowing-machines and concrete garden-rollers, some of them chugging along in little Austin Sevens. And all the soul-savers and Nosey Parkers, the people whom you've never seen but who rule your destiny all the same, the Home Secretary, Scotland Yard, the Temperance League, the Bank of England, Lord Beaverbrook, Hitler and Stalin on a tandem bicycle, the bench of Bishops, Mussolini, the Pope—they were all of them after me. I could almost hear them shouting:

'There's a chap who thinks he's going to escape! There's a chap who says he won't be streamlined! He's going back to Lower Binfield! After him! Stop him!'

It's queer. The impression was so strong that I actually took a peep through the little window at the back of the car to make sure I wasn't being followed. Guilty conscience, I suppose. But there was nobody. Only the dusty white road and the long line of the elms dwindling out behind me.

I trod on the gas and the old car rattled into the thirties. A few minutes later I was past the Westerham turning. So that was that. I'd burnt my boats. This was the idea which, in a dim sort of way, had begun to form itself in my mind the day I got my new false teeth.

PART IV

I CAME TOWARDS LOWER BINFIELD over Chamford Hill. There are four roads into Lower Binfield, and it would have been more direct to go through Walton. But I'd wanted to come over Chamford Hill, the way we used to go when we biked home from fishing in the Thames. When you get just past the crown of the hill the trees open out and you can see Lower Binfield lying in the valley below you.

It's a queer experience to go over a bit of country you haven't seen in twenty years. You remember it in great detail, and you remember it all wrong. All the distances are different, and the landmarks seem to have moved about. You keep feeling, surely this hill used to be a lot steeper—surely that turning was on the other side of the road? And on the other hand you'll have memories which are perfectly accurate, but which only belong to one particular occasion. You'll remember, for instance, a corner of a field, on a wet day in winter, with the grass so green that it's almost blue, and a rotten gatepost covered with lichen and a cow standing in the grass and looking at you. And you'll go back after twenty years and be surprised because the cow isn't standing in the same place and looking at you with the same expression.

As I drove up Chamford Hill I realised that the picture I'd had of it in my mind was almost entirely imaginary. But it was a fact that certain things had changed. The road was tarmac, whereas in the old days it used to be macadam (I remember the bumpy feeling of it under the bike), and it seemed to have got a lot wider. And there were far less trees. In the old days there used to be huge beeches growing in the hedgerows, and in places their boughs met across the road and made a kind of arch. Now they were all gone. I'd nearly got to the top of the hill when I came on something which was certainly new. To the right of the road there was a whole lot of fake-picturesque houses, with overhanging eaves and rose pergolas and what-not. You know the kind of houses that are just a little too high-class to stand in a row, and so they're dotted about in a kind of colony, with private roads leading up to them. And at the entrance to one of the private roads there was a huge white board which said:

THE KENNELS
PEDIGREE SEALYHAM PUPS
DOGS BOARDED

Surely *that* usen't to be there?

I thought for a moment. Yes, I remembered! Where those houses stood there used to be a little oak plantation, and the trees grew too close together, so that they were very tall and thin, and in spring the ground underneath them used to be smothered in anemones. Certainly there were never any houses as far out of the town as this.

I got to the top of the hill. Another minute and Lower Binfield would be in sight. Lower Binfield! Why should I pretend I wasn't excited? At the very thought of seeing it again an extraordinary feeling that started in my guts crept upwards and did something to my heart. Five seconds more and I'd be seeing it. Yes, here we are! I declutched, trod on the footbrake, and—Jesus!

Oh, yes, I know *you* knew what was coming. But *I* didn't. You can say I was a bloody fool not to expect it, and so I was. But it hadn't even occurred to me.

The first question was, where *was* Lower Binfield?

I don't mean that it had been demolished. It had merely

been swallowed. The thing I was looking down at was a good-sized manufacturing town. I remember—Gosh, how I remember! and in this case I don't think my memory is far out—what Lower Binfield used to look like from the top of Chamford Hill. I suppose the High Street was about a quarter of a mile long, and except for a few outlying houses the town was roughly the shape of a cross. The chief landmarks were the church tower and the chimney of the brewery. At this moment I couldn't distinguish either of them. All I could see was an enormous river of brand-new houses which flowed along the valley in both directions and half-way up the hills on either side. Over to the right there were what looked like several acres of bright red roofs all exactly alike. A big Council housing estate, by the look of it.

But where was Lower Binfield? Where was the town I used to know? It might have been anywhere. All I knew was that it was buried somewhere in the middle of that sea of bricks. Of the five or six factory chimneys that I could see, I couldn't even make a guess at which belonged to the brewery. Towards the eastern end of the town there were two enormous factories of glass and concrete. That accounts for the growth of the town, I thought, as I began to take it in. It occurred to me that the population of this place (it used to be about two thousand in the old days) must be a good twenty-five thousand. The only thing that hadn't changed, seemingly, was Binfield House. It wasn't much more than a dot at that distance, but you could see it on the hillside opposite, with the beech trees round it, and the town hadn't climbed that high. As I looked a fleet of black bombing planes came over the hill and zoomed across the town.

I shoved the clutch in and started slowly down the hill. The houses had climbed half-way up it. You know those very cheap small houses which run up a hillside in one continuous row, with the roofs rising one above the other like a flight of steps, all exactly the same. But a little before I got to the houses I stopped again. On the left of the road there was something else that was quite new. The cemetery. I stopped opposite the lych-gate to have a look at it.

It was enormous, twenty acres, I should think. There's always a kind of jumped-up unhomelike look about a new cemetery, with its raw gravel paths and its rough green sods, and the machine-made marble angels that look like something off a wedding-cake. But what chiefly struck me at the moment was that in the old days this place hadn't existed. There was no separate cemetery then, only the churchyard. I could vaguely remember the farmer these fields used to belong to—Blackett, his name was, and he was a dairy-farmer. And somehow the raw look of the place brought it home to me how things have changed. It wasn't only that the town had grown so vast that they needed twenty acres to dump their corpses in. It was their putting the cemetery out here, on the edge of the town. Have you noticed that they always do that nowadays? Every new town puts its cemetery on the outskirts. Shove it away—keep it out of sight! Can't bear to be reminded of death. Even the tombstones tell you the same story. They never say that the chap underneath them 'died', it's always 'passed away' or 'fell asleep'. It wasn't so in the old days. We had our churchyard plumb in the middle of the town, you passed it every day, you saw the spot where your grandfather was lying and where some day you were going to lie yourself. We didn't mind looking at the dead. In hot weather, I admit, we also had to smell them, because some of the family vaults weren't too well sealed.

I let the car run down the hill slowly. Queer! You can't imagine how queer! All the way down the hill I was seeing ghosts, chiefly the ghosts of hedges and trees and cows. It was as if I was looking at two worlds at once, a kind of thin bubble of the thing that used to be, with the thing that actually existed shining through it. There's the field where the bull chased Ginger Rogers! And there's the place where the horse-mushrooms used to grow! But there weren't any fields or any bulls or any mushrooms. It was houses, houses everywhere, little raw red houses with their grubby window-curtains and their scraps of back-garden that hadn't anything in them except a patch of rank grass or a few larkspurs straggling among the weeds. And blokes walking up and down, and women shaking out mats, and snotty-nosed kids playing along the pavement. All strangers! They'd all come crowding in while my back was turned. And yet it was they who'd have looked on me as a stranger, they didn't know anything about the old Lower Binfield, they'd never heard of Shooter and Wetherall, or Mr Grimmett and Uncle Ezekiel, and cared less, you bet.

It's funny how quickly one adjusts. I suppose it was five minutes since I'd halted at the top of the hill, actually a bit out of breath at the thought of seeing Lower Binfield again. And already I'd got used to the idea that Lower Binfield had been swallowed up and buried like the lost cities of Peru. I braced up and faced it. After all, what else do you expect? Towns have got to grow, people have got to live somewhere. Besides, the old town hadn't been annihilated. Somewhere or other it still existed, though it had houses round it instead of fields. In a few minutes I'd be seeing it again, the church and the brewery chimney and Father's shop-window and the horse-trough in the market-place. I got to the bottom of the hill, and the road forked. I took the left-hand turning, and a minute later I was lost.

I could remember nothing. I couldn't even remember whether it was hereabouts that the town used to begin. All I knew was that in the old days this street hadn't existed. For hundreds of yards I was running along it—a rather mean, shabby kind of street, with the houses giving straight on the pavement and here and there a corner grocery or a dingy little pub—and wondering where the hell it led to. Finally I pulled up beside a woman in a dirty apron and no hat who was walking down the pavement. I stuck my head out of the window.

'Beg pardon—can you tell me the way to the market-place?'

She 'couldn't tell'. Answered in an accent you could cut with a spade. Lancashire. There's lots of them in the south of England now. Overflow from the distressed areas. Then I saw a bloke in overalls with a bag of tools coming along and tried again. This time I got the answer in Cockney, but he had to think for a moment.

'Market-place? Market-place? Lessee, now. Oh—you mean the *Ole* Market?'

I suppose I did mean the Old Market.

'Oh, well—you take the right 'and turning——'

It was a long way. Miles, it seemed to me, though really it wasn't a mile. Houses, shops, cinemas, chapels, football grounds—new, all new. Again I had that feeling of a kind of enemy invasion having happened behind my back. All these people flooding in from Lancashire and the London suburbs, planting themselves down in this beastly chaos, not even bothering to know the chief landmarks of the town by name. But I grasped presently why what we used to call the market-place was now known as the Old Market. There was a big square, though you couldn't properly call it a square, because it was no particular shape, in the middle of the new town, with traffic-lights and a huge bronze statue of a lion worrying an eagle—the war memorial, I suppose. And the newness of everything! The raw, mean look! Do you know the look of these new towns that have suddenly swelled up like balloons in the last few years, Hayes, Slough, Dagenham and so forth? The kind of chilliness, the bright red brick everywhere, the temporary-looking shop-windows full of cut-price chocolates and radio parts. It was just like that. But suddenly I swung into a street with older houses. Gosh! The High Street!

After all my memory hadn't played tricks on me. I knew every inch of it now. Another couple of hundred yards and I'd be in the market-place. The old shop was down the other end of the High Street. I'd go there after lunch—I was going to put up at the George. And every inch a memory! I knew all the shops, though all the names had changed, and the stuff they dealt in had mostly changed as well. There's Lovegrove's! And there's Todd's! And a big dark shop with beams and dormer windows. Used to be Lilywhite's the draper's, where Elsie used to work. And Grimmett's! Still a grocer's, apparently. Now for the horse-trough in the market-place. There was another car ahead of me and I couldn't see.

It turned aside as we got into the market-place. The horse-trough was gone.

There was an AA man on traffic-duty where it used to stand. He gave a glance at the car, saw that it hadn't the AA sign and decided not to salute.

I turned the corner and ran down to the George. The horse-trough being gone had thrown me out to such an extent that I hadn't even looked to see whether the brewery chimney was still standing. The George had altered too, all except the name. The front had been dolled up till it looked like one of those riverside hotels, and the sign was different. It was curious that although till that moment I hadn't thought of it once in twenty years, I suddenly found that I could remember every detail of the old sign, which had swung there ever since I could remember. It was a crude kind of picture, with St George on a very thin horse trampling on a very fat dragon, and in the corner, though it was cracked and faded, you could read the little signature,

'Wm Sandford, Painter & Carpenter'. The new sign was kind of artistic-looking. You could see it had been painted by a real artist. St George looked a regular pansy. The cobbled yard, where the farmers' traps used to stand and the drunks used to puke on Saturday nights, had been enlarged to about three times its size and concreted over, with garages all round it. I backed the car into one of the garages and got out.

One thing I've noticed about the human mind is that it goes in jerks. There's no emotion that stays by you for any length of time. During the last quarter of an hour I'd had what you could fairly describe as a shock. I'd felt it almost like a sock in the guts when I stopped at the top of Chamford Hill and suddenly realised that Lower Binfield had vanished, and there'd been another little stab when I saw that the horse-trough was gone. I'd driven through the streets with a gloomy, Ichabod kind of feeling. But as I stepped out of the car and hitched my trilby hat onto my head I suddenly felt that it didn't matter a damn. It was such a lovely sunny day, and the hotel yard had a kind of summery look, with its flowers in green tubs and what-not. Besides, I was hungry and looking forward to a spot of lunch.

I strolled into the hotel with a consequential kind of air, with the boots, who'd already nipped out to meet me, following with the suitcase. I felt pretty prosperous, and probably I looked it. A solid businessman, you'd have said, at any rate if you hadn't seen the car. I was glad I'd come in my new suit—blue flannel with a thin white stripe, which suits my style. It has what the tailor calls a 'reducing effect'. I believe that day I could have passed for a stockbroker. And say what you like it's a very pleasant thing, on a June day when the sun's shining on the pink geraniums in the window-boxes, to walk into a nice country hotel with roast lamb and mint sauce ahead of you.

Not that it's any treat to me to stay in hotels, Lord knows I see all too much of them—but ninety-nine times out of a hundred it's those godless 'family and commercial' hotels, like Rowbottom's, where I was supposed to be staying at present, the kind of places where you pay five bob for bed and breakfast, and the sheets are always damp and the bath taps never work. The George had got so smart I wouldn't have known it. In the old days it had hardly been a hotel, only a pub, though it had a room or two to let and used to do a farmers' lunch (roast beef and Yorkshire, suet dumpling and Stilton cheese) on market days. It all seemed different except for the public bar, which I got a glimpse of as I went past, and which looked the same as ever. I went up a passage with a soft carpet, and hunting prints and copper warming-pans and such-like junk hanging on the walls. And dimly I could remember the passage as it used to be, the hollowed-out flags underfoot, and the smell of plaster mixed up with the smell of beer. A smart-looking young woman, with frizzed hair and a black dress, who I suppose was the clerk or something, took my name at the office.

'You wish for a room, sir? Certainly, sir. What name shall I put down, sir?'

I paused. After all, this was my big moment. She'd be pretty sure to know the name. It isn't common, and there are a lot of us in the churchyard. We were one of the old Lower Binfield families, the Bowlings of Lower Binfield. And though in a way it's painful to be recognised, I'd been rather looking forward to it.

'Bowling,' I said very distinctly. 'Mr George Bowling.'

'Bowling, sir. B-O-A—oh! B-O-W? Yes, sir. And you are coming from London, sir?'

No response. Nothing registered. She'd never heard of me. Never heard of George Bowling, son of Samuel Bowling—Samuel Bowling who, damn it! had had his half-pint in this same pub every Saturday for over thirty years.

II

The dining-room had changed, too.

I could remember the old room, though I'd never had a meal there, with its brown mantelpiece and its bronzy-yellow wallpaper—I never knew whether it was meant to be that colour, or had just got like that from age and smoke—and the oil painting, also by Wm Sandford, Painter & Carpenter, of the battle of Tel-el-Kebir. Now they'd got the place up in a kind of medieval style. Brick fireplace with inglenooks, a huge beam across the ceiling, oak panelling on the walls, and every bit of it a fake that you could have spotted fifty yards away. The beam was genuine oak, came out of some old sailing-ship, probably, but it didn't hold anything up, and I had my suspicions of the panels as soon as I set eyes on them. As I sat down at my table, and the slick young waiter came towards me fiddling with his napkin, I tapped the wall behind me. Yes! Thought so! Not even wood. They fake it up with some kind of composition and then paint it over.

But the lunch wasn't bad. I had my lamb and mint sauce, and I had a bottle of some white wine or other with a French name which made me belch a bit but made me feel happy. There was one other person lunching there, a woman of about thirty with fair hair, looked like a widow. I wondered whether she was staying at the George, and made vague plans to get off with her. It's funny how your feelings get mixed up. Half the time I was seeing ghosts. The past was sticking out into the present. Market day, and the great solid farmers throwing their legs under the long table, with their hobnails grating on the stone floor, and

working their way through a quantity of beef and dumpling you wouldn't believe the human frame could hold.
And then the little tables with their shiny white cloths and
wine glasses and folded napkins, and the faked-up decorations and the general expensiveness would blot it out again.
And I'd think, 'I've got twelve quid and a new suit. I'm
little Georgie Bowling, and who'd have believed I'd ever
come back to Lower Binfield in my own motor-car?' And
then the wine would send a kind of warm feeling upwards
from my stomach, and I'd run an eye over the woman
with fair hair and mentally take her clothes off.

It was the same in the afternoon as I lay about in the
lounge—fake-medieval again, but it had streamlined
leather armchairs and glass-topped tables—with some
brandy and a cigar. I was seeing ghosts, but on the whole
I was enjoying it. As a matter of fact I was a tiny bit boozed
and hoping that the woman with fair hair would come
in so that I could scrape acquaintance. She never showed
up, however. It wasn't till nearly tea-time that I went out.

I strolled up to the market-place and turned to the left.
The shop! It was funny. Twenty-one years ago, the day of
Mother's funeral, I'd passed it in the station fly, and seen
it all shut up and dusty, with the sign burnt off with a
plumber's blowflame, and I hadn't cared a damn. And
now, when I was so much further away from it, when there
were actually details about the inside of the house that I
couldn't remember, the thought of seeing it again did
things to my heart and guts. I passed the barber's shop. Still
a barber's, though the name was different. A warm, soapy,
almondy smell came out of the door. Not quite so good
as the old smell of bay rum and latakia. The shop—our
shop—was twenty yards further down. Ah!

An arty-looking sign—painted by the same chap as did
the one at the George, I shouldn't wonder—hanging out
over the pavement:

WENDY'S TEA-SHOP
MORNING COFFEE
HOME-MADE CAKES

A tea-shop!

I suppose if it had been a butcher's or an ironmonger's, or anything else except a seedsman's, it would have given me the same kind of jolt. It's absurd that because you happen to have been born in a certain house you should feel that you've got rights over it for the rest of your life, but so you do. The place lived up to its name, all right. Blue curtains in the window, and a cake or two standing about, the kind of cake that's covered with chocolate and has just one walnut stuck somewhere on the top. I went in. I didn't really want any tea, but I had to see the inside.

They'd evidently turned both the shop and what used to be the parlour into tea-rooms. As for the yard at the back where the dustbin used to stand and Father's little patch of weeds used to grow, they'd paved it all over and dolled it up with rustic tables and hydrangeas and things. I went through into the parlour. More ghosts! The piano and the texts on the wall, and the two lumpy old red armchairs where Father and Mother used to sit on opposite sides of the fireplace, reading the *People* and the *News of the World* on Sunday afternoons! They'd got the place up in an even more antique style than the George, with gate-leg tables and a hammered-iron chandelier and pewter plates hanging on the wall and what-not. Do you notice how dark they always manage to make it in these arty tea-rooms? It's part of the antiqueness, I suppose. And instead of an ordinary waitress there was a young woman in a kind of print wrapper who met me with a sour expression. I asked her for tea, and she was ten minutes getting it. You know the kind of tea—China tea, so weak that you could think it's water till you put the milk in. I was sitting almost exactly where Father's armchair used to stand. I could almost hear his voice, reading out a 'piece', as he used to call it, from the *People*, about the new flying machines, or the chap who was swallowed by a whale, or something. It gave me a most peculiar feeling that I was there on false pretences and they could kick me out if they discovered who I was, and yet simultaneously I had a kind of longing to tell somebody that I'd been born here, that I belonged to this house, or rather (what I really felt) that the house belonged to me. There was nobody else having tea. The girl in the print wrapper was hanging about by the window, and I could see that if I hadn't been there she'd have been picking her teeth. I bit into one of the slices of cake she'd brought me. Home-made cakes! You bet they were. Home-made with margarine and egg-substitute. But in the end I had to speak. I said:

'Have you been in Lower Binfield long?'

She started, looked surprised, and didn't answer. I tried again:

'I used to live in Lower Binfield myself, a good while ago.'

Again no answer, or only something that I couldn't hear. She gave me a kind of frigid look and then gazed out of the window again. I saw how it was. Too much of a lady to go in for back-chat with customers. Besides, she probably thought I was trying to get off with her. What was the good of telling her I'd been born in this house? Even if she believed it, it wouldn't interest her. She'd never heard of Samuel Bowling, Corn & Seed Merchant. I paid the bill and cleared out.

I wandered up to the church. One thing that I'd been half afraid of, and half looking forward to, was being recognised by people I used to know. But I needn't have worried, there wasn't a face I knew anywhere in the streets. It seemed as if the whole town had got a new population.

When I got to the church I saw why they'd had to have a new cemetery. The churchyard was full to the brim, and half the graves had names on them that I didn't know. But the names I did know were easy enough to find. I wandered round among the graves. The sexton had just scythed the grass and there was a smell of summer even there. They were all gone, all the older folks I'd known. Gravitt the butcher, and Winkle the other seedsman, and Trew, who used to keep the George, and Mrs Wheeler from the sweet-shop—they were all lying there. Shooter and Wetherall were opposite one another on either side of the path, just as if they were still singing at each other across the aisle. So Wetherall hadn't got his hundred after all. Born in '43 and 'departed this life' in 1928. But he'd beaten Shooter, as usual. Shooter died in '26. What a time old Wetherall must have had those last two years when there was nobody to sing against him! And old Grimmett under a huge marble thing shaped rather like a veal-and-ham pie, with an iron railing round it, and in the corner a whole batch of Simmonses under cheap little crosses. All gone to dust. Old Hodges with his tobacco-coloured teeth, and Lovegrove with his big brown beard, and Lady Rampling with the coachman and the tiger, and Harry Barnes's aunt who had a glass eye, and Brewer of the Mill Farm with his wicked old face like something carved out of a nut— nothing left of any of them except a slab of stone and God knows what underneath.

I found Mother's grave, and Father's beside it. Both of them in pretty good repair. The sexton had kept the grass clipped. Uncle Ezekiel's was a little way away. They'd levelled a lot of the older graves, and the old wooden headpieces, the ones that used to look like the end of a bedstead, had all been cleared away. What do you feel when you see your parents' graves after twenty years? I don't know what you ought to feel, but I'll tell you what I did feel, and that was nothing. Father and Mother have never faded out of my mind. It's as if they existed somewhere or other in a kind of eternity, Mother behind the brown teapot, Father with his bald head a little mealy, and his spectacles and his grey moustache, fixed for ever like people in a picture, and yet in some way alive. Those boxes of bones lying in the ground there didn't seem to have anything to do with them. Merely, as I stood there, I began to wonder what you feel like when you're underground, whether you care much and how soon you cease to care, when suddenly a heavy shadow swept across me and gave me a bit of a start.

I looked over my shoulder. It was only a bombing plane which had flown between me and the sun. The place seemed to be creeping with them.

I strolled into the church. For almost the first time since I got back to Lower Binfield I didn't have the ghostly feeling, or rather I had it in a different form. Because nothing had changed. Nothing, except that all the people were gone. Even the hassocks looked the same. The same dusty, sweetish corpse-smell. And by God! the same hole in the window, though, as it was evening and the sun was round the other side, the spot of light wasn't creeping up the aisle. They'd still got pews—hadn't changed over to chairs. There was our pew, and there was the one in front where Wetherall used to bellow against Shooter. Sihon king of the Amorites and Og the king of Bashan! And the worn stones in the aisle where you could still half-read the epitaphs of the blokes who lay beneath them. I squatted down to have a look at the one opposite our pew. I still knew the readable bits of it by heart. Even the pattern they made seemed to have stuck in my memory. Lord knows how often I'd read them during the sermon.

> Here .... *ſon, Gent.,*
> *of this pariſh* .... *his juſt*
> *& upright* ....
> ....
> *To his* .... *manifold private bene*
> *volences he added a diligent* ....
> ....
> .... *beloved wife*
> *Amelia, by* .... *iſſue ſeven*
> *daughters* ....

I remembered how the long S's used to puzzle me as a kid. Used to wonder whether in the old days they pronounced their S's as F's, and if so, why.

There was a step behind me. I looked up. A chap in a cassock was standing over me. It was the vicar.

But I mean *the* vicar! It was old Betterton, who'd been vicar in the old days—not, as a matter of fact, ever since I could remember, but since 1904 or thereabouts. I recognised him at once, though his hair was quite white.

He didn't recognise me. I was only a fat tripper in a blue suit doing a bit of sightseeing. He said good evening and promptly started on the usual line of talk—was I interested in architecture, remarkable old building this, foundations go back to Saxon times and so on and so forth. And soon he was doddering round, showing me the sights, such as they were—Norman arch leading into the vestry, brass effigy of Sir Roderick Bone who was killed at the Battle of Newbury. And I followed him with the kind of whipped-dog air that middle-aged businessmen always have when they're being shown round a church or a picture-gallery. But did I tell him that I knew it all already? Did I tell him that I was Georgie Bowling, son of Samuel Bowling—he'd have remembered my father even if he didn't remember me—and that I'd not only listened to his sermons for ten years and gone to his confirmation classes, but even belonged to the Lower Binfield Reading Circle and had a go at *Sesame and Lilies* just to please him? No, I didn't. I merely followed him round, making the kind of mumble that you make when somebody tells you that this or that is five hundred years old and you can't think what the hell to say except that it doesn't look it. From the moment that I set eyes on him I'd decided to let him think I was a stranger. As soon as I decently could I dropped sixpence in the Church Expenses box and bunked.

But why? Why not make contact, now that at last I'd found somebody I knew?

Because the change in his appearance after twenty years had actually frightened me. I suppose you think I mean that he looked older. But he didn't! He looked *younger*. And it suddenly taught me something about the passage of time.

I suppose old Betterton would be about sixty-five now, so that when I last saw him he'd have been forty-five—my own present age. His hair was white now, and the day he buried Mother it was a kind of streaky grey, like a shaving-brush. And yet as soon as I saw him the first thing that struck me was that he looked younger. I'd thought of him as an old, old man, and after all he wasn't so very old. As a boy, it occurred to me, all people over forty had seemed to me just worn-out old wrecks, so old that there was hardly any difference between them. A man of forty-five had seemed to me older then than this old dodderer of sixty-five seemed now. And Christ! I was forty-five myself. It frightened me.

So that's what I look like to chaps of twenty, I thought as I made off between the graves. Just a poor old hulk. Finished. It was curious. As a rule I don't care a damn about my age. Why should I? I'm fat, but I'm strong and healthy. I can do everything I want to do. A rose smells the same to me now as it did when I was twenty. Ah, but do I smell the same to the rose? Like an answer a girl, might have been eighteen, came up the churchyard lane. She had to pass within a yard or two of me. I saw the look she gave me, just a tiny momentary look. No, not frightened, not hostile. Only kind of wild, remote, like a wild animal when you catch its eye. She'd been born and grown up in those twenty years while I was away from Lower Binfield. All my memories would have been meaningless to her. Living in a different world from me, like an animal.

I went back to the George. I wanted a drink, but the bar didn't open for another half-hour. I hung about for a bit, reading a *Sporting and Dramatic* of the year before, and presently the fair-haired dame, the one I thought might be a widow, came in. I had a sudden desperate yearning to get off with her. Wanted to show myself that there's life in the old dog yet, even if the old dog does have to wear false teeth. After all, I thought, if she's thirty and I'm forty-five, that's fair enough. I was standing in front of the empty fireplace, making believe to warm my bum, the way you do on a summer day. In my blue suit I didn't look so bad. A bit fat, no doubt, but distingué. A man of the world. I could pass for a stockbroker. I put on my toniest accent and said casually:

'Wonderful June weather we're having.'

It was a pretty harmless remark, wasn't it? Not in the same class as 'Haven't I met you somewhere before?'

But it wasn't a success. She didn't answer, merely lowered for about half a second the paper she was reading and gave me a look that would have cracked a window. It was awful. She had one of those blue eyes that go into you like a bullet. In that split second I saw how hopelessly I'd got her wrong. She wasn't the kind of widow with dyed hair who likes being taken out to dance-halls. She was upper-middle-class, probably an admiral's daughter, and been to one of those good schools where they play hockey.

And I'd got myself wrong too. New suit or no new suit, I *couldn't* pass for a stockbroker. Merely looked like a commercial traveller who'd happened to get hold of a bit of dough. I sneaked off to the private bar to have a pint or two before dinner.

The beer wasn't the same. I remember the old beer, the good Thames Valley beer that used to have a bit of taste in it because it was made out of chalky water. I asked the barmaid:

'Have Bessemers' still got the brewery?'

'Bessemers'? Oo, *no*, sir! They've gorn. Oo, years ago –long before we come 'ere.'

She was a friendly sort, what I call the elder-sister type of barmaid, thirty-fivish, with a mild kind of face and the fat arms they develop from working the beer-handle. She told me the name of the combine that had taken over the brewery. I could have guessed it from the taste, as a matter of fact. The different bars ran round in a circle with compartments in between. Across in the public bar two chaps were playing a game of darts, and in the Jug and Bottle there was a chap I couldn't see who occasionally put in a remark in a sepulchral kind of voice. The barmaid leaned her fat elbows on the bar and had a talk with me. I ran over the names of the people I used to know, and there wasn't a single one of them that she'd heard of. She said she'd only been in Lower Binfield five years. She hadn't even heard of old Trew, who used to have the George in the old days.

'I used to live in Lower Binfield myself,' I told her. 'A good while back, it was, before the war.'

'Before the war? Well, now! You don't look that old.'

'See some changes, I dessay,' said the chap in the Jug and Bottle.

'The town's grown,' I said. 'It's the factories, I suppose.'

'Well, of course they mostly work at the factories.

There's the gramophone works, and then there's Truefitt Stockings. But of course they're making bombs nowadays.'

I didn't altogether see why it was of course, but she began telling me about a young fellow who worked in Truefitt's factory and sometimes came to the George, and he'd told her that they were making bombs as well as stockings, the two, for some reason I didn't understand, being easy to combine. And then she told me about the big military aerodrome near Walton—that accounted for the bombing planes I kept seeing—and the next moment we'd started talking about war, as usual. Funny. It was exactly to escape the thought of war that I'd come here. But how can you, anyway? It's in the air you breathe.

I said it was coming in 1941. The chap in the Jug and Bottle said he reckoned it was a bad job. The barmaid said it gave her the creeps. She said:

'It don't seem to do much good, does it, after all's said and done? And sometimes I lie awake at night and hear one of those great things going overhead, and I think to myself, "Well, now, suppose that was to drop a bomb right down on top of me!" And all this ARP, and Miss Todgers, she's the Air Warden, telling you it'll be all right if you keep your head and stuff the windows up with newspaper, and they say they're going to dig a shelter under the Town Hall. But the way I look at it is, how could you put a gas-mask on a baby?'

The chap in the Jug and Bottle said he'd read in the paper that you ought to get into a hot bath till it was all over. The chaps in the public bar overheard this and there was a bit of by-play on the subject of how many people could get into the same bath, and both of them asked the barmaid if they could share her bath with her. She told them not to get saucy, and then she went up to the other end of the bar and hauled them out a couple more pints of old and mild. I took a suck at my beer. It was poor stuff. Bitter, they call it. And it was bitter, right enough, too bitter, a kind of sulphurous taste. Chemicals. They say no English hops ever go into beer nowadays, they're all made into chemicals. Chemicals, on the other hand, are made into beer. I found myself thinking about Uncle Ezekiel, what he'd have said to beer like this, and what he'd have said about ARP and the buckets of sand you're supposed to put the thermite bombs out with. As the barmaid came back to my side of the bar I said:

'By the way, who's got the Hall nowadays?'

We always used to call it the Hall, though its name was Binfield House. For a moment she didn't seem to understand.

'The Hall, sir?'

''E means Binfield 'Ouse,' said the chap in the Jug and Bottle.

'Oh, Binfield House! Oo, I thought you meant the Memorial Hall. It's Dr Merrall's got Binfield House now.'

'Dr Merrall?'

'Yes, sir. He's got more than sixty patients up there, they say.'

'Patients? Have they turned it into a hospital, or something?'

'Well—it's not what you'd call an ordinary hospital. More of a sanatorium. It's mental patients, reely. What they call a Mental Home.'

A loony-bin!

But after all, what else could you expect?

III

I crawled out of bed with a bad taste in my mouth and my bones creaking.

The fact was that, what with a bottle of wine at lunch

and another at dinner, and several pints in between, besides a brandy or two, I'd had a bit too much to drink the day before. For several minutes I stood in the middle of the carpet, gazing at nothing in particular and too done-in to make a move. You know that god-awful feeling you get sometimes in the early morning. It's a feeling chiefly in your legs, but it says to you clearer than any words could do, 'Why the hell do you go on with it? Chuck it up, old chap! Stick your head in the gas oven!'

Then I shoved my teeth in and went to the window. A lovely June day, again, and the sun was just beginning to slant over the roofs and hit the house-fronts on the other side of the street. The pink geraniums in the window-boxes didn't look half bad. Although it was only about half-past eight and this was only a side-street off the market-place there was quite a crowd of people coming and going. A stream of clerky-looking chaps in dark suits with despatch-cases were hurrying along, all in the same direction, just as if this had been a London suburb and they were scooting for the Tube, and the school-kids were straggling up towards the market-place in twos and threes. I had the same feeling that I'd had the day before when I saw the jungle of red houses that had swallowed Chamford Hill. Bloody interlopers! Twenty thousand gate-crashers who didn't even know my name. And here was all this new life swarming to and fro, and here was I, a poor old fatty with false teeth, watching them from a window and mumbling stuff that nobody wanted to listen to about things that happened thirty and forty years ago. Christ! I thought, I was wrong to think that I was seeing ghosts. I'm the ghost myself. I'm dead, and they're alive.

But after breakfast—haddock, grilled kidneys, toast and marmalade and a pot of coffee—I felt better. The frozen dame wasn't breakfasting in the dining-room, there was a nice summery feeling in the air, and I couldn't get rid of the feeling that in that blue flannel suit of mine I looked just a little bit distingué. By God! I thought, if I'm a ghost, I'll *be* a ghost! I'll walk. I'll haunt the old places. And maybe I can work a bit of black magic on some of these bastards who've stolen my home town from me.

I started out, but I'd got no further than the market-place when I was pulled up by something I hadn't expected to see. A procession of about fifty school-kids was marching down the street in column of fours—quite military, they looked—with a grim-looking woman marching alongside of them like a sergeant-major. The leading four were carrying a banner with a red, white and blue border and BRITONS PREPARE on it in huge letters. The barber on the corner had come out onto his doorstep to have a look at them. I spoke to him. He was a chap with shiny black hair and a dull kind of face.

'What are those kids doing?'

'It's this here air-raid practice,' he said vaguely. 'This here ARP. Kind of practising, like. That's Miss Todgers, that is.'

I might have guessed it was Miss Todgers. You could see it in her eye. You know the kind of tough old devil with grey hair and a kippered face that's always put in charge of Girl Guide detachments, YWCA hostels and what-not. She had on a coat and skirt that somehow looked like a uniform and gave you a strong impression that she was wearing a Sam Browne belt, though actually she wasn't. I knew her type. Been in the WAACs in the war, and never had a day's fun since. This ARP was jam to her. As the kids swung past I heard her letting out at them with the real sergeant-major yell, 'Monica! Lift your feet up!' and I saw that the rear four had another banner with a red, white and blue border, and in the middle:

WE ARE READY. ARE YOU?

'What do they want to march them up and down for?' I said to the barber.

'I dunno. I s'pose it's kind of propaganda, like.'

I knew, of course. Get the kids war-minded. Give us all the feeling that there's no way out of it, the bombers are coming as sure as Christmas, so down to the cellar you go and don't argue. Two of the great black planes from Walton were zooming over the eastern end of the town. Christ! I thought, when it starts it won't surprise us any more than a shower of rain. Already we're listening for the first bomb. The barber went on to tell me that thanks to Miss Todgers's efforts the school-kids had been served with their gas-masks already.

Well, I started to explore the town. Two days I spent just wandering round the old landmarks, such of them as I could identify. And all that time I never ran across a soul that knew me. I was a ghost, and if I wasn't actually invisible, I felt like it.

It was queer, queerer than I can tell you. Did you ever read a story of H. G. Wells's about a chap who was in two places at once—that's to say, he was really in his own home, but he had a kind of hallucination that he was at the bottom of the sea? He'd be walking round his room, but instead of the tables and chairs he'd see the wavy water-weed and the great crabs and cuttlefish reaching out to get him. Well, it was just like that. For hours on end I'd be walking through a world that wasn't there. I'd count my paces as I went down the pavement and think, 'Yes, here's where so-and-so's field begins. The hedge runs across the street and slap through that house. That petrol pump is really an elm tree. And here's the edge of the allotments. And this street (it was a dismal little row of semi-detached houses called Cumberledge Road, I remember) is the lane where we used to go with Katie Simmons, and the nut-bushes grew on both sides.' No doubt I got the distances wrong, but the general directions were right. I don't believe anyone who hadn't happened to be born here would have believed that these streets were fields as little as twenty years ago. It was as though the countryside had been buried by a kind of volcanic eruption from the outer suburbs. Nearly the whole of what used to be old Brewer's land had been swallowed up in the Council housing estate. The Mill Farm had vanished, the cow-pond where I caught my first fish had been drained and filled up and built over, so that I couldn't even say exactly where it used to stand. It was all houses, houses, little red cubes of houses all alike, with privet hedges and asphalt paths leading up to the front door. Beyond the Council estate the town thinned out a bit, but the jerry-builders were doing their best. And there were little knots of houses dumped down here and there, wherever anybody had been able to buy a plot of land, and makeshift roads leading up to the houses, and empty lots with builders' boards, and bits of ruined fields covered with thistles and tin cans.

In the centre of the old town, on the other hand, things hadn't changed much, so far as the buildings went. A lot of the shops were still doing the same line of trade, although the names were different. Lilywhite's was still a draper's, but it didn't look too prosperous. What used to be Gravitt's, the butcher's, was now a shop that sold radio parts. Mother Wheeler's little window had been bricked over. Grimmett's was still a grocer's, but it had been taken over by the International. It gives you an idea of the power of these big combines that they could even swallow up a cute old skinflint like Grimmett. But from what I know of him—not to mention that slap-up tombstone in the churchyard—I bet he got out while the going was good and had ten or fifteen thousand quid to take to heaven with him. The only shop that was still in the same hands was Sarazins', the people who'd ruined Father. They'd swollen to enormous dimensions, and they had another huge branch in the new part of the town. But they'd turned into a kind of general store and sold furniture, drugs, hardware and ironmongery as well as the old garden stuff.

For the best part of two days I was wandering round, not actually groaning and rattling a chain, but sometimes feeling that I'd like to. Also I was drinking more than was good for me. Almost as soon as I got to Lower Binfield I'd started on the booze, and after that the pubs never seemed to open quite early enough. My tongue was always hanging out of my mouth for the last half-hour before opening time.

Mind you, I wasn't in the same mood all the time. Sometimes it seemed to me that it didn't matter a damn if Lower Binfield had been obliterated. After all, what had I come here for, except to get away from the family? There was no reason why I shouldn't do all the things I wanted to do, even go fishing, if I felt like it. On the Saturday afternoon I even went to the fishing-tackle shop in the High Street and bought a split-cane rod (I'd always pined for a split-cane rod as a boy—it's a little bit dearer than a greenheart) and hooks and gut and so forth. The atmosphere of the shop cheered me up. Whatever else changes, fishing-tackle doesn't—because, of course, fish don't change either. And the shopman didn't see anything funny in a fat middle-aged man buying a fishing-rod. On the contrary, we had a little talk about the fishing in the Thames and the big chub somebody had landed the year before last on a paste made of brown bread, honey and minced boiled rabbit. I even—though I didn't tell him what I wanted them for, and hardly even admitted it to myself—bought the strongest salmon trace he'd got, and some No. 5 roach-hooks, with an eye to those big carp at Binfield House, in case they still existed.

Most of Sunday morning I was kind of debating it in

my mind – should I go fishing, or shouldn't I? One moment I'd think, why the hell not, and next moment it would seem to me that it was just one of those things that you dream about and don't ever do. But in the afternoon I got the car out and drove down to Burford Weir. I thought I'd just have a look at the river, and tomorrow, if the weather was right, maybe I'd take my new fishing-rod and put on the old coat and grey flannel bags I had in my suitcase, and have a good day's fishing. Three or four days, if I felt like it.

I drove over Chamford Hill. Down at the bottom the road turns off and runs parallel to the towpath. I got out of the car and walked. Ah! A knot of little red and white bungalows had sprung up beside the road. Might have expected it, of course. And there seemed to be a lot of cars standing about. As I got nearer the river I came into the sound – yes, plonk-tiddle-tiddle-plonk! – yes, the sound of gramophones.

I rounded the bend and came in sight of the towpath. Christ! Another jolt. The place was black with people. And where the water-meadows used to be – tea-houses, penny-in-the-slot machines, sweet-kiosks and chaps selling Wall's Ice-Cream. Might as well have been at Margate. I remember the old towpath. You could walk along it for miles, and except for the chaps at the lock gates, and now and again a bargeman mooching along behind his horse, you'd meet never a soul. When we went fishing we always had the place to ourselves. Often I've sat there a whole afternoon, and a heron might be standing in the shallow water fifty yards up the bank, and for three or four hours on end there wouldn't be anyone passing to scare him away. But where had I got that idea that grown-up men don't go fishing? Up and down the bank, as far as I could see in both directions, there was a continuous chain of men fishing, one every five yards. I wondered how the hell they could all have got there until it struck me that they must be some fishing-club or other. And the river was crammed with boats—rowing-boats, canoes, punts, motor-launches, full of young fools with next to nothing on, all of them screaming and shouting and most of them with a gramophone aboard as well. The floats of the poor devils who were trying to fish rocked up and down on the wash of the motor-boats.

I walked a little way. Dirty, choppy water, in spite of the fine day. Nobody was catching anything, not even minnows. I wondered whether they expected to. A crowd like that would be enough to scare every fish in creation. But actually, as I watched the floats rocking up and down among the ice-cream tubs and the paper bags, I doubted whether there were any fish to catch. Are there still fish in the Thames? I suppose there must be. And yet I'll swear the Thames water isn't the same as it used to be. Its colour is quite different. Of course you think that's merely my imagination, but I tell you it isn't so. I know the water has changed. I remember the Thames water as it used to be, a kind of luminous green that you could see deep into, and the shoals of dace cruising round the reeds. You couldn't see three inches into the water now. It's all brown and dirty, with a film of oil on it from the motor-boats, not to mention the fag-ends and the paper bags.

After a bit I turned back. Couldn't stick the noise of the gramophones any longer. Of course it's Sunday, I thought. Mightn't be quite so bad on a weekday. But after all, I knew I'd never come back. God rot them, let 'em keep their bloody river. Wherever I go fishing it won't be in the Thames.

The crowds swarmed past me. Crowds of bloody aliens, and nearly all of them young. Boys and girls larking along in couples. A troop of girls came past, wearing bell-bottom trousers and white caps like the ones they wear in the

American Navy, with slogans printed on them. One of them, seventeen she might have been, had PLEASE KISS ME. I wouldn't have minded. On an impulse I suddenly turned aside and weighed myself on one of the penny-in-the-slot machines. There was a clicking noise somewhere inside it—you know those machines that tell your fortune as well as your weight—and a typewritten card came sliding out.

'*You are the possessor of exceptional gifts,*' I read, '*but owing to excessive modesty you have never received your due reward. Those about you underrate your abilities. You are too fond of standing aside and allowing others to take the credit for what you have done yourself. You are sensitive, affectionate and always loyal to your friends. You are deeply attractive to the opposite sex. Your worst fault is generosity. Persevere, for you will rise high!*'
'*Weight: 14 stone 11 pounds.*'

I'd put on four pounds in the last three days, I noticed. Must have been the booze.

IV

I drove back to the George, dumped the car in the garage and had a late cup of tea. As it was Sunday the bar wouldn't open for another hour or two. In the cool of the evening I went out and strolled up in the direction of the church.

I was just crossing the market-place when I noticed a woman walking a little way ahead of me. As soon as I set eyes on her I had a most peculiar feeling that I'd seen her somewhere before. You know that feeling. I couldn't see her face, of course, and so far as her back view went there was nothing I could identify, and yet I could have sworn I knew her.

She went up the High Street and turned down one of the side-streets to the right, the one where Uncle Ezekiel used to have his shop. I followed. I don't quite know why—partly curiosity, perhaps, and partly as a kind of precaution. My first thought had been that here at last was one of the people I'd known in the old days in Lower Binfield, but almost at the same moment it struck me that it was just as likely that she was someone from West Bletchley. In that case I'd have to watch my step, because if she found out I was here she'd probably split to Hilda. So I followed cautiously, keeping at a safe distance and examining her back view as well as I could. There was nothing striking about it. She was a tallish, fattish woman, might have been forty or fifty, in a rather shabby black dress. She'd no hat on, as though she'd just slipped out of her house for a moment, and the way she walked gave you the impression that her shoes were down at heel. All in all, she looked a bit of a slut. And yet there was nothing to identify, only that vague something which I knew I'd seen before. It was something in her movements, perhaps. Presently she got to a little sweet- and paper-shop, the kind of little shop that always keeps open on a Sunday. The woman who kept it was standing in the doorway, doing something to a stand of postcards. My woman stopped to pass the time of day.

I stopped too, as soon as I could find a shop window which I could pretend to be looking into. It was a plumber's and decorator's, full of samples of wallpaper and bathroom fittings and things. By this time I wasn't fifteen yards away from the other two. I could hear their voices cooing away in one of those meaningless conversations that women have when they're just passing the time of day. 'Yes, that's jest about it. That's jest where it is. I said to him myself, I said, "Well, what else do you expect?" I said. It don't seem right, do it? But what's the use, you might as well talk to a stone. It's a shame!' and so on and so forth. I was getting warmer. Obviously my woman was a small shopkeeper's wife, like the other. I was just wondering whether she mightn't be one of the people I'd known in Lower Binfield after all, when she turned almost towards me and I saw three-quarters of her face. And Jesus Christ! It was Elsie!

Yes, it was Elsie. No chance of mistake. Elsie! That fat hag!

It gave me such a shock—not, mind you, seeing Elsie, but seeing what she'd grown to be like—that for a moment things swam in front of my eyes. The brass taps and ball-stops and porcelain sinks and things seemed to fade away into the distance, so that I both saw them and didn't see them. Also for a moment I was in a deadly funk that she might recognise me. But she'd looked bang in my face and hadn't made any sign. A moment more, and she turned and went on. Again I followed. It was dangerous, she might spot I was following her, and that might start her wondering who I was, but I just had to have another look at her. The fact was that she exercised a kind of horrible fascination on me. In a manner of speaking I'd been watching her before, but I watched her with quite different eyes now.

It was horrible, and yet I got a kind of scientific kick out of studying her back view. It's frightening, the things that twenty-four years can do to a woman. Only twenty-four years, and the girl I'd known, with her milky-white skin and red mouth and kind of dull-gold hair, had turned into this great round-shouldered hag, shambling along on twisted heels. It made me feel downright glad I'm a man. No man ever goes to pieces quite so completely as that. I'm fat, I grant you. I'm the wrong shape, if you like. But at least I'm *a* shape. Elsie wasn't even particularly fat, she was merely shapeless. Ghastly things had happened to her hips.

217

As for her waist, it had vanished. She was just a kind of soft lumpy cylinder, like a bag of meal.

I followed her a long way, out of the old town and through a lot of mean little streets I didn't know. Finally she turned in at the doorway of another shop. By the way she went in, it was obviously her own. I stopped for a moment outside the window. 'G. Cookson, Confectioner and Tobacconist.' So Elsie was Mrs Cookson. It was a mangy little shop, much like the other one where she'd stopped before, but smaller and a lot more flyblown. Didn't seem to sell anything except tobacco and the cheapest kinds of sweets. I wondered what I could buy that would take a minute or two. Then I saw a rack of cheap pipes in the window, and I went in. I had to brace my nerve up a little before I did it, because there'd need to be some hard lying if by any chance she recognised me.

She'd disappeared into the room behind the shop, but she came back as I tapped on the counter. So we were face to face. Ah! No sign. Didn't recognise me. Just looked at me the way they do. You know the way small shopkeepers look at their customers—utter lack of interest.

It was the first time I'd seen her full face, and though I half expected what I saw, it gave me almost as big a shock as that first moment when I'd recognised her. I suppose when you look at the face of someone young, even of a child, you ought to be able to foresee what it'll look like when it's old. It's all a question of the shape of the bones. But if it had ever occurred to me, when I was twenty and she was twenty-two, to wonder what Elsie would look like at forty-seven, it wouldn't have crossed my mind that she could ever look like *that*. The whole face had kind of sagged, as if it had somehow been drawn downwards. Do you know that type of middle-aged woman that has a face just like a bulldog? Great underhung jaw, mouth turned down at the corners, eyes sunken, with pouches underneath. Exactly like a bulldog. And yet it was the same face, I'd have known it in a million. Her hair wasn't completely grey, it was a kind of dirty colour, and there was much less of it than there used to be. She didn't know me from Adam. I was just a customer, a stranger, an uninteresting fat man. It's queer what an inch or two of fat can do. I wondered whether I'd changed even more than she had, or whether it was merely that she wasn't expecting to see me, or whether—what was the likeliest of all—she'd simply forgotten my existence.

'Devening,' she said, in that listless way they have.

'I want a pipe,' I said fatly. 'A briar pipe.'

'A pipe. Now jest lemme see. I know we gossome pipes somewhere. Now where did I—ah! 'Ere we are.'

She took a cardboard box full of pipes from somewhere under the counter. How bad her accent had got! Or maybe I was just imagining that, because my own standards had changed? But no, she used to be so 'superior', all the girls at Lilywhite's were so 'superior', and she'd been a member of the vicar's Reading Circle. I swear she never used to drop her aitches. It's queer how these women go to pieces once they're married. I fiddled among the pipes for a moment and pretended to look them over. Finally I said I'd like one with an amber mouthpiece.

'Amber? I don't know as we got any——' she turned towards the back of the shop and called: 'Ge-orge!'

So the other bloke's name was George too. A noise that sounded something like 'Ur!' came from the back of the shop.

'Ge-orge! Where ju put that other box of pipes?'

George came in. He was a small stoutish chap, in shirtsleeves, with a bald head and a big gingery-coloured soup-strainer moustache. His jaw was working in a ruminative kind of way. Obviously he'd been interrupted in the middle of his tea. The two of them started poking round

219

in search of the other box of pipes. It was about five minutes before they ran it to earth behind some bottles of sweets. It's wonderful, the amount of litter they manage to accumulate in these frowzy little shops where the whole stock is worth about fifty quid.

I watched old Elsie poking about among the litter and mumbling to herself. Do you know the kind of shuffling, round-shouldered movements of an old woman who's lost something? No use trying to describe to you what I felt. A kind of cold, deadly, desolate feeling. You can't conceive it unless you've had it. All I can say is, if there was a girl you used to care about twenty-five years ago, go and have a look at her now. Then perhaps you'll know what I felt.

But as a matter of fact, the thought that was chiefly in my mind was how differently things turn out from what you expect. The times I'd had with Elsie! The July nights under the chestnut trees! Wouldn't you think it would leave some kind of after-effect behind? Who'd have thought the time would ever come when there would be just no feeling whatever between us? Here was I and here was she, our bodies might be a yard apart, and we were just as much strangers as though we'd never met. As for her, she didn't even recognise me. If I told her who I was, very likely she wouldn't remember. And if she did remember, what would she feel? Just nothing. Probably wouldn't even be angry because I'd done the dirty on her. It was as if the whole thing had never happened.

And on the other hand, who'd ever have foreseen that Elsie would end up like this? She'd seemed the kind of girl who's bound to go to the devil. I know there'd been at least one other man before I had her, and it's safe to bet there were others between me and the second George. It wouldn't surprise me to learn that she'd had a dozen altogether. I treated her badly, there's no question about that, and many a time it had given me a bad half-hour.

She'll end up on the streets, I used to think, or stick her head in the gas oven. And sometimes I felt I'd been a bit of a bastard, but other times I reflected (what was true enough) that if it hadn't been me it would have been somebody else. But you see the way things happen, the kind of dull pointless way. How many women really end up on the streets? A damn sight more end up at the mangle. She hadn't gone to the bad, or to the good either. Just ended up like everybody else, a fat old woman muddling about a frowzy little shop, with a gingery-moustached George to call her own. Probably got a string of kids as well. Mrs George Cookson. Lived respected and died lamented— and might die this side of the bankruptcy court, if she was lucky.

They'd found the box of pipes. Of course there weren't any with amber mouthpieces among them.

'I don't know as we got any amber ones jest at present, sir. Not amber. We gossome nice vulcanite ones.'

'I wanted an amber one,' I said.

'We gossome nice pipes 'ere.' She held one out. 'That's a nice pipe, now. 'Alf a crown, that one is.'

I took it. Our fingers just touched. No kick, no reaction. The body doesn't remember. And I suppose you think I bought the pipe, just for old sake's sake, to put half a crown in Elsie's pocket. But not a bit of it. I didn't want the thing. I don't smoke a pipe, I'd merely been making a pretext to come into the shop. I turned it over in my fingers and then put it down on the counter.

'Doesn't matter, I'll leave it,' I said. 'Give me a small Player's.'

Had to buy something, after all that fuss. George the second, or maybe he was the third or fourth, routed out a packet of Player's, still munching away beneath his moustache. I could see he was sulky because I'd dragged him away from his tea for nothing. But it seemed too damn silly to waste half a crown. I cleared out, and that was the last I ever saw of Elsie.

I went back to the George and had dinner. Afterwards I went out with some vague idea of going to the pictures, if they were open, but instead I landed up in one of the big noisy pubs in the new part of the town. There I ran into a couple of chaps from Staffordshire who were travelling in hardware, and we got talking about the state of trade, and playing darts and drinking Guinness. By closing time they were both so boozed that I had to take them home in a taxi, and I was a bit under the weather myself, and the next morning I woke up with a worse head than ever.

V

But I had to see the pool at Binfield House.

I felt really bad that morning. The fact was that ever since I struck Lower Binfield I'd been drinking almost continuously from every opening time to every closing time. The reason, though it hadn't occurred to me till this minute, was that really there'd been nothing else to do. That was all my trip had amounted to so far—three days on the booze.

The same as the other morning, I crawled over to the window and watched the bowler hats and school caps hustling to and fro. My enemies, I thought. The conquering army that's sacked the town and covered the ruins with fag-ends and paper bags. I wondered why I cared. You think, I dare say, that if it had given me a jolt to find Lower Binfield swollen into a kind of Dagenham, it was merely because I don't like to see the earth getting fuller and country turning into town. But it isn't that at all. I don't mind towns growing, so long as they do grow and don't merely spread like gravy over a tablecloth. I know that people have got to have somewhere to live, and that if a factory isn't in one place it'll be in another. As for the picturesqueness, the sham countrified stuff, the oak panels and pewter dishes and copper warming-pans and what-not, it merely gives me the sick. Whatever we were in the old days, we weren't picturesque. Mother would never have seen any sense in the antiques that Wendy had filled our house with. She didn't like gate-leg tables—she said they 'caught your legs'. As for pewter, she wouldn't have it in the house. 'Nasty greasy stuff', she called it. And yet, say what you like, there was something that we had in those days and haven't got now, something that you probably can't have in a streamlined milk-bar with the radio playing. I'd come back to look for it, and I hadn't found it. And yet somehow I half believed in it even now, when I hadn't yet got my teeth in and my belly was crying out for an aspirin and a cup of tea.

And that started me thinking again about the pool at Binfield House. After seeing what they'd done to the town, I'd had a feeling you could only describe as fear about going to see whether the pool still existed. And yet it might, there was no knowing. The town was smothered under red brick, our house was full of Wendy and her junk, the Thames was poisoned with motor-oil and paper bags. But maybe the pool was still there, with the great black fish still cruising round it. Maybe, even, it was still hidden in the woods and from that day to this no one had dis-covered it existed. It was quite possible. It was a very thick bit of wood, full of brambles and rotten brushwood (the beech trees gave way to oaks round about there, which made the undergrowth thicker), the kind of place most people don't care to penetrate. Queerer things have happened.

I didn't start out till late afternoon. It must have been about half-past four when I took the car out and drove on to the Upper Binfield road. Half-way up the hill the houses thinned out and stopped and the beech trees began. The road forks about there and I took the right-hand fork, meaning to make a detour round and come back to Binfield House on the road. But presently I stopped to have a look at the copse I was driving through. The beech trees seemed just the same. Lord, how they were the same! I backed the car onto a bit of grass beside the road, under a fall of chalk, and got out and walked. Just the same. The same stillness, the same great beds of rustling leaves that seem to go on from year to year without rotting. Not a creature stirring except the small birds in the tree tops which you couldn't see. It wasn't easy to believe that that great noisy mess of a town was barely three miles away. I began to make my way through the little copse, in the direction of Binfield House. I could vaguely remember how the paths went. And Lord! Yes! The same chalk hollow where the Black Hand went and had catapult shots, and Sid Lovegrove told us how babies were born, the day I caught my first fish, pretty near forty years ago!

As the trees thinned out again you could see the other road and the wall of Binfield House. The old rotting wooden fence was gone, of course, and they'd put up a high brick wall with spikes on top, such as you'd expect to see round a loony-bin. I'd puzzled for some time about how to get into Binfield House until finally it had struck me that I'd only to tell them my wife was mad and I was looking for somewhere to put her. After that they'd be quite ready to show me round the grounds. In my new suit I probably looked prosperous enough to have a wife in a private asylum. It wasn't till I was actually at the gate that it occurred to me to wonder whether the pool was still inside the grounds.

The old grounds of Binfield House had covered fifty acres, I suppose, and the grounds of the loony-bin weren't likely to be more than five or ten. They wouldn't want a great pool of water for the loonies to drown themselves in. The lodge, where old Hodges used to live, was the same as ever, but the yellow brick wall and the huge iron gates were new. From the glimpse I got through the gates I wouldn't have known the place. Gravel walks, flower-beds, lawns, and a few aimless-looking types wandering about—loonies, I suppose. I strolled up the road to the right. The pool—the big pool, the one where I used to fish—was a couple of hundred yards behind the house. It might have been a hundred yards before I got to the corner of the wall. So the pool was outside the grounds. The trees seemed to have got much thinner. I could hear children's voices. And Gosh! there was the pool.

I stood for a moment, wondering what had happened to it. Then I saw what it was—all the trees were gone from round its edge. It looked all bare and different, in fact it looked extraordinarily like the Round Pond in Kensington Gardens. Kids were playing all round the edge, sailing boats and paddling, and a few rather older kids were rushing about in those little canoes which you work by turning a handle. Over to the left, where the old rotting boat-house used to stand among the reeds, there was a sort of pavilion and a sweet kiosk, and a huge white notice saying UPPER BINFIELD MODEL YACHT CLUB.

I looked over to the right. It was all houses, houses, houses. One might as well have been in the outer suburbs. All the woods that used to grow beyond the pool, and grew so thick that they were like a kind of tropical jungle, had been shaved flat. Only a few clumps of trees still standing round the houses. They were arty-looking houses, another of those sham-Tudor colonies like the one I'd seen the first day at the top of Chamford Hill, only more so. What a fool I'd been to imagine that these woods were still the same! I saw how it was. There was just one tiny bit of copse, half a dozen acres perhaps, that hadn't been cut down, and it was pure chance that I'd walked through it on my way here. Upper Binfield, which had been merely a name in the old days, had grown into a decent-sized town. In fact it was merely an outlying chunk of Lower Binfield.

I wandered up to the edge of the pool. The kids were splashing about and making the devil of a noise. There seemed to be swarms of them. The water looked kind of dead. No fish in it now. There was a chap standing watching the kids. He was an oldish chap with a bald head and a few tufts of white hair, and pince-nez and a very sunburnt face. There was something vaguely queer about his appearance. He was wearing shorts and sandals and one of those celanese shirts open at the neck, I noticed, but what really struck me was the look in his eye. He had very blue eyes that kind of twinkled at you from behind his spectacles. I could see that he was one of those old men who've never grown up. They're always either health-food cranks or else they have something to do with the Boy Scouts—in either case they're great ones for Nature and the open air. He was looking at me as if he'd like to speak.

'Upper Binfield's grown a great deal,' I said.

He twinkled at me.

'Grown! My dear sir, we never allow Upper Binfield to grow. We pride ourselves on being rather exceptional people up here, you know. Just a little colony of us all by ourselves. No interlopers—te-hee!'

'I meant compared with before the war,' I said. 'I used to live here as a boy.'

'Oh-ah. No doubt. That was before my time, of course. But the Upper Binfield Estate is something rather special in the way of building estates, you know. Quite a little world of its own. All designed by young Edward Watkin, the architect. You've heard of him, of course. We live in the midst of Nature up here. No connection with the town down there'—he waved a hand in the direction of Lower Binfield—'the dark satanic mills—te-hee!'

He had a benevolent old chuckle, and a way of wrinkling his face up, like a rabbit. Immediately, as though I'd asked him, he began telling me all about the Upper Binfield Estate, and young Edward Watkin, the architect, who had such a feeling for the Tudor, and was such a wonderful fellow at finding genuine Elizabethan beams in old farmhouses and buying them at ridiculous prices. And such an interesting young fellow, quite the life and soul of the nudist parties. He repeated a number of times that they were very exceptional people in Upper Binfield, quite different from Lower Binfield, they were determined to enrich the countryside instead of defiling it (I'm using his own phrase), and there weren't any public houses on the estate.

'They talk of their Garden Cities. But we call Upper Binfield the Woodland City—te-hee! Nature!' He waved a hand at what was left of the trees. 'The primeval forest brooding round us. Our young people grow up amid surroundings of natural beauty. We are nearly all of us enlightened people, of course. Would you credit that three-quarters of us up here are vegetarians? The local butchers don't like us at all—te-hee! And some quite eminent people live here. Miss Helena Thurloe, the novelist—you've heard of her, of course. And Professor Woad, the psychic research worker. Such a poetic character! He goes wandering out into the woods and the family can't find him at mealtimes. He says he's walking among the fairies. Do you believe in fairies? I admit—te-hee!—I am just a wee bit sceptical. But his photographs are most convincing.'

I began to wonder whether he was someone who'd escaped from Binfield House. But no, he was sane enough, after a fashion. I knew the type. Vegetarianism, simple life, poetry, Nature-worship, roll in the dew before breakfast. I'd met a few of them years ago in Ealing. He began to show me round the estate. There was nothing left of the woods. It was all houses, houses – and what houses! Do you know these faked-up Tudor houses with the curly roofs and the buttresses that don't buttress anything, and the rock-gardens with concrete bird-baths and those red plaster elves you can buy at the florists'? You could see in your mind's eye the awful gang of food-cranks and spook-hunters and simple-lifers with £1,000 a year that lived there. Even the pavements were crazy. I didn't let him take me far. Some of the houses made me wish I'd got a hand-grenade in my pocket. I tried to damp him down by asking whether people didn't object to living so near the lunatic asylum, but it didn't have much effect. Finally I stopped and said:

'There used to be another pool, besides the big one. It can't be far from here.'

'Another pool? Oh, surely not. I don't think there was ever another pool.'

'They may have drained it off,' I said. 'It was a pretty deep pool. It would leave a big pit behind.'

For the first time he looked a bit uneasy. He rubbed his nose.

'Oh-ah. Of course, you must understand our life up here is in some ways primitive. The simple life, you know. We prefer it so. But being so far from the town has its inconveniences, of course. Some of our sanitary arrangements are not altogether satisfactory. The dust-cart only calls once a month, I believe.'

'You mean they've turned the pool into a rubbish-dump?'

'Well, there *is* something in the nature of a——' he shied at the word rubbish-dump. 'We have to dispose of tins and so forth, of course. Over there, behind that clump of trees.'

We went across there. They'd left a few trees to hide it. But yes, there it was. It was my pool, all right. They'd drained the water off. It made a great round hole, like an enormous well, twenty or thirty feet deep. Already it was half full of tin cans.

I stood looking down at the tin cans.

'It's a pity they drained it,' I said. 'There used to be some big fish in that pool.'

'Fish? Oh, I never heard anything about that. Of course we could hardly have a pool of water here among the houses. The mosquitoes, you know. But it was before my time.'

'I suppose these houses have been built a good long time?' I said.

'Oh—ten or fifteen years, I think.'

'I used to know this place before the war,' I said. 'It was all woods then. There weren't any houses except Binfield House. But that little bit of copse over there hasn't changed. I walked through it on my way here.'

'Ah, that! That is sacrosanct. We have decided never to build in it. It is sacred to the young people. Nature, you know.' He twinkled at me, a kind of roguish look, as if he was letting me into a little secret: 'We call it the Pixy Glen.'

The Pixy Glen. I got rid of him, went back to the car and drove down to Lower Binfield. The Pixy Glen. And they'd filled my pool up with tin cans. God rot them and bust them! Say what you like—call it silly, childish, anything—but doesn't it make you puke sometimes to see what they're doing to England, with their bird-baths and their plaster gnomes, and their pixies and tin cans, where the beech woods used to be?

Sentimental, you say? Anti-social? Oughtn't to prefer trees to men? I say it depends what trees and what men.

Not that there's anything one can do about it, except to wish them the pox in their guts.

One thing, I thought as I drove down the hill, I'm finished with this notion of getting back into the past. What's the good of trying to revisit the scenes of your boyhood? They don't exist. Coming up for air! But there isn't any air. The dustbin that we're in reaches up to the stratosphere. All the same, I didn't particularly care. After all, I thought, I've still got three days left. I'd have a bit of peace and quiet, and stop bothering about what they'd done to Lower Binfield. As for my idea of going fishing— that was off, of course. Fishing, indeed! At my age! Really, Hilda was right.

I dumped the car in the garage of the George and walked into the lounge. It was six o'clock. Somebody had switched on the wireless and the news-broadcast was beginning. I came through the door just in time to hear the last few words of an SOS. And it gave me a bit of a jolt, I admit. For the words I heard were:

'—where his wife, Hilda Bowling, is seriously ill.'

The next instant the plummy voice went on: 'Here is another SOS. Will Percival Chute, who was last heard of——', but I didn't wait to hear any more. I just walked straight on. What made me feel rather proud, when I thought it over afterwards, was that when I heard those words come out of the loudspeaker I never turned an eyelash. Not even a pause in my step to let anyone know that I was George Bowling, whose wife Hilda Bowling was seriously ill. The landlord's wife was in the lounge, and she knew my name was Bowling, at any rate she'd seen it in the register. Otherwise there was nobody there except a couple of chaps who were staying at the George and who didn't know me from Adam. But I kept my head. Not a sign to anyone. I merely walked on into the private bar, which had just opened, and ordered my pint as usual.

I had to think it over. By the time I'd drunk about half the pint I began to get the bearings of the situation. In the first place, Hilda *wasn't* ill, seriously or otherwise. I knew that. She'd been perfectly well when I came away, and it wasn't the time of year for 'flu or anything of that kind. She was shamming. Why?

Obviously it was just another of her dodges. I saw how it was. She'd got wind somehow—trust Hilda!—that I wasn't really at Birmingham, and this was just her way of getting me home. Couldn't bear to think of me any longer with that other woman. Because of course she'd take it for granted that I was with a woman. Can't imagine any other motive. And naturally she assumed that I'd come rushing home as soon as I heard she was ill.

But that's just where you've got it wrong, I thought to myself as I finished off the pint. I'm too cute to be caught that way. I remembered the dodges she'd pulled before, and the extraordinary trouble she'll take to catch me out. I've even known her, when I'd been on some journey she was suspicious about, check it all up with a Bradshaw and a road-map, just to see whether I was telling the truth about my movements. And then there was that time when she followed me all the way to Colchester and suddenly burst in on me at the Temperance Hotel. And that time, unfortunately, she happened to be right—at least, she wasn't, but there were circumstances which made it look as if she was. I hadn't the slightest belief that she was ill. In fact, I knew she wasn't, though I couldn't exactly say how.

I had another pint, and things looked better. Of course there was a row coming when I got home, but there'd have been a row anyway. I've got three good days ahead of me, I thought. Curiously enough, now that the things I'd come to look for had turned out not to exist, the idea of having a bit of a holiday appealed to me all the more. Being away from home—that was the great thing. Peace perfect peace with loved ones far away, as the hymn puts it. And suddenly I decided that I *would* have a woman if I felt like it. It would serve Hilda right for being so dirty-minded, and besides, where's the sense of being suspected if it isn't true?

But as the second pint worked inside me, the thing began to amuse me. I hadn't fallen for it, but it was damned ingenious all the same. I wondered how she'd managed about the SOS. I've no idea what the procedure is. Do you have to have a doctor's certificate, or do you just send your name in? I felt pretty sure it was the Wheeler woman who'd put her up to it. It seemed to me to have the Wheeler touch.

But all the same, the cheek of it! The lengths that women will go! Sometimes you can't help kind of admiring them.

VI

After breakfast I strolled out into the market-place. It was a lovely morning, kind of cool and still, with a pale yellow light like white wine playing over everything. The fresh smell of the morning was mixed up with the smell of my cigar. But there was a zooming noise from behind the houses, and suddenly a fleet of great black bombers came whizzing over. I looked up at them. They seemed to be bang overhead.

The next moment I heard something. And at the same moment, if you'd happened to be there, you'd have seen an interesting instance of what I believe is called conditioned reflex. Because what I'd heard—there wasn't any question of mistake—was the whistle of a bomb. I hadn't heard such a thing for twenty years, but I didn't need to be told what it was. And without taking any kind of thought I did the right thing. I flung myself on my face.

After all I'm glad you didn't see me. I don't suppose I looked dignified. I was flattened out on the pavement like a rat when it squeezes under a door. Nobody else had been half as prompt. I'd acted so quickly that in the split second while the bomb was whistling down I even had time to be afraid that it was all a mistake and I'd made a fool of myself for nothing.

But the next moment—ah!

BOOM—BRRRRR!

A noise like the Day of Judgment, and then a noise like a ton of coal falling onto a sheet of tin. That was falling bricks. I seemed to kind of melt into the pavement. 'It's started,' I thought. 'I knew it! Old Hitler didn't wait. Just sent his bombers across without warning.'

And yet here's a peculiar thing. Even in the echo of that awful, deafening crash, which seemed to freeze me up from top to toe, I had time to think that there's something grand about the bursting of a big projectile. What does it sound like? It's hard to say, because what you hear is mixed up with what you're frightened of. Mainly it gives you a vision of bursting metal. You seem to see great sheets of iron bursting open. But the peculiar thing is the feeling it gives you of being suddenly shoved up against reality. It's like being woken up by somebody shying a bucket of water over you. You're suddenly dragged out of your dreams by a clang of bursting metal, and it's terrible, and it's real.

There was a sound of screams and yells, and also of car brakes being suddenly jammed on. The second bomb which I was waiting for didn't fall. I raised my head a little. On every side people seemed to be rushing round and screaming. A car was skidding diagonally across the road. I could hear a woman's voice shrieking, 'The Germans! The Germans!' To the right I had a vague impression of a man's round white face, rather like a wrinkled paper bag, looking down at me. He was kind of dithering:

'What is it? What's happened? What are they doing?'

'It's started,' I said. 'That was a bomb. Lie down.'

But still the second bomb didn't fall. Another quarter of a minute or so, and I raised my head again. Some of the people were still rushing about, others were standing as if they'd been glued to the ground. From somewhere behind the houses a huge haze of dust had risen up, and through it a black jet of smoke was streaming upwards. And then I saw an extraordinary sight. At the other end of the market-place the High Street rises a little. And down this little hill a herd of pigs was galloping, a sort of huge flood of pig-faces. The next moment, of course, I saw what it was. It wasn't pigs at all, it was only the schoolchildren in their gas-masks. I suppose they were bolting for some cellar where they'd been told to take cover in case of air-raids. At the back of them I could even make out a taller pig who was probably Miss Todgers. But I tell you that for a moment they looked exactly like a herd of pigs.

I picked myself up and walked across the market-place. People were calming down already, and quite a little crowd had begun to flock towards the place where the bomb had dropped.

Oh, yes, you're right, of course. It wasn't a German aeroplane after all. The war hadn't broken out. It was only an accident. The planes were flying over to do a bit of bombing practice—at any rate, they were carrying bombs—and somebody had put his hand on the lever by mistake. I expect he got a good ticking off for it. By the time that the postmaster had rung up London to ask whether there was a war on, and been told that there wasn't, everyone had grasped that it was an accident. But there'd been a space of time, something between a minute and five minutes, when several thousand people believed we were at war. A good job it didn't last any longer. Another quarter of an hour and we'd have been lynching our first spy.

I followed the crowd. The bomb had dropped in a little side-street off the High Street, the one where Uncle Ezekiel used to have his shop. It wasn't fifty yards from where the shop used to be. As I came round the corner I could hear voices murmuring 'Oo-oo!'—a kind of awed noise, as if they were frightened and getting a big kick out of it. Luckily I got there a few minutes before the ambulance and the fire-engine, and in spite of the fifty people or so that had already collected I saw everything.

At first sight it looked as if the sky had been raining bricks and vegetables. There were cabbage leaves everywhere. The bomb had blown a greengrocer's shop out of existence. The house to the right of it had had part of its roof blown off, and the roof beams were on fire, and all the houses round had been more or less damaged and had their windows smashed. But what everyone was looking at was the house on the left. Its wall, the one that joined the greengrocer's shop, was ripped off as neatly as if someone had done it with a knife. And what was extraordinary was that in the upstairs rooms nothing had been touched. It was just like looking into a doll's house. Chests-of-drawers, bedroom chairs, faded wallpaper, a bed not yet made and a jerry under the bed—all exactly as it had been lived in, except that one wall was gone. But the lower rooms had caught the force of the explosion. There was a frightful smashed-up mess of bricks, plaster, chair-legs, bits of a varnished dresser, rags of tablecloth, piles of broken plates and chunks of a scullery sink. A jar of marmalade had rolled across the floor, leaving a long streak of marmalade behind, and running side by side with it there was a ribbon of blood. But in among the broken crockery there was lying a leg. Just a leg, with the trouser still on it and a black boot with a Wood-Milne rubber heel. This was what the people were oo-ing and ah-ing at.

I had a good look at it and took it in. The blood was beginning to get mixed up with the marmalade. When the fire-engine arrived I cleared off to the George to pack my bag.

This finishes me with Lower Binfield, I thought. I'm going home. But as a matter of fact I didn't shake the dust off my shoes and leave immediately. One never does. When anything like that happens, people always stand about and discuss it for hours. There wasn't much work done in the old part of Lower Binfield that day, everyone was too busy talking about the bomb, what it sounded like and what they thought when they heard it. The barmaid at the George said it fair gave her the shudders. She said she'd never sleep sound in her bed again, and what did you expect, it just showed that with these here bombs you never knew. A woman had bitten off part of her tongue owing to the jump the explosion gave her. It turned out that whereas at our end of the town everyone had imagined it was a German air-raid, everyone at the other end had taken it for granted that it was an explosion at the stocking factory. Afterwards (I got this out of the news-paper) the Air Ministry sent a chap to inspect the damage, and issued a report saying that the effects of the bomb were 'disappointing'. As a matter of fact it had only killed three people, the greengrocer, Perrott his name was, and an old couple who lived next door. The woman wasn't much smashed about, and they identified the old man by his boots, but they never found any trace of Perrott. Not even a trouser-button to read the burial service over.

In the afternoon I paid my bill and hooked it. I didn't have much more than three quid left after I'd paid the bill. They know how to cut it out of you at these dolled-up country hotels, and what with drinks and other odds and ends I'd been shying money about pretty freely. I left my new rod and the rest of the fishing tackle in my bedroom. Let 'em keep it. No use to me. It was merely a quid that I'd chucked down the drain to teach myself a lesson. And I'd learnt the lesson all right. Fat men of forty-five can't go fishing. That kind of thing doesn't happen any longer, it's just a dream, there'll be no more fishing this side the grave.

It's funny how things sink into you by degrees. What had I really felt when the bomb exploded? At the actual moment, of course, it scared the wits out of me, and when I saw the smashed-up house and the old man's leg I'd had the kind of mild kick that you get from seeing a street accident. Disgusting, of course. Quite enough to make me fed-up with this so-called holiday. But it hadn't really made much impression.

But as I got clear of the outskirts of Lower Binfield and turned the car eastward, it all came back to me. You know how it is when you're in a car alone. There's something either in the hedges flying past you, or in the throb of the engine, that gets your thoughts running in a certain rhythm. You have the same feeling sometimes when you're in the train. It's a feeling of being able to see things in better perspective than usual. All kinds of things that I'd been doubtful about I felt certain about now. To begin with, I'd come to Lower Binfield with a question in my mind. What's ahead of us? Is the game really up? Can we get back to the life we used to live, or is it gone for ever? Well, I'd had my answer. The old life's finished, and to go about looking for it is just waste of time. There's no way back to Lower Binfield, you can't put Jonah back into the whale. I *knew*, though I don't expect you to follow my train of thought. And it was a queer thing I'd done by coming here. All those years Lower Binfield had been tucked away somewhere or other in my mind, a sort of quiet corner that I could step back into when I felt like it, and finally I'd stepped back into it and found that it didn't exist. I'd chucked a pineapple into my dreams, and lest there should be any mistake the Royal Air Force had followed up with five hundred pounds of TNT.

War is coming. 1941, they say. And there'll be plenty of broken crockery, and little houses ripped open like packing-cases, and the guts of the chartered accountant's clerk plastered over the piano that he's buying on the never-never. But what does that kind of thing matter, anyway? I'll tell you what my stay in Lower Binfield had taught me, and it was this. *It's all going to happen.* All the things you've got at the back of your mind, the things you're terrified of, the things that you tell yourself are just a nightmare or only happen in foreign countries. The bombs, the food-queues, the rubber truncheons, the barbed wire, the coloured shirts, the slogans, the enormous faces, the machine-guns squirting out of bedroom windows. It's all going to happen. I know it—at any rate, I knew it then. There's no escape. Fight against it if you like, or look the other way and pretend not to notice, or grab your spanner and rush out to do a bit of face-smashing along with the others. But there's no way out. It's just something that's got to happen.

I trod on the gas, and the old car whizzed up and down the little hills, and the cows and elm trees and fields of wheat rushed past till the engine was pretty nearly red-hot. I felt in much the same mood as I'd felt that day in January when I was coming down the Strand, the day I got my new false teeth. It was as though the power of prophecy had been given me. It seemed to me that I could see the whole of England, and all the people in it, and all the things that'll happen to all of them. Sometimes, of course, even then, I had a doubt or two. The world is very large, that's a thing you notice when you're driving about in a car, and in a way it's reassuring. Think of the enormous stretches of land you pass over when you cross a corner of a single English county. It's like Siberia. And the fields and beech-spinneys and farmhouses and churches, and the villages with their little grocers' shops and the parish hall and the ducks walking across the green. Surely it's too big to be changed? Bound to remain more or less the same. And presently I struck into outer London and followed the Uxbridge Road as far as Southall. Miles and miles of ugly houses, with people living dull decent lives inside them. And beyond it London stretching on and on, streets, squares, back-alleys, tenements, blocks of flats, pubs, fried-fish shops, picture-houses, on and on for twenty miles, and all the eight million people with their little private lives which they don't want to have altered. The bombs aren't made that could smash it out of existence. And the chaos of it! The privateness of all those lives! John Smith cutting out the football coupons, Bill Williams swapping stories in the barber's, Mrs Jones coming home with the supper beer. Eight million of them! Surely they'll manage somehow, bombs or no bombs, to keep on with the life that they've been used to?

Illusion! Baloney! It doesn't matter how many of them there are, they're all for it. The bad times are coming, and the streamlined men are coming too. What's coming after-wards I don't know, it hardly even interests me. I only know that if there's anything you care a curse about, better say good-bye to it now, because everything you've ever known is going down, down, into the muck, with the machine-guns rattling all the time.

VII

But when I got back to the suburb my mood suddenly changed.

It suddenly struck me—and it hadn't even crossed my mind till that moment—that Hilda might really be ill after all.

That's the effect of environment, you see. In Lower Binfield I'd taken it absolutely for granted that she wasn't ill and was merely shamming in order to get me home. It had seemed natural at the time, I don't know why. But as I drove into West Bletchley and the Hesperides Estate closed round me like a kind of red brick prison, which is what it is, the ordinary habits of thought came back. I had that kind of Monday morning feeling when everything seems bleak and sensible. I saw what bloody rot it was, this business that I'd wasted the last five days on. Sneaking off to Lower Binfield to try and recover the past, and then, in the car coming home, thinking a lot of prophetic baloney about the future. The future! What's the future got to do with chaps like you and me? Holding down our jobs—that's our future. As for Hilda, even when the bombs are dropping she'll still be thinking about the price of butter.

And suddenly I saw what a fool I'd been to think she'd do a thing like that. Of course the SOS wasn't a fake! As though she'd have the imagination! It was just the plain cold truth. She wasn't shamming at all, she was really ill. And Gosh! at this moment she might be lying somewhere in ghastly pain, or even dead, for all I knew. The thought sent a most horrible pang of fright through me, a sort of dreadful cold feeling in my guts. I whizzed down Ellesmere Road at nearly forty miles an hour, and instead of taking the car to the lock-up garage as usual I stopped outside the house and jumped out.

So I'm fond of Hilda after all, you say? I don't know what you mean by fond. Are you fond of your own face? Probably not, but you can't imagine yourself without it. It's part of you. Well, that's how I felt about Hilda. When things are going well I can't stick the sight of her, but the thought that she might be dead or even in pain sent the shivers through me.

I fumbled with the key, got the door open, and the familiar smell of old mackintoshes hit me.

'Hilda!' I yelled. 'Hilda!'

No answer. For a moment I was yelling 'Hilda! Hilda!' into utter silence, and some cold sweat started out on my backbone. Maybe they'd carted her away to hospital already—maybe there was a corpse lying upstairs in the empty house.

I started to dash up the stairs, but at the same moment the two kids, in their pyjamas, came out of their rooms on either side of the landing. It was eight or nine o'clock, I suppose—at any rate the light was just beginning to fail. Lorna hung over the banisters.

'Oo, Daddy! Oo, it's Daddy! Why have you come back today, Daddy? Mummy said you weren't coming till Friday.'

'Where's your mother?' I said.

'Mummy's out. She went out with Mrs Wheeler. Why have you come home today, Daddy?'

'Then your mother hasn't been ill?'

'No. Who said she'd been ill? Daddy! Have you been in Birmingham?'

'Yes. Get back to bed, now. You'll be catching cold.'

'But where's our presents, Daddy?'

'What presents?'

'The presents you've brought us from Birmingham.'

'You'll see them in the morning,' I said.

'Oo, Daddy! Can't we see them tonight?'

'No. Dry up. Get back to bed or I'll wallop the pair of you.'

So she wasn't ill after all. She *had* been shamming. And really I hardly knew whether to be glad or sorry. I turned back to the front door, which I'd left open, and there, as large as life, was Hilda coming up the garden path.

I looked at her as she came towards me in the last of the evening light. It was queer to think that less than three minutes earlier I'd been in the devil of a stew, with actual cold sweat on my backbone, at the thought that she might be dead. Well, she wasn't dead, she was just as usual. Old Hilda with her thin shoulders and her anxious face, and the gas bill and the school fees, and the mackintoshy smell and the office on Monday—all the bedrock facts that you invariably come back to, the eternal verities as old Porteous calls them. I could see that Hilda wasn't in too good a temper. She darted me a little quick look, like she does sometimes when she's got something on her mind, the kind of look some little thin animal, a weasel for instance, might give you. She didn't seem surprised to see me back, however.

'Oh, so you're back already, are you?' she said.

It seemed pretty obvious that I was back, and I didn't answer. She didn't make any move to kiss me.

'There's nothing for your supper,' she went on promptly. That's Hilda all over. Always manages to say something depressing the instant you set foot inside the house. 'I wasn't expecting you. You'll just have to have bread and cheese—but I don't think we've got any cheese.'

I followed her indoors, into the smell of mackintoshes. We went into the sitting-room. I shut the door and switched on the light. I meant to get my say in first, and I knew it would make things better if I took a strong line from the start.

'Now,' I said, 'what the bloody hell do you mean by playing that trick on me?'

She'd just laid her bag down on top of the radio, and for a moment she looked genuinely surprised.

'What trick? What do you mean?'

'Sending out that SOS!'

'What SOS? What are you *talking* about, George?'

'Are you trying to tell me you didn't get them to send out an SOS saying you were seriously ill?'

'Of course I didn't! How could I? I wasn't ill. What would I do a thing like that for?'

I began to explain, but almost before I began I saw what had happened. It was all a mistake. I'd only heard the last few words of the SOS and obviously it was some other Hilda Bowling. I suppose there'd be scores of Hilda Bowlings if you looked the name up in the directory. It was just the kind of dull stupid mistake that's always happening. Hilda hadn't even showed that little bit of imagination I'd credited her with. The sole interest in the whole affair had been the five minutes or so when I thought she was dead, and found that I cared after all. But that was over and done with. While I explained she was watching me, and I could see in her eye that there was trouble of some kind coming. And then she began questioning me in what I call her third-degree voice, which isn't, as you might expect, angry and nagging, but quiet and kind of watchful.

'So you heard this SOS in the hotel at Birmingham?'

'Yes. Last night, on the National Broadcast.'

'When did you leave Birmingham, then?'

'This morning, of course.' (I'd planned out the journey in my mind, just in case there should be any need to lie my way out of it. Left at ten, lunch at Coventry, tea at Bedford—I'd got it all mapped out.)

'So you thought last night I was seriously ill, and you didn't even leave till this morning?'

'But I tell you I didn't think you were ill. Haven't I explained? I thought it was just another of your tricks. It sounded a damn sight more likely.'

'Then I'm rather surprised you left at all!' she said with so much vinegar in her voice that I knew there was

243

something more coming. But she went on more quietly: 'So you left this morning, did you?'

'Yes. I left about ten. I had lunch at Coventry——'

'Then how do you account for *this?*' she suddenly shot out at me, and in the same instant she ripped her bag open, took out a piece of paper and held it out as if it had been a forged cheque, or something.

I felt as if someone had hit me a sock in the wind. I might have known it! She'd caught me after all. And there was the evidence, the dossier of the case. I didn't even know what it was, except that it was something that proved I'd been off with a woman. All the stuffing went out of me. A moment earlier I'd been kind of bullying her, making out to be angry because I'd been dragged back from Birmingham for nothing, and now she'd suddenly turned the tables on me. You don't have to tell me what I looked like at that moment. I know. Guilt written all over me in big letters—I know. And I wasn't even guilty! But it's a matter of habit. I'm used to being in the wrong. For a hundred quid I couldn't have kept the guilt out of my voice as I answered:

'What do you mean? What's that thing you've got there?'

'You read it and you'll see what it is.'

I took it. It was a letter from what seemed to be a firm of solicitors, and it was addressed from the same street as Rowbottom's Hotel, I noticed.

'Dear Madam,' I read, 'With reference to your letter of the 18th inst., we think there must be some mistake. Rowbottom's Hotel was closed down two years ago and has been converted into a block of offices. No one answering the description of your husband has been here. Possibly——'

I didn't read any further. Of course I saw it all in a flash. I'd been a little bit too clever and put my foot in it. There was just one faint ray of hope—young Saunders might have forgotten to post the letter I'd addressed from Rowbottom's, in which case it was just possible I could brazen it out. But Hilda soon put the lid on that idea.

'Well, George, you see what the letter says? The day you left here I wrote to Rowbottom's Hotel—oh, just a little note, asking them whether you'd arrived there. And you see the answer I got! There isn't even any such place as Rowbottom's Hotel. And the same day, the very same post, I got your letter saying you were at the hotel. You got someone to post it for you, I suppose. *That* was your business in Birmingham!'

'But look here, Hilda! You've got this all wrong. It isn't what you think at all. You don't understand.'

'Oh, yes, I do, George. I understand *perfectly*.'

'But look here, Hilda——'

Wasn't any use, of course. It was a fair cop. I couldn't even meet her eye. I turned and tried to make for the door.

'I'll have to take the car round to the garage,' I said.

'Oh, no George! You don't get out of it like that. You'll stay here and listen to what I've got to say, please.'

'But, damn it! I've got to switch the lights on, haven't I? It's past lighting-up time. You don't want us to get fined?'

At that she let me go, and I went out and switched the car lights on, but when I came back she was still standing there like a figure of doom, with the two letters, mine and the solicitor's, on the table in front of her. I'd got a little of my nerve back, and I had another try:

'Listen, Hilda. You've got hold of the wrong end of the stick about this business. I can explain the whole thing.'

'I'm sure *you* could explain anything, George. The question is whether I'd believe you.'

'But you're just jumping to conclusions! What made you write to these hotel people, anyway?'

'It was Mrs Wheeler's idea. And a very good idea too, as it turned out.'

'Oh, Mrs Wheeler, was it? So you don't mind letting that blasted woman into our private affairs?'

'She didn't need any letting in. It was she who warned me what you were up to this week. Something seemed to tell her, she said. And she was right, you see. She knows all about you, George. She used to have a husband *just* like you.'

'But, Hilda——'

I looked at her. Her face had gone kind of white under the surface, the way it does when she thinks of me with another woman. A woman! If only it had been true!

And Gosh! what I could see ahead of me! You know what it's like. The weeks on end of ghastly nagging and sulking, and the catty remarks after you think peace has been signed, and the meals always late, and the kids wanting to know what it's all about. But what really got me down was the kind of mental squalor, the kind of mental atmosphere in which the real reason why I'd gone to Lower Binfield wouldn't even be conceivable. That was what chiefly struck me at the moment. If I spent a week explaining to Hilda *why* I'd been to Lower Binfield, she'd never understand. And who *would* understand, here in Ellesmere Road? Gosh! did I even understand myself? The whole thing seemed to be fading out of my mind. Why had I gone to Lower Binfield? *Had* I gone there? In this atmosphere it just seemed meaningless. Nothing's real in Ellesmere Road except gas bills, school fees, boiled cabbage and the office on Monday.

One more try:

'But look here, Hilda! I know what you think. But you're absolutely wrong. I swear to you you're wrong.'

'Oh, no, George. If I was wrong why did you have to tell all those lies?'

No getting away from that, of course.

I took a pace or two up and down. The smell of old mackintoshes was very strong. Why had I run away like that? Why had I bothered about the future and the past, seeing that the future and the past don't matter? Whatever motives I might have had, I could hardly remember them now. The old life in Lower Binfield, the war and the after-war, Hitler, Stalin, bombs, machine-guns, food-queues, rubber truncheons—it was fading out, all fading out. Nothing remained except a vulgar low-down row in a smell of old mackintoshes.

One last try:

'Hilda! Just listen to me a minute. Look here, you don't know where I've been all this week, do you?'

'I don't want to know where you've been. I know *what* you've been doing. That's quite enough for me.'

'But dash it——'

Quite useless, of course. She'd found me guilty and now she was going to tell me what she thought of me. That might take her a couple of hours. And after that there was further trouble looming up, because presently it would occur to her to wonder where I'd got the money for this trip, and then she'd discover that I'd been holding out on her about the seventeen quid. Really there was no reason why this row shouldn't go on till three in the morning. No use playing injured innocence any longer. All I wanted was the line of least resistance. And in my mind I ran over the three possibilities, which were:

A. To tell her what I'd really been doing and somehow make her believe me.

B. To pull the old gag about losing my memory.

C. To let her go on thinking it was a woman, and take my medicine.

But, damn it! I knew which it would have to be.